Saving Mattie

Saving Mattie
Copyright © 2008, Philip S. Dunlap
All rights reserved

Cover model: Bailey Hertweck
Copyright ©2008
All rights reserved

Location courtesy of:
Kelley Agricultural Historical Museum
Sharpsville, IN 46068

Photography
Copyright ©2008, Philip S. Dunlap

Sundowners and MountainView Publishing
Divisions of
Treble Heart Books
1284 Overlook Dr.
Sierra Vista, AZ 85635-5512

Published and Printed in the U.S.A.

The characters and events in this book are fictional, and any resemblance to persons, whether living or dead, is strictly coincidental.

All rights reserved. No part of this book may be reproduced or transmitted in any form by any means, electronic or mechanical, including photocopying, recording, scanning to a computer disk, or by any informational storage and retrieval system, without express permission in writing from the publisher.

ISBN: 978-1-932695-73-1

Thank you for
Choosing a
Sundowners
&
MountainView Publishing
Crossover novel

Saving Mattie

by

Phil Dunlap

Sundowners

&

MountainView Publishing

are Divisions of

Treble Heart Books

Dedication

I dedicate this book to my loving wife, Judy, who has faithfully supported, and participated in, my love of the old west.

Chapter 1

I had been riding for hours when I first spotted the ranch house. I reined in several yards from the porch, preparing to announce my arrival, when I was suddenly braced by a skinny moppet with a cut-down scattergun, the barrel of which I was none too happy to be staring down. The aforesaid moppet was but a waif of a girl, blond-headed and feisty, yet it was clear she was scared out of her wits. Staring up at a tall, rangy, unshaven cowpoke wearing a slouch hat, tan trail duster, and a Colt on his hip didn't do much to instill confidence in her safety, either.

"What'cha doin' here, mister?" she said with a note of defiance in her voice. "What d'ya want?"

"Well, missy, if you'll point that cannon somewhere else, I'll tell you."

She seemed to be giving that some thought as I sat stone still atop my roan mare, hands stacked on the pommel. I wasn't about to give her any reason to squeeze the trigger. I saw no one else around, no sounds that would normally accompany a working ranch, no nickering horses, no bellowing cattle. Not even a hen clucking as she pecked at the grassless yard. Finally, after a few minutes, she let the shotgun barrel droop slightly toward the ground, but still kept a firm grip on it just in case this dust-encrusted drover turned out to be someone to fear.

"Okay, mister, but you better be tellin' me quick or you get a belly full of buckshot. I can use this thing. My pa taught me."

"I'm sure you can, missy. Say, what's your name? And how old are you, anyway?"

"Name's Mattie. Mattie Slaughter. I live here. And I'm twelve, if it's any of your business. Now be sayin' what's on your mind or be movin' on."

"I go by Rawhide Smith, and if it wouldn't be too much trouble, Mattie who is twelve, could you call your pa out so I can ask him for a job? Tell him I'm real good with horses. And I'm down to my last two dollars."

"We don't need any help. We're doin' just fine with what we got. Now you best be ridin' on."

I looked around, keeping my hands in plain sight lest she start getting an itchy trigger finger again. The air was hot and still. And, with the exception of a slight breeze that whistled around the corner of the farmhouse occasionally, flapping some loose siding, the place was quiet. Too quiet. I was getting a strange feeling that this little girl was in trouble, but she wasn't going to let on that she needed help. Any sudden move on my part could land me on my back in the dirt with a thousand little balls of lead decorating my body. Child or no child, it was easy to see she meant business. Folks who are fearful can easily be pushed to the brink of something they might regret later. I didn't want to be the victim of that possibility.

"I don't suppose you'd at least allow me to water my horse, maybe have a sip for myself. It's been a long ride from Ellettsville and a mighty dry one, too."

She thought about that. I could see she was troubled by the prospect of my getting down, but at the same time, she didn't want to deny a man, or his horse, a drink of water. A squinty-eyed frown wrinkled her forehead.

"Could I just talk to your pa for a spell? You could keep the shotgun on me if you want. But I'm not here to cause your folks any grief. I'm just lookin' for a job, and if you don't have a need, I'll be glad to mosey on out of here. A little water would sure be helpful before I go, though."

She took a step backward, and eased the gun back up.

"He's out back, they all are."

"All?"

"Pa, Ma, and my brother. There, out back. You can talk to them if you want. I do. But I doubt you'll get any more answers than I have."

"Is it okay if I get down off my horse?"

"Keep your hands where I can see 'em, and I reckon it'll be okay." She scooted around behind me as I dismounted. That way, she had me dead in her sights if I should make any fast moves. I had no intention of doing any such thing.

When we reached the back porch, I looked around for any of the folks she said I would find, but there was no one there. I walked farther out, puzzled by the complete absence of anything or anyone, two legs or four. I looked back at Mattie with a questioning look.

"Mattie, I don't see anyone. Where's your Pa?"

"Right there, by the shed," she replied in a cold, soft voice. "The sun gets so hot sometimes, I thought it best if they could rest in the shade at least a bit of the time."

I walked to the shed. There, in the shade were three

mounds of dirt each topped with a crudely crafted cross of lashed-together twigs. I turned to Mattie and found her sitting on the ground crossed-legged with her small face buried in her hands, quietly sobbing, the shotgun lay beside her.

"What happened here, Mattie? How did they die?" I squatted beside her and put my hand on her shoulder.

She looked up with tear-stained eyes. "They was murdered, you know, shot down like they was no more use than a coyote raiding the chickens. I buried 'em proper and said some words over 'em, too. Ma would have liked what I said about her. Pa, too. Maybe not so much my brother, but—"

"When did this happen? How long have you been here alone?"

"I-I think it was about a week ago, maybe more, maybe less. I don't know. I ain't that good with my days, and such. I'm best at readin'."

"How did you escape bein' killed, yourself?"

She hung her head. "I was where I shouldn't a'been, down by the creek pokin' at frogs with a stick. Pa's told me a bunch of times that I shouldn't ought to do that 'cause I could fall in and drown. But I did it anyway. I like frogs."

"Did you see who did this?"

"It was them Venable brothers. Meaner'n snakes, they are."

"Why did they do it?"

"Wanted money, I reckon. I could hear them all the way down at the creek. They were yellin' at Pa, sayin' he'd better cough up some money or they'd shoot the lot of 'em. Pa said no, and the Venables started blastin' away. By the time I got all the way up the hill, they was already in the house lookin' for money. I hid out behind the barn 'till they rode off."

"Did they find any?"

"Naw. Pa hid what little money we had in a secret place. The Venables ain't smart enough to look there."

I was at a loss for words, heartbroken and furious all at the same time. A little voice in my head began to pester me. What if this pitiful child was my own little sister? What if, what if? My conscience had a tight grip on me, leaving no room for doubt: Mattie Slaughter had just become my responsibility. What I was going to do with a twelve-year-old child was a puzzlement. I knew I couldn't leave her alone with no one to care for her. At the very least I had to find a place that would take her in, and care for her properly. I reckon I was too busy figuring out her future when she brought me back to reality.

"Mister Smith, you got anything to eat in them saddlebags?"

Her question as to whether I had any food told me she wasn't just scared, she was hungry, too. Well, she wasn't alone on that score.

I helped Mattie to her feet and walked her to the house. She tried to carry the shotgun, which was by now getting pretty heavy, and half carried, half dragged it in the dirt. I can't say I was too happy about that since it invited an accidental discharge, the blast of which could have gone about anywhere, but I kept my mouth shut and tried to stay clear of any possible line of fire.

"Mattie, would it be okay if I come inside?" I asked.

"I'll think on it."

I waited for her to make up her mind. She was a suspicious little thing, although I reckon after what had befallen her family, maybe she had a right to be. She stopped and looked at me with a scowl.

"You didn't answer me, Mister Smith. Do you have anything to eat or not?"

Saving Mattie

"Call me Rawhide, and no, little lady, I'm afraid I don't. Ate the last I had last night, or the night before, I can't rightly remember. Does that mean you have no food left, either?"

"That's about it, Mister Rawhide. Boy that sure is a strange name." Then she snickered. That was the first time I'd seen a hint of a smile on her pretty little freckled face.

"What happened to your stock? Didn't you have some cattle, horses, something?"

"The Venables drove off what few cattle we had, took our two horses and shot the chickens. They stole everything a soul might be able to eat. Guess they figured dead folks don't need food, huh?"

"Well, then you can't stay here. We'll double up on my horse and light out for Fort Stockton. I'm certain we'll find some nice folks that will be right pleased to put a little lady up in a nice home."

"Nope."

"Uh, nope what?"

"Nope, I ain't goin' nowhere. This is my place, now, and I'm stayin' on." defiance blazed in her eyes. "I ain't leavin' my family."

"But, Mattie, your family is dead. You need someone to tend to your needs, feed you regular, buy you clothes, put you in school."

"That way they win."

"Who wins?"

"Them Venables. That's what they wanted all along, to drive us off our land."

"But—"

She crossed her arms and planted her feet firmly in the dirt. "I said nope, and I meant it."

If I wanted to get the stubborn youngster to safety, the

only way I could see would be to pick her up and forcibly carry her across about a hundred miles of harsh country, foraging for food along the way. Not a very appealing prospect.

"Okay, Mattie, just how do you suggest we keep from starving to death if we stay here? I don't see any beefsteak trees growing out there."

She pouted for several minutes without saying anything. She was obviously pondering her options, and not reaching any logical conclusions. She was hungry, and deep down, she knew I was right. That didn't mean she would begin to see things my way. Not by a long shot.

"In the evenings, sometimes, when I go down by the stream, I see mule deer come to drink. Maybe we could shoot one."

Killing and dressing-out a deer held little appeal for me, but I had to admit that, in the short term, it was a solution. The afternoon sun was hot and it would be at least three hours before there was any chance of a deer coming out to drink and feed on the grass shoots along the creek. It made sense to use that time to look the place over for any other possibilities.

"Okay, Mattie, we'll try to bag us a deer. But for now, we need to see if we can't find some other food, like beans or coffee, somewhere. Do you know where your ma kept things like that?"

"Of course, I'm not a child, you know. I can cook and everything."

"That's great. Where do we start looking?"

"They took it all. Everything is gone. They took our flour, beans, coffee. Everything. I already told you."

Being scolded by a twelve-year-old was something I wasn't used to, and the temptation to swat her little bottom did present itself to me. But, I refrained in the interest of maintaining good relations with her. Besides, I wasn't certain she wouldn't try to punch me back.

"We'll look around anyway, just in case they got careless and overlooked something," I said, without waiting for her to give me the bad news all over again, for the third time. She fell in behind with a great sigh of resignation as I headed for the front door. It was clear she had resigned herself to letting this foolish grown-up find out the hard way that she had been right all along.

I looked through the cabinet near the stove, finding only a few bowls and wooden spoons for mixing biscuits, which would be helpful if I were to find any flour. There was no flour. Nor were there any beans. No potatoes, either, in the root cellar. No cans of peaches or tomatoes, and no coffee. The Venables had cleaned the place out good and proper, leaving a twelve-year-old to starve. A real nice bunch of folks. Of course, if the Venables had known she was there, watching their every move, seeing them gun down innocent folks for no reason, she would also have been dead. The killers didn't seem too particular into whom they fired their bullets.

There I was, faced with my only two options: put Mattie on my horse and force her to go to Fort Stockton, or hope a mule deer would find its way into the sights of my Winchester. Of course, to do either, I first had to admit Mattie was right about the lack of anything edible on the premises.

"What'd I tell you, Mister Rawhide? Didn't I say there wasn't nothin' to eat?" She stood with her hands on her hips—what little she had in the way of hips—with a look of righteousness that stung. She had a body that resembled a stick, and no food for a week wasn't helping her gain any weight.

"Yep, little lady, I reckon you did say something like that. So, it looks as if we're either goin' to Fort Stockton, or we hunt down a deer."

"I already told you, I ain't goin' nowhere."

I patted my mare's neck as I climbed into the saddle, pulled Mattie up behind me, shotgun and all, and told her to aim me towards the creek.

Chapter 2

As the late afternoon shadows gathered about us, Mattie and I huddled behind a thicket of sagebrush and weeds. The heat of day was dwindling and a slight breeze began to ruffle what little grass there was. My horse had wandered off behind a small hillock to graze. Fortunately, we were downwind so any deer that happened by wouldn't catch our scent and skedaddle. From a nearby tree, a blue jay scolded us for invading his territory. We had waited for nearly an hour and a half when there came the sound of splashing water from downstream. We waited in hopes that it would be a deer, and that it would wander into the open, and be within rifle range. The splashing grew louder.

Two riders came into view from up the creek, their horse's hooves splashing as they crossed. They stopped, let their mounts drink, then continued on past us, oblivious to our being within a few feet of their course. I can't say why I didn't stand up and ask if they happened to have any food they'd be willing to share, but something told me that wouldn't be a good idea. Perhaps it was their scruffy look, or the way they wore their revolvers, that made me cautious. Then I looked at Mattie. Her eyes were wide with fear, coupled with anger. I could see she was about to jump up and confront these two. She had the shotgun tightly gripped in her small hands, her thumb was on one hammer, preparing to cock it. I quickly grabbed her, pulled the shotgun from her, and put my hand over her mouth, shaking my head to let her know that whatever she was thinking would be a bad idea.

When the riders were well past our position, I let Mattie go. Whatever the cause, the anger inside her was about to boil over. I didn't want to be the recipient of whatever had sparked her outrage.

"What is it, Mattie? Do you know those two?"

"It's them! It's the Venables! They was the ones that killed my family." Tears were now streaming down her cheeks. She was shaking with sorrow, anger, and overcome with fear all at the same time. "Why didn't you shoot them?"

"I didn't know who they were, and I don't go around shooting people for no reason. In fact, I don't shoot people for any reason if I can help it. It ain't right."

I pulled her close to give her whatever comfort I could, as something inside me akin to a need for revenge was growing, also, regardless of what I'd just told her about not bein' proper to go around shootin' folks.

"We'll get the horse and follow them. See what they're up to." She nodded her agreement and we went over the hill to find Chigger, my strawberry roan mare. As soon as I spotted Chigger, I knew I should have hobbled her. She had wandered off nearly a quarter mile. It would take us several minutes to catch her. I tried whistling her back, but to no avail. About five acres of fresh grass and sweet clover along the creek were more of a distraction to her than her owner's need for a ride. Bees buzzed about the sweet flowers.

After nearly a half hour of trying, we finally corralled the mare, got mounted and headed out to find the Venable boys. When we came to the top of a hill where we could see the Slaughter farm, we were both shocked by what we saw. The ranch house was engulfed in flames and the two Venables were mounting up to ride away. Their laughter could be heard all the way to the hill where we huddled in dismay. Now, we not only had no food, we had no place to sleep, either, unless the ramshackle shed could be counted. I felt Mattie shudder as she leaned closer. The two men had stopped by the side of the shed and were looking down at the three graves. I'd have bet money they were thinking the same thing I was, "Who buried these folks. Did we leave someone alive that could identify us?"

That *must* have been what they had been thinking because they dismounted and started looking around for signs of more people. They looked inside the shed, then the barn, then around the corral. None of the structures were sturdily built, and a strong wind or a large man could have pushed any of them down. Finally, after several minutes of fruitless searching, they mounted up and tore hell bent for leather to the west, in the direction of a dismal little cow town called Bradleyville. I knew of it, had heard stories of how wicked it was, and had decided not to take Mattie there because of its bad reputation. It was no place for a child, and there would certainly be no one who would be able to care for her.

After we were certain we wouldn't be seen sneaking back onto Slaughter land, we mounted up and slowly descended the hill, keeping a very cautious eye out for any surprises that might come our way. Mattie spoke her first words since seeing the Venables set fire to her home.

"Why'd those rattlesnakes burn our house?"

"Probably for the same reason they shot your family. They

were sending a warning to other settlers that it isn't healthy to farm this land. I figure they're cattlemen, and they likely work for a big spread somewhere nearby. Folks comin' in, buyin' some land, and then using some of the free range, maybe raising a few milk cows or sheep, just don't set well with them. They also don't like the idea of fences bein' put up so folks can grow crops."

"They didn't have to kill my pa and ma, did they?"

"Mattie, the world is full of evil. You just happened onto some of it at a very young age, that's all. It's been here all along. I'm sorry you had to taste it so long before you're full grown."

"Do you think they went off to kill some more families?"

"I don't know. Are there any more settlers off in the direction they went?"

"Yeah. There's the Brewsters over that way. Oh, and the Johnsons, too. The Brewsters raise sheep, I think. Pa said he didn't want any sheep 'cause they eat up all the grass and it don't grow back," she said with a youthful authority in her voice. I doubted the truthfulness of her father's admonition about sheep, but kept it to myself.

I pondered our next move. Should I try to warn those other families about the Venables, or take Mattie directly to Fort Stockton? Having a girl along would sure make any confrontation that much more difficult. I made up my mind that Mattie's safety was the most important thing.

"We have little choice, now, Mattie. We might as well mount up and get started for Fort Stockton."

"Aren't we gonna warn the Brewsters and the Johnsons?"

I felt my face grow hot from the embarrassment I felt at having a child remind me of the right thing to do. Reluctant as I was to let her accompany me into any potential danger, I had to acknowledge that her inherent goodness outweighed my caution.

"Yeah. Reckon we should, at that. What about the money you said your pa kept safe. Shouldn't you take that along? You'll be needin' a stake before long, I'll wager."

Mattie looked at me like I was one of the Venables trying to steal what little she had left. She was thinking on it real hard for a minute or two.

"How do I know you ain't aimin' to try getting your hands on my pa's money?"

"Mattie, I swear to you I have no intention of stealin' your money. It's yours, rightful. But don't you figure there'd be no sense to leavin' it here for the coyotes."

"It'll be all right where it is. I'll be comin' back, anyway."

"In the mean time, the Venables might come lookin' to dig up whatever they can find. You don't want them to get it, do you?"

She pondered that some more, then slipped off the horse and ran around the house to the shed. When she returned several minutes later, she carried a glass jar with the lid screwed on tightly. Inside, I could see a wad of greenbacks and a handful of coins. I took her outstretched hand and pulled her up behind me. She held the jar close to her chest as if it could take flight at any moment. I carried her shotgun across the saddle in front of me.

"Okay, little lady, which way are we headed?"

"The Brewster's place is that way." She pointed to the west. "Maybe they'll have some food."

The direction she was indicating would also take us closer to Bradleyville, a town I wasn't eager to visit. Something in her voice convinced me we were doing the right thing.

***

Nightfall was upon us before we reached the Brewster homestead. We found a nice clearing by a stream to camp, with trees to help ward off the early morning dew. I unsaddled Chigger, and hobbled her this time. I had two blankets tied behind the cantle, not hotel comfort, but enough to keep us each warm. I built a fire for little more reason than the warmth it would bring, since we had no food to cook over it. Mattie wrapped her blanket around her and tucked it under her bare feet. I hadn't bothered to ask if she owned any shoes. If she did, it made little difference since shoes would have been in the house, and the house was now a pile of ashes, along with everything in it.

As she sat staring into the dancing flames, I went to my saddlebags and drew out my most treasured possession, which immediately caught her attention.

"What's that?" The fire put a sparkle in her eyes.

"The Good Book."

"What's so good about it? It's just like any other book, ain't it?"

"Nope. This one's special. I take it with me wherever I go."

"How can a book be special? I've seen books, even learned to read some of them, but I never saw one I'd call *special*. Just stories, that's all." She tried to appear ambivalent about the well-worn, leather-bound book I held, but her eyes revealed more than mere curiosity. This child was a natural learner, and I figured she would hound me until I told her what she wanted to know.

"It's special in many ways. This book is filled with stories about God, and history, and how we should live, and even what's to come."

"Who's God? I never heard tell about him before. Is he important, or something?"

I was stunned by her question. I'd never run into anyone before who didn't know who God was. And I wasn't sure just how to answer her.

"Well, God is who created this whole world. He created the stars and the moon and everything we see around us, all the animals, all the people, everything."

"Did he create the Venables?"

"Well, yes he did. He created us all."

"*Why* did he create the Venables?"

This child was obviously going to ask more questions than I could answer. Her mind seemed to grasp the basics of right and wrong, but she'd never been taught that there is more to it than that. I was in trouble and I knew it. I was beginning to think I should have never pulled my Bible from the saddlebags.

"God desires man to follow a path of goodness, but not all men do. Some follow a path of evil, like the Venables. That's why there are good men and bad men. The good let God guide their lives. The bad just wander around doin' what they want."

"If a person don't know about this God, does that mean they're bad?"

"No, but—"

"My pa didn't know anyone named God. But he wasn't bad, was he? Is that why the Venables shot him?"

"Mattie, I don't have answers to all your questions. Sorry."

"But I want answers. I want to know why my pa and my ma and my brother were killed. Was it because they done somethin' wrong? Was they bad, like you said?"

"No, it ain't like that at all. I'm sure your folks were real fine people. Real fine. After all, they brought you into this world, didn't they? No one that was bad coulda done that. It was the Venables that were bad. They did the killin', didn't they?"

Mattie hung her head. "Uh-huh. I reckon I see what you mean. But I don't understand why this fella named God didn't stop them before they did what they did."

"Look, how 'bout I read some of the stories in this here book to you, then maybe you'll understand even more."

"Okay, but can it wait? I'm getting' awful sleepy."

"Sure, Mattie, it can wait. You snuggle down under that blanket and I'll see you in the morning."

"G'night, Mister Rawhide." She was asleep in about a minute, surrounded by a cricket serenade.

I bolted upright, throwing off my blanket, as I was rudely awakened by the sound of gunfire. It seemed to be coming from just over a series of low hills to the west, from the direction we were headed. I saddled Chigger and we gathered our things and climbed aboard. I spurred the horse to a gallop. By the time we reached the top of the first rise, I could see two men hiding behind some rocks pouring lead into a crudely built farmhouse. Whoever was inside was returning fire. I counted only one rifle sticking out a window. Whoever was shooting at their attackers didn't seem to be hitting anything worthwhile.

"It's them Venables, Mister Rawhide. I can tell from here. Can we go get them?"

"I can't take a child into the middle of a gun battle. We'll sit here and see what happens."

"What'll happen is they'll kill the Brewsters while we're sittin' around thinkin' what to do. I'm goin' down there. Give me my shotgun now!"

I was torn between Mattie's safety and the truthfulness

of her statement. All of a sudden, I felt guilty for not doing the right thing without further thought.

"I'll go down there and see if I can draw some of their fire. But you aren't leavin' this very spot. Do you understand? 'Cause if you do, first I'll tan your hide, then I'll leave you out here for the wolves to gnaw on. Now get down and hide over yonder behind them shrubs, and don't make a sound."

I helped her off Chigger and watched her run to the shrubs I'd pointed to. I wasn't sure whether to leave her shotgun with her, but decided if I got gunned down, she'd need some way to protect herself. I spurred the mare down the hill and toward what I felt certain would be a big mistake. I pulled my rifle from its scabbard, swung it in a circle by the lever to chamber a round and cock it. Took a one-handed aim at the closest man hiding behind the rocks. My shot ricocheted off the boulder, missing my target, but scaring him into scooting for cover next to the other man. They stopped firing, then took only a second to decide riding away was better than being caught in a crossfire. I was thankful they had at least a modicum of good sense. I reined up and watched as they tore across the range like their britches was afire, which if they'd hung around a few more minutes, they might have been.

I turned Chigger around and rode back uphill to collect Mattie before going down to the farmhouse to see if anyone had been wounded. She was standing atop the hill cheering me as I rode up. I reached down, grabbed her by the wrist and hauled her up behind me once more.

"That was great, Mister Rawhide. Them Venables was surely scared off. I wish you had been around when they killed my folks. Let's go see to the Brewsters."

"Mattie, would you mind leavin' off this Mister stuff. Call me Rawhide."

"Okay, M— Er, Rawhide. I'll try to remember. Now, let's get going. Time's a'wastin'."

Chapter 3

As we approached the Brewster place, a wretchedly thin woman in a bedraggled and worn cotton dress stood in the doorway pointing a rifle in our direction. Her eyes were ringed with dark circles, and her face was lined with worry. She was a pitiful sight. Clearly, life on the prairie hadn't been kind to her.

"Hello, the house. We're friendly. No need for the rifle, ma'am." I hoped the sound of an unthreatening voice might ease her fears. The rifle remained pointed at us. I heard a weak voice coming from inside the cabin that seemed to be calling for help.

She looked around, then eased the rifle to point at the ground. Her shoulders slumped as if the last vestiges of hope had vanished and she might just as well give in to whatever was to befall her. Mattie came to the rescue.

"Missus Brewster, it's me, Mattie Slaughter," she said peering around me. "You remember my pa and ma. This here's my friend Mister Rawhide. We come to be of help. Would it be okay to get down off'n this nag?"

Saving Mattie

"Nag?" I was offended. I was glad that Chigger didn't understand such words or I'm sure we'd both have been dumped on our backsides right about then.

"Mattie, child, I'm so sorry I didn't see you there. Of course, you get right down from there and come inside. You come at a time when we could use all the help we can get."

I took Mattie's hand and helped ease her down off Chigger, and we followed Mrs. Brewster inside a dark, depressing house made of logs and mud chinking. A cow lay dead in the yard, bullet ridden, as did several chickens. The Venables had done a fair job of shooting out the only three windows, too, and the door was about to come clean off its leather hinges from being slammed into numerous times by .44 rounds.

Near a window lay a man, moaning. He was bleeding from a shoulder wound. I knelt beside him to take a look. The bullet had probably busted the shoulder, but if we could get the lead out, the man would probably live. I'd seen much worse wounds where a man had lived to fight another day.

"Ma'am, I think we need to get this bullet out, pronto. If you got a skinnin' knife, and some whiskey, I'll get at it."

The lady scurried around, pulling a drawer from a hutch and fumbling through the several utensils therein. She found a knife, almost worn down to nothing from being sharpened over and over. It was quite sharp and looked as if it would do the job.

"I'll put a pot on for hot water. We'll need to clean him up after you go carvin' on him. I'll fetch my needle and thread, too, seal up the hole with a right fancy stitch."

I had to grin at her description of the imminent operation. Over the years, I had patched up cowboys on many an occasion. During cattle drives, young drovers would get knocked off their mounts, half-trampled by skittish cattle, or shot up while on a drunk in some wild and wooly town. I was no stranger to fishing around for a hunk of lead in a man's flesh. Not that I ever looked forward to it, however.

Mister Brewster gritted his teeth and groaned some as I fished around to find the bullet. I got it out with a minimum of damage to his muscle tissue, but there was blood aplenty, and I was seriously thinking of cauterizing the wound instead of sewing him up. But Mrs. Brewster shouldered me aside just as I finished and began cleaning the wound with a hot cloth and some sort of foul smelling salve. She already had the needle in hand and the thread strung, ready for the task at hand. I decided not to push the hot poker idea, and scooted out of her way.

"Is he going to be all right?" Mattie asked, her eyes bulging at the sight. She had dutifully watched every gruesome moment with a minimum of flinching and gasping. I was proud of her. Of course, I should have expected no less of a child who'd been forced to bury her whole family.

"I think he'll be fine after a few days of healing."

"That's good," Mattie said.

When Mrs. Brewster had finished, I helped her carry him to a cot in the corner of the room. She covered him with a blanket, then turned to Mattie.

"How's your folks, child? I ain't seen them in a coon's age."

"They was both killed by them two we saw shootin' up your place. It was them Venables. Why was they here?"

Mrs. Brewster got a wistful look on her face. "The big ranchers want us off our land. They say we're interfering with their cattle grazing. Didn't seem to be of any difference that we own this land, all legal like. Told us if we didn't pack up and leave peaceable like, they'd bury us right here where we stand. Either way, we'd be gone."

"They wanted money from my pa, and when he said no, they shot him and Ma and my brother, too."

"Mercy, Mattie, I'm so sorry. You poor child."

"Mrs. Brewster, I know it probably ain't none of my business, but why haven't you called in the law? What these boys're doin' ain't legal. And a man surely can't get away with gunnin' down another soul just for refusin' to go along with such unlawful demands."

"Like they did my folks?" Mattie asked.

"Just like."

"There ain't no law hereabouts, Mister Rawhide. The closest thing we got is a constable over in Bradleyville. But he ain't got no authority outside the town. The County Sheriff never comes around except to collect taxes, and the army over in Fort Stockton has their hands full with the Kiowa and Comanche raidin' homesteads and stealin' cattle," Mrs. Brewster said.

"How about the Rangers?"

"Rangers got Comanche troubles, too," said Mrs. Brewster. "When you're out here in the middle of nowhere, you take the hand that's dealt you. We got dealt some cattlemen who don't want smaller ranches comin' in. They say it cuts down their free range, or somethin' like that. I never did understand how folks could lay claim to land they never paid a dime for."

"But you did pay for your land, that right?"

"Four sections. Got a deed and everything. Yes, sir, and we aim to stay right here. They can come with their threats and their gunslingers, but you can tell 'em for me, the Brewsters ain't leavin' without a fight," Mr. Brewster said, struggling to sit on the edge of the cot. He was pale and drawn from the loss of blood and the pain of being carved on by an amateur.

"Well, if they come back today, you can add my gun to yours."

"If you can stay awhile, I'll get some food on. I'll bet you two are hungry after your ride," Mrs. Brewster said.

"Mattie in particular. I ain't sure she's eaten anything for a week, ever since her folks were killed. And me, well, I reckon I could handle a bite, too. Thanks."

"Think nothin' of it. Sit yourselves down and tell me about what happened to your folks, Mattie."

"Did the Venables shoot your cow?" Mattie asked, not wanting to delve into her folks' killing at that moment.

"Yep, 'bout an hour ago."

"It's still fresh enough to cut a few steaks off before it goes bad. I'd be obliged if you'd allow me that task in payment for your generous offer of a meal."

"Go to it, son. You got my blessing. I only hope they didn't go down by the creek and shoot up the rest of our meager herd."

"I'll ride out and check on them as soon as I butcher the cow."

"Bless you, son."

As soon as I offered to carve up that dead cow, I regretted it. The sun was getting higher in the sky and bound to be blistering by one o'clock. I figured I'd probably melt away from perspiration before I got to eat anything, and that was the least of my troubles. Being elbow deep in blood and guts wasn't my idea of the way to enjoy the day. But I'd opened my mouth, and I couldn't turn back now. I wrapped a rope around the critter's hind legs, tied it to my saddle, and dragged it to the barn. I threw the rope over a beam and then hauled the cow up with Chigger's help. Once up, I removed the hide and bled her so the meat would taste better and last longer. As soon as I began to quarter the beast, I was joined by an inquisitive Mattie, who squatted in the dust nearby, sighed, and appeared ready to add to my torment with more questions than I knew I'd have answers for. But, my first assumption proved in error, as she surprised me with a completely unexpected conversation.

"Mister Rawhide, what's going to happen to me?"

"What do you mean?"

"I mean since my house has been burned down, and my pa and ma are dead, where'll I go. What'll I do?"

I was right about being stumped by her questions, but not in the way I'd figured. True, I had no real good answers, but these were serious questions and deserved a thoughtful answer. Right then, I didn't have one.

"You surely don't think I would abandon you to the wolves, do you?"

"No, but you could ask the Brewsters to take me in, or give me to some family in Bradleyville."

"In the first place, it looks to me like the Brewsters have their hands full just takin' care of themselves, especially if they have to live with the constant threat of being run off or shot by the Venables."

"Does that mean you aren't going to ask them to take me in?"

"That's what that means."

"What about when we get to Bradleyville? You thinkin' of givin' me to a Chinaman or something?"

"A Chinaman? Whatever gave you such an idea?"

"That's what my pa always said whenever I'd do something he didn't like. He'd say, 'Mattie, if you don't behave, I'm going to sell you to the first Chinaman who stops by.'"

I nearly burst out laughing at her imitation of her father's voice, but controlled the impulse.

"I assume no Chinaman ever stopped at your ranch."

"I reckon not, although I never was real certain I'd know one if he did."

She was a pleasant, if inquisitive, little girl, with a dimpled smile, and eyes that flashed with a certain youthful wisdom. I had to chuckle at her innocence. But I could see the point she was trying to make. I was an itinerant cowpoke, without much prospect for gainful employment, and probably by any legal standard, not fit to be a guardian of a twelve-year-old. And yet, I could feel myself growing fond of her. And she was clinging to the only hope she saw at the time for her future: me.

Just then, Mr. Brewster appeared in the doorway. He was pale and unsteady, but at least he was standing. His voice was weak and raspy.

"Mister Rawhide, could you come closer for a moment. I don't think I can make it out there."

I was glad to put down that skinning knife, if only for a brief time.

"Yes, Mister Brewster. How can I help?" I got up and met him at the door. He turned to go back inside, nearly losing his balance in the process. I grabbed his arm and guided him to an old rocker. "What is it I can do for you?"

"You done more'n a man could ask already. I'm downright grateful you come along when you did. I doubt I'd still be alive if you hadn't."

"Happy to be able to lend a hand, Mister Brewster."

"Call me Joshua. My wife is Anna. I figure with all we owe you, we ought to be callin' one another by our Christian names."

I reached over to shake his good hand. His grip was surprisingly strong for having gone through what he had endured in only a few short hours.

"We'll be sittin' down to dinner in a few minutes, Mister Rawhide. You two best be washin' up," said Anna.

I acknowledged her invitation and motioned for Mattie

to follow me outside to the well. When we got there, a ceramic bowl, towel, and a bar of soap sat on a sideboard. I drew a bucket of water and poured some in the bowl.

"Get to scrubbin' those dirty paws of yours, Mattie."

She scowled at me, then gingerly dipped her hands into the water, drew them out rapidly and grabbed the towel. I stopped her before she could soil the towel with hands that looked like they hadn't been washed in years.

"What'd you do that for?"

"See that bar of soap? Do you know what that's for?"

"Yeah."

"Use it. Soap up good and get some of that grime off. Then you can wipe on the towel."

"But—"

"But nothing. The Good Book says that cleanliness is next to Godliness. It's true."

"I suppose that means I gotta wash my hands?"

"That's exactly what it means, young lady."

"That book of yours sure does seem to have a lot of rules," she grumbled. She did as she was told, however, and we went back inside to be greeted by the delicious smell of fresh-baked bread and the sizzle of beef frying in a skillet.

We had no more than sat down than Mattie stood up, placed a hand on the table, leaned over and reached across to stab a piece of bread with her knife. I grabbed her thin arm, and gently pulled her back. She gave me a questioning frown. Anna Brewster came to my rescue.

"We say grace around our table before we eat, Mattie. I think that's what Mister Rawhide was suggesting," Anna said.

"Who's Grace?" said Mattie, looking at me like she was caught in the middle of a tug-o-war.

"Grace is when we give thanks to God for his goodness and love. And for the food he has provided."

"He didn't provide nothin' that I can see. Miz Brewster done it. I saw her."

"Yes, child, but if it weren't for the Lord, we wouldn't be able to grow our food, and if he hadn't sent you two here just when he did, we'd likely have both perished. You're here because that was God's will."

"I don't reckon I understand, but could somebody go ahead and say that grace thing so we can eat? I'm starved near to death."

We all three chuckled as Joshua Brewster made short work of saying Grace. Mattie's lessons in religion were coming faster than she could digest them. But as soon as she was let loose, she devoured meat, bread, and a bowl of beans faster than a fella could say howdy.

Chapter 4

After we'd finished eating, and I was full almost to bursting, Joshua leaned forward on his one good arm and looked at me with sorrowful eyes. Anna saw this and said she and Mattie would clear the table, while the men folk talked. Mattie groaned at the thought of being roped into washing dishes or something equally as disgusting, but she followed Anna to the back porch where a large copper tub sat on a short harvest table. I overheard Anna tell Mattie to crank up a bucket of water from the well to heat over the fireplace.

"Mister Rawhide, I owe you my life, and I ain't about to forget it. I can see you're down on your luck and I'd like to help out. Although I ain't got any money, I can feed you for a spell, give you two a place to rest your weary bones."

"That's real generous of you, Joshua. But I was raised not to accept handouts. I'll eat your food but only in exchange for work."

"Don't hear that kind of talk from many young people, nowadays. Stirs the soul, it does. All right, I reckon we can dig up a few chores that could use some attendin' to. Why don't you put your blankets in the shed. You should be comfortable there till we can figure out somethin' else. The child can sleep in here with us. How's that sound?"

"You got yourself a cowhand, Joshua. Now where can I find your herd?"

"Don't rightly have what you could call a herd, Mister Rawhide, more like a flock."

Since the only critters I ever heard of that came in a flock were sheep, I sat stunned by the revelation. I could only hope Joshua didn't hear my groan. I hated sheep. The smell, probably from that oily stuff they got in their wool, and when it's time for sheering. What a nasty chore. While I'd never done it, myself, from everything I'd heard, sheering had to be tough work. What had I gotten myself into? It was awhile before I could speak.

"Uh, where would I find this, er, flock, Joshua?"

Just over the rise to the back. That is, if them Venables didn't find them on their way out of here. They'd have shot 'em down out of pure spite. Evil men, they are."

"I'll have to agree with that. I reckon I'll go outside and finish cuttin' up your milk cow. Too bad they shot her." I got up from the table while Mattie and Anna went back and forth, clearing the dishes and washing them up. I was happy to see Mattie busying herself with something besides worry and the thoughts of her family lying dead no more than five miles away.

"I got a couple of goats tied up out back, so I reckon we'll be drinkin' goat's milk for a while. You ever had goats milk?"

"Can't say that I have, Joshua. Taste much different than a cow's milk?"

"Well I will say a body needs to acquire a taste for it. Once done, though, it's fine."

First sheep, and now goat's milk. I was beginning to feel like I'd ridden into some strange foreign land. And it looked like I'd have to acquire a taste for more than just milk from a cantankerous goat that'd just as soon eat the pants off me as sit still for a milking. I suspect my attitude was showing as I sauntered outside to commence my task.

They had a barn of sorts, although it was obviously meant as a temporary structure. The side slats were far enough apart to let birds fly through without hitting a thing. Joshua had some hay stored in there, a few tools, and a single bottom plow and harness. I saw no signs of a horse, so it was hard to imagine just how he expected to even plow up a garden. Glancing about, it was obvious he didn't. What little garden I saw had been hand dug with a spade, broken down with a hoe, and then raked smooth. For feeding only two people, it probably worked reasonably well. But with four mouths to feed, even for the short time we'd likely be under the Brewster's roof, it appeared to me that the pickings could get mighty slim in a very short time.

I returned to carving out some steaks from the cow's hindquarters. We could let them age for a couple days wrapped and hanging in the barn, or salted down in a large wooden barrel I found sitting idle in the corner. I cut lots of strips for drying into jerky. I also cut some meat up in smaller pieces for stewing. As I wiped perspiration from my forehead, I saw Mattie coming out the door.

"I'll bet Anna liked having your help cleaning up."

"Yeah, I suppose. I had to help my ma so it wasn't anything new. I don't mind, not really. Ma kept saying I'd better get used to it, like it or not, because it was women's work. And someday, I'd be a woman."

"Your ma was right. You'll be a woman, and it won't be that long, either. Why I know girls who have married at sixteen or seventeen. Four or five years from now and you'll be swamped with boys wantin' to marry up with you."

"What if I don't want to, get married, that is?"

"It'll be your choice. No one else's. Your life is yours to live any way you want."

She seemed to accept my answer with a glad heart, but I could see she was quickly conjuring up another set of questions for me. Even though I was almost done with the cow, I tried to look very busy hoping that would deter her from distracting me. It didn't work.

"Mister Rawhide, how long do you figure we'll be stayin' on here?"

I muttered something about having to think on it, and kept on carving out those steaks.

"If we was to leave too soon, wouldn't the Venables try to run the Brewsters off their place again?"

"I reckon that's a possibility, but we can't stay forever. One of these days, Joshua will be able to get back to work and there'll be no need for an extra hand, and two more mouths to feed."

She mulled that over for a minute, then said, "I think we need to find them Venables and shoot 'em. That way, nobody will have to worry about gettin' run off their place."

"That'd be against the law, Mattie, and we can't bust the law just because we don't like someone. Those boys will get their comeuppance sooner or later, without us having to gun 'em down and maybe get hanged in the process."

"Don't the law want to do what's right?"

"Of course. But they want to do it themselves, not have cowboys and little girls gunnin' folks down, even if they do deserve it."

She turned with a pensive look and started back for the house. "I s'pose, but I intend to keep my shotgun handy, just in case I run across a Venable."

I didn't say it, but I felt the same way.

Saving Mattie

* * *

The next morning I awoke to the sound of Anna Brewster drawing water from the well. I rolled out from under my blanket, yawned, and pulled on my boots. I tucked in my shirt and came to the door of the shed.

"Good mornin', Anna."

She acknowledged my presence with a smile and a nod. She poured the water into a bucket and struggled with it, water sloshing from side to side, as she walked back to the house. Before she went inside, she turned to say, "Breakfast in about ten minutes. Don't be late."

Unless there was a band of Comanches between me and that food, she could count on my being on time. I went over to the tub where Anna and Mattie had washed the dishes the evening before and poured some water into a bowl to wash up. I picked up a bar of lye soap, smelled it, then replaced it where I'd found it. I figured water doesn't really need any help from such foul smelling stuff, as I splashed some on my face. The water was cold, but it felt good to be clean again. Cowboys aren't known for their cleanliness, and I didn't figure it was any different with me. I'd been on the range most all of my life, at least from the time I left home at sixteen or so. Of course, I couldn't let Mattie know that I held her up to a slightly different standard.

I remember my ma standing over me with a hickory switch, telling me that the next time I came to her table looking like I'd been wallowing with the pigs, she'd whip me to within an inch of my life. I didn't like all that soap and water, but I favored no whipping even more.

After breakfast, I headed out to find Joshua's flock of sheep. I saddled Chigger and mounted up. Joshua came outside and pointed in the general direction where he hoped

I'd find them. He handed me a burlap bag about a quarter full of something that smelled strangely like some of what I'd cut off that dead cow.

"Here, take this out to George."

"George?"

"You'll meet up when you find the flock."

I shrugged my acceptance, as he obviously wasn't going into any further detail. I urged the mare to a trot toward a low hill line to the north. We'd gone about a mile when the unmistakable sound of sheep reached my ears. Just over a rise I looked down on about fifty of the wooly critters. They appeared safe. The Venables hadn't found them. If they had, there would undoubtedly be a lot of carcasses spread out all over the grasslands. I went down to take a look at my new charges. Chigger balked at wading in amongst them, so I dismounted and led her through the flock. The sheep seemed unperturbed by our presence, staying close together as they cropped the grass. The area they were in appeared to be as safe as anywhere, and they were a little farther from the main house than I felt prudent. But since I knew little or nothing about sheep, I figured Joshua knew best.

All of a sudden, I saw a black and white blur coming around the flock. At first I thought it might be a wolf, or maybe a Comanche stalking his next meal. I was surprised to see that it was a dog that seemed to be taking responsibility for keeping the sheep together. The dog was in almost constant motion as he was instantly alert to any individual sheep wandering away from the rest, nipping at the heels of any that were obstinate, and barking at any insubordination he perceived. I'd seen herding dogs before, but not this well trained. I stood watching in fascination as he worked the flock. Then it hit me. This busy mutt was George. I called his name. He stopped dead in his tracks, then cautiously began to come

Saving Mattie

toward me. I leaned down and opened the bag. Looking inside, I found I had been right about what I'd been carrying. It was packed with scraps of meat from the cow carcass. George sniffed the bag, then dragged some chunks out on the grass and began gnawing on it. I don't know whether I'd just made a friend or not, but it was clear he was hungry.

From all the stories I'd heard about the problems caused by herds of woolies cropping the grass to nothing and pulling it out by the roots so it wouldn't grow back, I was surprised at seeing no evidence of such behavior. Maybe all those tales were just to give cattlemen an excuse to drive them off the range. If the Venables ever caught wind of their presence, though, I knew Joshua would be in for the fight of his life, if he wasn't already. And I figured I might be in it with him if those rowdies decided to return any time soon.

I sat in the grass on the side of a low hill and watched as the sheep lazily wandered around, nipping grass here and there, then occasionally stopping to lie down or wander off on their own until the dog, George, came to chase them back into the fold. It was peaceful and quiet. The sky was full of large white clouds that signaled a possibility of rain soon. The smell of moisture was making the air heavy. Rain would be more than welcome as the weather had been dry and hot for too long. A creek barely trickled along around the bases of the intermittent hills, the only evidence of moisture anywhere. I walked down and held my canteen under the surface for a minute, then lifted it to my mouth. The water was cool and clear. From somewhere nearby I heard the distinctive sound of a mule baying. I mounted Chigger and went off to see where the sound was coming from. Around a hill I found a white-faced mule tangled up in some barbed wire that had been ripped from its posts and trampled into the dirt. It looked like the Venables had taken their vengeance out on some of Brewster's fencing around a field of about twenty acres of corn. Brewster had obviously put up the fence to keep cattle from either eating or trampling his crop. I looked to see how much fence was down and saw it would take a couple days to get enough of it back up to be useful.

    I knew why the cattlemen didn't want smaller ranchers coming in and fencing off range they had considered theirs to use free and clear, even if they held no title to it. They ran large herds of longhorns, fattening them up on government land, then driving them to markets like Abilene or Fort Worth. There was a big profit to be made, especially if the cattlemen had only the expense of hiring cowboys to keep rustlers away. They often considered these smaller ranchers no better than rustlers, since sometimes a yearling might wander into another herd before it could be branded. It didn't happen often, and the small rancher could avoid trouble by fencing off some land if he had only a small herd himself. This practice made the big ranchers a mite hard to get along with. That seemed to be what was happening with Joshua Brewster and the Venables. I knew I couldn't just stand by and let a couple of greedy hotheads kill another family just so they could keep getting free grazing. Brewster said he paid for his land. Had a bill of sale, and all. I hadn't seen it, but I didn't figure he would lie about a thing like that.

Chapter 5

After freeing the mule from its barbed wire trap, I rode back to the Brewster house, leading the stubborn animal behind on a rope. Its balkiness wasn't lost on Chigger who seemed to have little patience with half-breeds with an attitude. The mare lurched forward several times whenever the mule decided it was time for a rest. The mule complied grudgingly by letting out a hee-haw every now and then.

When we got to the house, Joshua was sitting on the porch, half asleep in a rickety rocker that he had adapted from a handmade ladder-back. He looked up and waved weakly. I still held the rope leading the mule.

"Where would you like this grumpy old fleabag, Joshua? I found him all wound up in a tangle of wire. I figure the Venables pulled down some of your fence when they left, and your mule got himself caught up."

"Glad you found him. Thanks for bringing him in safe and sound. Be obliged if you'd put him in the corral behind the barn."

I complied with Joshua's wishes and returned a few minutes later to find Mattie standing on the porch, too. She was wearing one of those wistful, distant looks I'd seen on the faces of females before. Only thing was, she seemed a little young to be caught up in such thoughtful meanderings. Although, I reckoned it had something to do with losing her family, and all. I probably would have worn some of my feelings on my shirtsleeve, too, if I'd been through what she had.

"I coulda gone with you, Mister Rawhide. Maybe you coulda used some extra help," she said, almost pleading, and obviously bored with helping out in the house.

I leaned forward in the saddle, stacked my hands, and frowned a bit at my failure.

"I probably could have, at that, Mattie. I'm sorry I didn't think about it earlier, but I wanted to get a look at the woolies, make sure they were still on one piece. Reckon I was in too much of a hurry."

"What are 'Woolies?'"

"Sheep. Haven't you ever seen a sheep before?"

"Once, I think. But I never heard them called anything other than sheep."

"Well, the cattlemen call them woolies because they are, well, wooly, and that's where we get our wool for clothing."

"Oh."

She started tapping her toe and looking around as if she were growing quite impatient for some reason. Maybe young girls get bored easily. I had no idea what went through a young girl's mind, since I didn't even know one before meeting up with Mattie Slaughter. And I hadn't learned a whole lot from her. I figured I would if I hung around her much longer.

"Say, Joshua, George sure is a handy fella to have around. He keeps those sheep in line like they were his own personal property." Joshua nodded. But I'd gotten Mattie's attention.

"Who's George?"

"George is a sheep herdin' dog. Black and white and fast as the wind."

"Can we go see him, Mister Rawhide, please?"

"I don't see why it'd hurt anything. Come on, let me pull you up behind me and we'll go check him out."

She wasted no time bounding off the porch, running up to me with her arm outstretched. I pulled her up and told Joshua we'd be back in about a half hour. He just nodded, again, like we were wearing him out with too much conversation. We rode across country since there was no trail leading out to where the sheep were held in the shelter of several low hills that formed a kind of natural corral. That was probably why the Venables had missed them when they rode off.

I caught a whiff of the musky odor of the oil in the sheep's wool just as we topped one of the hills. Mattie's eyes grew wide at the sight of all those sheep, like cotton balls in a field of green, and a little black and white dog skulking around the periphery of the flock.

"Is that George?"

"Yep. George the sheepherder."

"Can I go see him?"

"Don't see why not." I eased her off the saddle and she wasted no time heading for the dog, almost as soon as her feet touched the ground. George slunk low to the ground, checking Mattie out to see if this strange little human could be trusted near his flock.

"Don't run up on him, Mattie. Stop where you are and sit down. Then call his name. He'll have to warm up to you until he knows you're a friend. Sorta the same as it is with people."

She stopped, curled her legs under her and called him.

At first he was hesitant, then slowly he eased closer, sniffing to see if the air carried any smells of danger. She waited patiently for him to get close enough to pet. I dismounted and walked over to where she sat and bent down, holding out my hand. He sensed I was the same one who'd brought him food earlier and he accepted my gesture eagerly. When he was close enough to run my hand over his head, he sat down. Mattie gently placed her small hand on his head and began stroking him. She was grinning from ear-to-ear as if she'd just discovered some lost treasure. George seemed to appreciate the attention. She looked over at me and gave me a look of satisfaction. The pact of friendship between girl and dog had been sealed.

"Doesn't he get lonely out here all day by himself?"

"I don't know. I haven't had a chance to ask him." I had to chuckle at my own wit. Mattie frowned thoughtfully.

"What does he do with them at night? They can't stay out here, can they? Wouldn't some wild animals eat them?"

Now it was my turn to frown. I hadn't really considered that. It was a good question, though. Then, a disquieting thought occurred to me. Was Joshua expecting *me* to camp out here at night to watch over the woolies? If so, my departure might be sooner than I thought. I had no intention of bedding down with a flock of sheep. As we sat in the peaceful afternoon sun, Mattie joyfully petted George, while I chewed my lip, figuring I'd better get straight with Joshua just what my temporary duties might be.

My thoughts drifted to the Bible stories I'd read about shepherds herding their sheep around with a staff to ward off predators, like wolves or wild dogs, and such. A picture popped into my head of me in a long robe poking and prodding at a bunch of sheep, trying to get them to do my bidding, chasing after those that failed to have the same respect for a human that they seemed to have for George, tripping over the hem of the robe and falling flat on my face. I popped out of my mental wanderings, suddenly quite thankful for the little black and white dog that lay at our feet.

Watching as Mattie buried her fingers in the dog's soft fur, I couldn't help wondering what was going through her mind at that moment, too.

Mattie was quiet as we rode back to the house. But I could feel her young mind swirling with thoughts. I wanted to ask her if she'd ever had a dog, but didn't want to upset her if, sometime in the past, she'd tragically lost a furry friend. I couldn't explain it, but I was growing quite protective of this little girl's feelings. As we pulled up in front of the house, she slid from the saddle, landing on the ground in a dusty cloud, and scampered into the house. Almost before the door slammed behind her, I could hear her jabbering to Joshua and Anna about George. My fears had been for nothing.

After unsaddling Chigger, I determined to hitch up my britches and head inside to have a little heart-to-heart with Joshua about sheep. I hung my slouch hat on a peg by the door. Anna was just putting some bowls on the table filled to the brim with something that smelled mighty good. It's difficult to have a serious conversation while your mouth is watering. Sheep talk would have to wait.

After finishing, I asked Joshua if we could step outside for some conversation. He nodded agreement and I helped him out the door and to the rocker on the porch. He sat back with a groan. The pain hadn't left him, yet. And probably wouldn't for a while.

"Joshua, I been meanin' to talk to you about those sheep.

The Good Book speaks a heap about sheep and shepherds and all, but the truth is, out here, the cattlemen don't like them. They'd just as soon shoot 'em as see 'em, and that's a fact. I wonder if they might be a part of your trouble with the rancher that the Venable boys work for."

"Can't say one way or the other. Fact is I've never spoken to Emmett Bradley, himself. He always sends around his hired hands to do his dirty work. Don't know whether he even knows about the sheep," said Joshua. "What I can't figure out is why he wants us off our land. We aren't in his way, and we don't free range what few cattle we got."

"Maybe he just figures he was here first and that gives him some sort of special rights."

"Hmm. Could be, I s'pose. I ain't sure a man should have a special right to kill folks, though. Take for instance Mattie's family. They never did anything to rile Bradley. Kept to themselves, and didn't take more'n they'd paid for. Bradley's the one who's spread out all over hell's half acre, and ain't never paid a dime for it, neither."

"Maybe there's some reason we don't know about," I said. I suppose I was frowning a bit because Joshua looked at me funny.

"What else could there be? None of us small ranchers got anything more'n you can see just standin' here."

"How many cattle do you figure Bradley is running?"

"Don't know for certain, mind you, but it's in the thousands, likely ten or more." Joshua looked at me as if to ask why I'd want to know that.

His uncertainty was as good an insight into Bradley's reasoning for wanting the prairie all to himself as anything I'd heard so far. With that many head of beef on the hoof, the cattleman's got a big investment to preserve. And when a man is greedy, it doesn't take a lot to make him lash out at anyone whom he figures might be placing his investment at risk. The problem with that thinking is that no one has the right to take another man's rightfully owned property, and certainly not a life. Greedy men are not known for exhibiting a high degree of moral behavior, however.

Now, here I was, unable to do anything but watch over a bunch of sheep till Joshua heals up enough to take care of himself, and even then I couldn't be sure he could defend himself with no help but a woman and a little girl. My hand seemed to have been dealt.

It was at that moment that I took it into my mind to go to Bradleyville to see for myself what these Venables looked like up close, and maybe gain some insight into what made Emmett Bradley so all-fired ornery. If it came to a showdown between them, and me, well that's a chance I'd have to take. I could only hope it would be worth it, whatever the outcome. But before I could put my plan into words, let alone any action, we were joined by Mattie with a proposition of her own. She stood off to one side where she had a good view of both Joshua and me.

"I been thinkin' on something,' Mister Rawhide. I figure it's time we look up them Venables and have a face-to-face talk." She stood straight with her hands on her skinny hips. Her lower jaw was set and her brow furled as if some very deep thoughts lurked therein.

I was taken aback by this child's bold willingness to face her adversary, armed with little more than determination, and an old sawed-off shotgun. And she'd probably attempt it all by herself if she couldn't find a willing companion with a similar intent. I took her stance to suggest I was expected to walk into the fiery furnace alongside her. How does an adult admit fear to a child? Since I had no previous experience with children, and in particular little girls, I felt ill equipped to deal with the situation. I had no qualms about venturing into Bradleyville alone, but accompanied by a scrawny twelve-year-old girl was an entirely different matter. I tried my best to think fast.

'Well, Mattie, I been thinkin' some on the very same idea, as well, and I think I've come up with a better solution."

"Uh-huh. I know what you're thinking.' You're about to say it's too dangerous for a girl in a town like Bradleyville, so I best stay behind till you clean up their mess, and then you'll come back here and tell me all about it. How you got to be a hero and all. Right?" Her eyes were bright with righteous indignation, daring me to deny her words. I couldn't, of course. How this spindly child could read my mind was most perplexing. Wise beyond her years was all I could think of in explanation. My words weren't easy in coming.

"Mattie, you have to understand. I can't allow you to show up in Bradleyville. Why, once those Venables come to the realization you saw them kill your family, they'd be bound to come after you before the law could lock 'em up. I'm thinkin' of you, child, and keepin' you safe. That's all."

Mattie stomped her foot, and crossed her arms. Her little mouth was set so hard you would think she had lockjaw. It was clear from her narrowed eyes and jutting chin she wasn't going to go along with my plan in any way, shape, or form. Any kind of reasonable response seemed remote at the time. We glared at each other for a time before I gave up and went to wash up for dinner.

Chapter 6

The next morning, I helped Joshua climb onto the old mule's back so we could have a look at the flock of woolies. He seemed to be feeling better, and I thought the opportunity to get him off where we could talk without Mattie overhearing, and butting in, would be a good idea. But as I was getting Chigger saddled Mattie came running out the front door waving her arms and shouting.

"Wait! Where are you going? Can I come?"

"We're going out to check on the sheep. Why don't you stay and help Anna. I know she'd like that. We'll be back in time for lunch."

"Promise?"

"I promise."

She hung her head, did a slow swing around, and went back to the house as if the weight of the world was on her shoulders. I swung into the saddle and rode off with Joshua to the grassy place he kept the flock. I looked over ever so often to make sure he was doing all right. He appeared to be bouncing back nicely, especially considering his age–which I put at close to sixty–and the severity of his wound. We rode in silence until we reached the hillocks where we could look down on his flock. We pulled up near the trees that Mattie and I had sat under while she got acquainted with George. The flock seemed to be all there and unharmed, and Joshua nodded with satisfaction.

"It looks like the Venables haven't yet discovered the flock, Joshua."

"If they had I 'spect we'd be lookin' down on a graveyard."

"I reckon the same."

He stacked his hands on the pommel and his expression turned sad.

"What is it, Joshua?"

"I ain't sure how long we can hold out here, Rawhide. Those boys will be back sooner or later for sure, probably when I'm out with what few cattle I got, or movin' the sheep to another field. Anna can't stand up to them owlhoots alone, and you'll be movin' on, so–"

"Now hold on, Joshua, I ain't said I'm leavin' anytime soon, at least not until you don't need me no more."

"And what's goin' to happen to the child? I don't rightly see how we can tend to her, and it's for sure she ain't up to a life of wanderin' from one cattle operation to the next, herdin' beeves, and such. She needs a home where she can get some schoolin' and a proper upbringing. A real home, not a blanket under the stars."

He was right and I didn't have an answer for any of it. I hadn't yet given any real thought to what I was going to do with Mattie. And it was beginning to gnaw at me.

"Joshua, I reckon I don't rightly know what the proper thing is, but I know I can't abandon her to some stranger. I'll figure it out. Might take a spell, but the answer will come to me, I know it. I have faith that it will. So, you needn't worry none about her. I'll take good care of her. You got my word on it."

He smiled and nodded, the sadness erased from his lined and weather-beaten face.

"I figured you for a stand-up sort, Rawhide. And I'm glad to know you're intendin' to do right by her. She's a sweet little thing. She deserves better'n she's gotten in this godforsaken land."

He reached out his bony hand and we shook on it. I figured I'd just made a commitment that I'd have to work on real hard to keep.

"It's comin' on lunchtime, so let's be headin' back to the house."

When we got back, Anna called out, "Vittles are on. Get washed up."

Mattie ran out to greet us.

"You're back. You kept your word."

"Didn't you think I would? I'm not in the habit of tellin' fibs, Mattie. You should know that by now."

She looked at the ground, drawing a circle in the dirt with one toe.

"How come?"

"How come what?"

"You don't tell fibs. My brother did it all the time. I think my pa even told ma a few things that weren't rightly true."

"Well, it ain't right, so I don't do it."

"How do you know it ain't right? Who does it hurt?"

I helped Joshua off the mule and held his arm to steady him till we got inside. Mattie followed along, determined to not let me get away without explaining my position on right and wrong. Joshua eased into a chair with a grunt while Anna began putting bowls on the table. I hung my hat on a peg and went out to wash up. When I returned and took a chair, myself, Mattie plopped down beside me, staring at me to let me know she was still there.

"It's right there in that book I showed you, Mattie. Tells all about it."

"The Good Book? That one?"

"Uh-huh."

"Where? Where's it say not to tell a fib?"

"It's one of the Ten Commandments."

"What're those? How come there're ten?"

"Tell you what. How about we eat first, then I'll show you in the book where it tells what the Ten Commandments are, and I'll try to explain why they're there. It ain't somethin' I can say in just one sitting, though. It's a very long story."

"I'm good at listening to stories. My ma always said so. She read to me lots." When she made reference to her ma, I could swear I saw a tear start to form, but she just sniffled once, then set to eating.

As I scooped up spoon-after-spoon of beans, and then wiped at my plate with a piece of fresh bread to soak up any left over gravy, I set to thinking about how in the world was I going to read to Mattie and make her understand all those thee's and thou's. Sometimes, I wasn't sure myself what was being said. Getting through to a twelve-year-old would be even harder. Anna saw the doubt on my face and came to my rescue.

"Mattie, somewhere in my trunk I still have a card with the Ten Commandments printed right on it. It has a picture of Moses, too. Would you like to help me find it after lunch?"

Mattie's eyes lit up at the prospect of digging around through the old wooden trunk she'd seen at the foot of Anna's bed. Then she got a puzzled look, and with a questioning frown, said, "Who's Moses?"

Anna and I looked across the table at each other for a brief moment. She grasped the complexity of teaching a child who obviously had no understanding of God or anything else of a Biblical nature. She saw, as I did, that the prospect of a quick schooling was out of the question, mainly because, while Mattie was very smart, she also questioned everything. I could see every answer providing fodder for twenty more questions. Anna once more saved me.

"Anybody want a piece of rhubarb pie? I just made it fresh this morning."

Late in the afternoon, when all the chores had been done, Mattie and Anna went rummaging through the trunk looking for the things Anna had promised to show Mattie. The young girl had never seen inside someone else's private belongings before and was giggling at almost every item Anna withdrew. The two of them had a great time, Anna reminiscing, and Mattie discovering new delights. Finally, Anna pulled out a card on which were printed the Ten Commandments. In the corner was an engraved drawing of a man in flowing robes, with a long white beard. Mattie's eyes grew wide as she noticed the stern look on Moses' face.

"He sure doesn't look friendly," she blurted out. Anna failed to keep from laughing out loud. "I wouldn't want him to be mad at me."

"I'm not sure God chose him for his looks," said Anna. She handed the card to Mattie and told her to take it to me. "Rawhide'll explain it all to you, child. Now you run along while I tidy up before supper."

Having overheard Anna's instructions to Mattie, I tried to look busy so I could put her off a while longer, not at all eager to tackle such an imposing task. But the child was so excited at the prospects of learning new things, I couldn't find it in my heart to stall further. I motioned for her to accompany me out to the porch. I drew out my black leather copy of the Bible, and we sat on the edge of the porch. She folded her skinny legs beneath her, cupped her chin in her hands and waited eagerly for me to start.

"What's that say?" she asked, pointing to the lettering on the cover.

"It says, 'The Holy Bible.'"

"I thought you said it was the 'Good Book.' You didn't tell a fib, did you?"

"No. Most everyone where I grew up called the Bible the Good Book because that's what it is. It's full of stories and history and lessons and, well, it's God's word. That's why it's called good. Because God is all that is good in the whole universe." I turned to an inside page, trying to find where I should start, when Mattie was already a step ahead of me.

"What's a uni, uh, uni—"

"Universe. That's what you see when you look up into the sky, all the stars and the moon and the sun. It goes on forever out there. There are planets and all sorts of—"

"What's a planet?"

I was in for a long, hard ride. I needed to find a way to slow this horse down.

"Mattie, I can't explain everything in the world to you all at once. It'll take lots of time to talk about, read, and understand what's in this book. It covers thousands of years, and you'll not be able to learn it all at one sitting. You'll have to be patient and hold off on some of your questions for a spell."

She gave me one of her dejected looks and shrugged her shoulders a little, keeping her inquisitive eyes directly on my face. While I was intrigued by her desire to learn, it was a bit unnerving to have her watching me so intensely.

"I understand. You go ahead whenever you've a mind to. If you like, it's okay to tell me in more than one sitting," she said quite seriously. I almost burst out laughing, but didn't because I was afraid she'd think I was making fun of her. The last thing I wanted was to do further damage to this fragile young girl.

"Maybe we should start at the beginning. Genesis tells about how the world was started and I figure if it's good enough for God to start there, it oughta be good enough for us. That all right with you?"

"Yep." She took on a very serious air about her, hugging her knees to her chest and peering over them as if to guard against any information that might not be to her liking. I wasn't all that certain how she would take the snake part, but I dove in as if it were a cool, clear pool of water on a blistering day.

I read, she listened, for nearly an hour. She asked a few questions, but for the most part she remained still and attentive. I hadn't gotten too far into Genesis when I heard Joshua calling from atop the old mule. He was returning from checking on the sheep. His voice was full of distress.

"Mister Rawhide, you gotta come quick. They done it. Them thievin' rattlers done what we was afraid they'd do. Hurry!"

I told Mattie we'd have to continue at another time. She seemed to understand as I handed her the book and rushed off to saddle Chigger. I met up with Joshua just before we reached the rise that would let us look down on the flock of sheep. He was shaking with anger, pounding the pommel, and cursing under his breath. When I reached his side, he pointed to where the flock had been grazing. There wasn't one sheep to be seen. I stood up in my stirrups and tried to look as far as I could see. There was nothing but grama grass, sagebrush, and a few scrub trees for what looked like miles. I was speechless for a minute as I tried to understand what I was seeing, or actually what I *wasn't* seeing.

"What say I ride out and see if I can pick up a trail. Maybe they just wandered off somewhere. I'll find them and bring them back, Joshua, don't you worry." I wanted to be optimistic, but I was having a hard time even convincing myself. He nodded his approval of my attempt, at least, although it was clear he wasn't much more hopeful than I was.

"Go ahead, son, you can give her a try. I'll just stay here in case I see something, myself." He seemed to slump in his saddle as if defeat and despair were his only companions. I couldn't let the old man down. Life had dealt with him harshly, and while I hoped for a miracle, I was beginning to question why God was allowing such evil to overwhelm the lives of these fine people.

I urged Chigger to a trot and followed the stream along through a tangle of bushes and cottonwoods to a place where the hills gave way to a wide, rolling green expanse. Joshua's sheep *could* have wandered out there, I supposed, but I was increasingly doubtful of finding them.

All of a sudden I spotted something that I had hoped I wouldn't find. Tracks. Lots of tracks. Horses carrying four, maybe five men, had ridden through here within the past day or so. In between the horse's trail were the prints of many sheep, enough to make up a whole flock almost the exact size of Joshua's. Clearly, his sheep had been rustled, and I figured I knew who was responsible. I knew it would be hard to break the news to the old man, as I choked back my own rage and rode back to join him, but he had to learn the truth. I hated being the messenger, though, of such bad news. Then something else struck me: Where was George? I hadn't seen anything of him.

As I rode, my anger building with every minute that passed, a plan was forming. The time had come for action. No more sitting and waiting. I meant to do something about those confounded Venables, myself, if need be, since neither the law nor God seemed so inclined.

Chapter 7

"They're gone, Joshua. Looks like several men just rode in and took 'em. I'm sorry." Joshua didn't say a word, just drooped in his saddle like a man who'd just taken a serious whupping.

I'd said all I could at the moment. The plan was still gathering momentum in my head, and needed more time to build up steam. Sometimes my ideas will take a whole week to put enough parts together to make sense, but this one was coming faster than that and I knew it. I was getting that strange feeling in my trigger finger again, like that time in Abilene when I had to exercise my Colt to the detriment of a drunken cowboy who was threatening to shoot a woman who'd dared refuse his advances on the boardwalk in front of the dry goods store. When he turned on me after I'd asked him as kindly as I could to leave off pestering the lady, his hand went for his Remington. In a blink of an eye both our fates were sealed. I reckon I became a gunslinger in many folk's eyes on that day. Of course, the drunk became a customer for the undertaker.

Saving Mattie

The sheriff ruled it a justifiable homicide, especially since the lady in question was his sister-in-law, and testified readily about my intervention, but I didn't hang around long enough to find out if the drunken stranger had any friends or relatives that might be interested in a little revenge. I hiked myself up on Chigger's back and skedaddled.

And that's how I came to be looking for a job at the Slaughter ranch the day I met Mattie. And here again, as fate would have it, it was looking very much like I had another lady in distress on my hands. I could only hope it wouldn't turn out the same as before, with one man dead in the street, and me riding for higher ground and safer surroundings. Cutting and running was not an option for me, so I figured it best to hone the edges of my plan to a fine point before committing to anything foolish or hasty. However, considering what I'd seen so far of the viciousness of the Venable brothers, I figured a little practice with my Colt might not be out of order.

The biggest problem as I saw it was what to do with Mattie while I go after the Venables? I didn't feel good about leaving her with Joshua and Anna. If they were attacked again, Mattie would again have to fend for herself, and I couldn't put her through that. This time, those rattlers might not miss. I needed to assure her safety above all else. But how?

Joshua was sullen as we approached the house. He must have been trying to find a way to tell Anna about their loss. It wouldn't be easy, especially since she'd been reluctant to come out here in the first place, or so she'd indicated on several occasions. I wanted to come up with some encouragement, but such words failed me right at that moment. As we reined in to the corral, and both dismounted, Joshua handed me the mule's reins and asked if I'd see to some food and water for the animal. I said I would be glad to.

I watched as he walked wearily to the front porch. Anna stepped out at hearing his footsteps on the creaky planking. They kept their voices low as he explained to her the likelihood that their quest to build a ranch of their own would most likely now fail. The loss of their sheep would be the final blow. They would probably have to pack up and move back to Kansas or at least somewhere east of Fort Worth. And they wouldn't have the money to buy good ground, so he'd have to find work elsewhere and work his way back up. I could tell by the slump in his shoulders that he was thinking he was too old and too tired to start all over again.

I unsaddled our mounts, fed and watered them, then wandered to the house to find Mattie. She was out back trying her best to haul up a bucket of water from the well, but finding it too full and too heavy. She was about to give up when I approached.

"Mattie, there is something we need to talk about. I need your opinion on a serious matter."

"Okay, Mister Rawhide, I'll listen just as soon as you take this bucket off my hands and take it in to Anna. She sent me out to fetch water and I think I filled it too full and now I can't get it up far enough to empty some out. Some fix, huh?"

"Yep. But we got a bigger problem than a too-full bucket." I hoisted the overflowing wooden bucket over the edge of the well and disconnected it from its rope.

"How big?" Mattie said with a puzzled look on her face. She was happy here. The color had returned to her cheeks and she seemed to thrive around a family and a home that exuded caring. I was thinking dark thoughts as I knew what I was about to suggest would be met with sorrow and a natural desire to resist. I was about to tell her we were going to leave this place. I sprung the idea on her just as we placed the bucket on the table out back, next to the washtub.

"Mattie, some bad things are happening around here. The Brewster's flock of sheep has been rustled, er, stolen, and I want to try to bring them back. That will mean I'm going to have to go into Bradleyville to try finding the Venable brothers."

"How about George? Is he okay? They didn't hurt him, did they?" The pain in her eyes was palpable.

"I didn't see hide nor hair of him. Maybe he followed to see where they took the flock. But I still have to go see for myself."

"Oh. Well, I'll just stay here with Joshua and Anna till you get back."

"Well, you see that's part of the problem. If the Venables take a notion to return here for a showdown with Joshua while I'm gone, I don't think you'd be safe. I can't let you stay."

"I'll be okay. I can take care of myself. Didn't I hold a shotgun on you until I saw that you was friendly? And don't forget, I still got that ol' gun."

"I know you do. And I figure most men would be scared to try anything with you pointin' those two fat barrels at 'em. But these coyotes aren't like most men. They're vicious animals. I'm figurin' on stoppin' them before they come back, but since I don't know where they are, I just naturally can't take any chances of you gettin' hurt. You do understand, don't you?"

Mattie hung her head. I could see a tear forming in her pretty eyes. From watching her react to what I'd told her, I could almost guarantee what her next question would be. I wasn't disappointed.

"How come this God fella that you keep talkin' about can't take care of me? If he can make a world, why don't he jus' stomp on those Venables?"

"It's not that simple, child. God takes care of us in so many ways, but he's not a gunslinger. Sometimes, there aren't any peaceful solutions to the evil that pops up every once in a while. This is one of those times. He's lettin' us handle this one ourselves. And I'm goin' to need your help. Okay?"

"O-okay." An unsure hesitation sounded in her voice. I gave her a hug and we went inside to share my plan with the Brewsters.

"Joshua, Anna, I got some talkin' to do and I'd like you to hear me out. It ain't gonna be easy for me to say."

Joshua didn't look up from his rocker. He nodded and waved a hand to indicate I was to proceed. Anna, still shaken by what Joshua had told her about their flock, took a chair across from him to steady herself. I cleared my throat and began.

"These animals have to be corralled. I don't think waitin' to see what they will do next is a good idea."

Joshua looked up. "What else can we do?"

"That's what I'm gettin' to. I figure the best thing would be for me to go into Bradleyville and look these boys up. Maybe get a handle on why they seem to have such a hatred for you small ranchers."

"Ain't no secret. They don't want us holdin' deeds to land that they used to be able to graze their cattle on for free. Fat cattle bring higher prices, and that's what it's all about. I figured you'd have seen that by now, son." He looked at me with a puzzled frown. But I wasn't through.

"Yes, Joshua. I do understand all that. But that can't be the whole of it. There has to be more. Who do they work for? And why not just offer a man a fair price for his spread and be done with it? Why, a man could slowly buy up all the land around here and end up a very rich rancher. Once he actually holds title, he wouldn't be bothered by folks movin' in."

"You're missin' it, son. Bradley don't want to *own* anything. He wants to use it for free like he's been doin' for years."

I couldn't help shaking my head. I knew the big ranches wanted free grazing, and that they would have already owned thousands of acres by now if they could have afforded it. But, to me, that wasn't the whole picture. And I had every intention of discovering what that was.

"So he hasn't ever offered to buy your land?"

Joshua stroked his chin. "Well, yeah, he did come by wantin' to buy me out, but I told him he was barkin' up the wrong tree. I didn't come all the way out here to turn around and go back, not by a long shot."

Just then Mattie spoke up. "That Mister Bradley, the one you're talkin' about, well he come by our place and talked to Pa about some sort of business, too. Pa sent him packing."

"Joshua, lay out for me where Bradleyville lies and where all the small ranches are in this area." I cleared the table so he could make a map of sorts with several saucers and cups that were setting off to one side. He rose from his rocker and came to the table, leaned over and began placing cups to represent the ranches. Then he put a plate near the edge to represent Bradleyville.

"This here is the Johnson place, then us, then the Slaughter's. Over here are the Brinegar's and the Olson's, then the Fulgate's up here." Then he sat back down and began rocking, again.

I immediately saw a distinct pattern. One that had me wondering if there wasn't a completely different reason why Bradley wanted the ranchers gone.

"Have these other ranchers had the same problems as you have?"

"Don't know, but I don't think so. Well, except for the Johnsons. Albert said he'd been offered a pittance for his land. He said he told Bradley the same as I did. And Mattie's folks, too."

I wasn't ready to carry my theory any further at the time. First, I had to let the Brewsters know what I planned to do with Mattie, and why.

"Joshua, I want to take Mattie to Bradleyville where I hope to find someone to watch over her while I try to flush out those sidewinders that are making your lives miserable. Someone has to stop them, and I think maybe I can help that along. Do you know anyone in town that might be able to take her in for a spell?"

"Oh, I'd hate to lose Mattie, Mister Rawhide. She's such a wonderful helper and a comfort to me. You know I never had any children. Mattie has sure filled an emptiness in my heart these past days. Isn't there any other way?" Anna said, barely above a whisper, her voice choked with sadness.

"I wish there was, Anna. But I think if she stays it would put an extra burden on the two of you if the Venables should come back before I get to them."

"The boy's right, Anna. We ain't gonna be able to put up much of a fight." Joshua sighed and shook his head. It hurt him to admit what he saw as his weakness: a grown man unable to protect a child from danger. I didn't see it that way, but knew I couldn't convince him otherwise.

"I reckon you're right. You always have had good instincts, Joshua, ever since we got hitched. So, what about that new preacher, Jericho Pike and his wife? They got neither kith nor kin, I hear. Maybe they'd look favorably on havin' a sweet child about for a spell."

Mattie brightened at being referred to so favorably.

"That's a fine idea, Anna. Son, you'll probably find the reverend working around the new church building. It sits at the west edge of town."

"Thank you both for understanding. I reckon we'll be lookin' to ride out early in the morning, if that's all right with you." Joshua and Anna glanced at each other, then nodded their acceptance. Anna looked away just as a tear started to fall on her cheek.

After supper, Mattie helped with the cleanup while Joshua explained the best way to get to Bradleyville, the easiest shortcut, and all the things in town to avoid, mainly the town's two saloons, which he considered evil incarnate. I asked him what he knew about this preacher and his wife and he said they were new to town, and this was likely their first church. They were young, and he seemed a little too soft-spoken for a preacher. But then Joshua allowed that his opinion might be tainted by his being raised in a hellfire and brimstone church back in Tennessee.

I tried to hold back a knowing grin, having come from a similar background myself.

That next morning, I pulled Mattie up behind me, along with her shotgun and a burlap bag Anna had given her to carry the new clothes Anna had sewn for her, and a sack lunch for when we got hungry between here and town. It smelled of fresh biscuits and salt pork. I could feel a can of pork and beans in there, too.

We said our goodbyes, wishing one another good health, and to be careful. Mattie was wistful as we rode away, looking back often to wave again and again. I'm certain Anna didn't go inside until we were well out of sight. Mattie clung to me tightly, as if I might somehow slip out of her grip, leaving her all alone in a very violent land once again.

Chapter 8

As we topped a low hillock about an hour's ride from the Brewster's place, we saw smoke rising in the west. I urged Chigger to a faster pace, fearful of what we might find. When we got to a fork in the road–what little road there was–I spotted three riders making a hasty retreat across a wide green meadow off toward the river about a mile away. But as we watched them ride off, we continued to get closer to the source of the smoke. We were soon greeted by the results of yet another attack on a small ranch house by what looked like the same men who had struck the Brewsters. And likely the same riders who had killed the Slaughters. Having Mattie see this horror all over again nearly broke my heart, yet it steeled my will to ferret out the lowlifes who preyed on others, and deal with them as harshly as they had their victims. That turned out to be the second part of my plan. The first was to get Mattie to safety.

I pulled Chigger up in front of the smoldering pile of timbers, flames still licking the branches of nearby trees, now stripped of their leaves by the intense fire. Off to one side, I spotted the body of a man face down in the dirt, a rifle several feet away. I hopped off Chigger, telling Mattie to stay where she was.

"I'm going to see if there's anything that can be done for that poor man, Mattie. You stay here on Chigger. Don't get off, understand?"

Her eyes were wide as she nodded a fearful agreement without so much as a word passing her lips.

When I reached the man, it was clear there was nothing I could do for him. He was dead from a bullet in the back. It appeared his rifle hadn't been fired. He must have seen the raiders coming and tried to get to the safety of one of the outbuildings. He'd been caught in the open.

I found a shovel and began digging a grave. Mattie remained atop Chigger watching my every move as if she was fearful that I might decide to run away and leave her. Even from twenty feet away I could see her trembling. I dug the hole and dragged the man's body to it, pushed him in, and began covering him with dirt. When finished, I patted the dirt down as much as possible, hoping some critter wouldn't come along and dig the corpse up. Then I began looking around for other victims. I found no one, so I climbed back aboard the horse, wheeled her around, and started back toward town. Mattie was the first to speak.

"That was the Johnson's ranch. Albert Johnson and his wife, Vera, live there. Don't know what they're goin' to do now, with it all burned up and all."

"I suspect it won't make any difference, Mattie. Mr. Johnson is dead. I don't know where his wife is, but it's likely she was burned up in the fire."

It was a couple of minutes before she responded. "That wasn't Mr. Johnson."

"What! Who was it?"

"My pa said Mr. Johnson had hired a man to help with his cattle. I don't know his name."

"You are sure that wasn't Johnson?"

"I said so, didn't I?"

"Yes, but you could have been mistaken. You probably didn't get a real good look at his face."

"Didn't need to."

"Oh, and why is that?"

"Pa said Mr. Johnson was in the big war. It was before I was born, you know."

"Uh, yes, I was pretty sure of that. But what difference does it make that Mr. Johnson was in the war?"

"He only had one leg. That man had two. Must have been the hired hand," Mattie said with an air of authority and satisfaction that she'd been able to tell a grown-up something he didn't know.

"I wonder where the Johnsons are, then." I reined in, stopping to consider the situation further before leaving the ranch boundary. Maybe I should go back and have a better look. There were some other buildings that had been spared. A barn, a small building probably used for smoking meat, and an outhouse. I hadn't looked in any of them. I decided to go back, just to make sure I hadn't overlooked the bodies of two more people, or maybe they were alive and needed help. This time Mattie insisted on helping me in my search.

As we wandered from building to building, I was struck by the absence of any animals, no horses, cattle, chickens, pigs. Nothing. Were they rounded up and driven off? Mattie noticed the same thing.

"They must have took off, the Johnsons I mean."

"Why do you say that?"

"When they came to visit my ma and pa, they came in a

buckboard. I don't see it anywhere. Mr. Johnson couldn't sit a horse very well, so he always used that buckboard."

"Since we haven't found any sign of either of the Johnsons, and the buckboard is gone, it seems safe to assume they left before the attack began. That's good news. Now all we have to do is find them."

"Maybe they went to town."

"Sounds reasonable. Probably needed supplies of some sort, and they left the hired hand to stay and take care of things while they were gone. That sorta puzzles me though."

"Why?"

"If it was the Venables that set the fire and shot that man down, did they wait for the Johnsons to leave before attacking? Why wait? Or did they just happen to get here while the Johnsons were away? Just by chance."

"Can't say as I have an answer for that, Mister Rawhide. But I do know I didn't see no signs of that God fella lendin' a hand at fendin' off the Venables."

"What kind of signs did you expect?"

"Seeing the Venables squashed like bugs out there in the yard, maybe."

"God doesn't work that way."

"What way does he work?"

Here I was, again, trapped by the innocent questions of a young child. Questions that had either no answer or answers that were so complex no twelve-year-old could understand were pelting me like a hailstorm. I knew I needed to respond, but I felt trapped, and totally inadequate to the task. I had no way to get through to her beyond those things I'd tried to teach her already. I wasn't the best reader and maybe my stumbling through the first few chapters of Genesis was more a confusion than a help. By most folks' standards, the Bible isn't an easy read, anyway. More than me have stumbled their way through it. And there was plenty I still didn't understand. Maybe I should have left off telling Mattie about God. How could I ever hope to explain those parts I didn't understand too well myself?

Then a thought struck me. Maybe this preacher in Bradleyville would take on the job of educating Mattie to the ways of the Lord. After all, isn't that what he'd been trained to do? That would get me off the hook, something I very badly wanted at that point. That idea was looking better and better.

We arrived in Bradleyville by mid-afternoon. The streets were mostly empty, except for a couple of wagons rumbling along straddling the ruts. I was about to stop in front of the constable's office when Mattie began tugging at my shirt.

"Mister Rawhide. He's here, and so's she. Look, over there." She pointed to three people coming out of the general store, two of them, a rangy, gray-haired, one-legged man and an older woman, were being helped with their packages by the second man.

"Who is that, Mattie?"

"Why that's Mr. and Mrs. Johnson and Mr. Barnes, the storeowner. They're okay, not shot down or nothing," she said with cheer in her voice.

"So that's not their hired hand?"

"Nope. I remember him. I'd sorta forgotten what he looked like, but now I remember. He looked like that dead fella out there at the Johnson place."

"Then it appears I'm going to have to give the Johnsons the bad news about the man with the bullet in his back that I buried at their ranch."

"Uh-huh. Let's go say hello." She ignored my obvious reluctance as she slipped from the saddle behind me and dropped to the ground. She scampered across the street and ran up to Mrs. Johnson. They gave each other a hug. Mr.

Johnson leaned on a crutch under his left shoulder, his left leg gone below the knee. Right about then is when I decided I'd better introduce myself and give the Johnsons the bad news, of which I figured they were not as yet aware. Not much sense in buying all those supplies if folks don't have a house to put them in.

I marched across the street, extended my hand to Mr. Johnson, and tried my darnedest to look cheery, even though I was anything but.

"Mr. Johnson, my name is Smith, Rawhide Smith. I'd like to talk a spell if you've got a minute. I think you're going to want to hear what I have to say. Can we step aside for a little privacy?"

While he looked slightly taken aback at my boldness, he nodded and we moved the few steps to the corner of the store, just out of earshot of Mattie and Mrs. Johnson. The man Mattie had identified as the storeowner, Barnes, continued to load items onto the buckboard.

"Well, Mr. Smith, just what is it you wanted to say?"

"Me and Mattie was ridin' to town when we saw smoke comin' from up ahead. When we got to where we could see what was burning, Mattie said it was your ranch house. There were some men ridin' hell bent for leather off to the west, probably trying to get away before they were seen. I'm afraid we got there too late to save anything. The house burned to the ground. I'm real sorry."

Johnson looked stricken. He swallowed hard before he spoke, steadying himself on the porch post. He began shaking his head.

"Them lousy vipers. It looks like they did just what they said they'd do if I didn't clear out. Vera's gonna be heartbroken. What'll we do now?"

He looked like he was trying to find a place to sit before

he fell down from the shock of it all. I guided him to a long bench outside the gunsmith's shop next door. He dropped heavily onto the rickety wooden seat, his crutch more hindrance than help at that point. I sat beside him.

"Mr. Johnson, I'm afraid I've got some more bad news."

"Good heavens, man, what could be worse than losing one's home?"

"I buried a man back there at your place. He'd been shot in the back. Mattie said it looked like a man you have working for you?"

"Oh, no. Not Morales. Are you sure? Who shot him?"

"I have no idea. We didn't get a real good look at those that burned the place, either. Just their backs. The dust they were kickin' up pretty much gave them cover for a clean getaway."

"I-I don't rightly know what we're goin' to do, now. Everything we owned was inside that house. Built it myself, one leg and all. And Morales, he was a hard workin', honest man. Wouldn't hurt no one. I'm goin' to miss that good-natured Mexican." The man's deeply lined face, darkened from years of exposure to sun, rain, and wind, turned even more dour as he considered his prospects. He clearly had no answers to his own questions.

"I wish I had been closer when it happened. Mighta been able to stop 'em. Same thing happened to the Brewsters, but then I *did* show up in time to help drive off the varmints."

"You say they hit the Brewsters' place, too?"

"Yep. 'Bout a week ago."

"How do you happen to have Mattie Slaughter with you. Why ain't she home with her folks?"

"When I rode up to the Slaughter spread, I was confronted by Mattie with a shotgun. I was looking for work. When she said her pa didn't need any help, I asked if I could speak to him, myself. That's when I saw the three graves that poor child had dug for her family. She said it was the Venable brothers that done it. Killed her folks and her brother. She had been down at the creek when they struck or she'd also be dead. I just naturally figured it was better for her to come along with me than stay out there by herself with no one to care for her."

"Well, you figured right, son. I reckon I better talk to the constable about this, not that he'll do a blamed thing. He'll say it ain't his problem if it's outside the town limits. He'll say the closest law is fifty miles away and not likely to have the time to make it over here."

"We could ask him to send a telegram to Fort Stockton, get the army to take a look, or get a U. S. Marshal from Fort Worth, or—"

"You'd be wastin' your breath. Constable Emory is in Emmett Bradley's hip pocket, and he ain't goin' to do anything to jeopardize that situation," Johnson said.

"Do the Venable brothers work for Bradley?"

"Yep. They do his bidding, every bit of it. They were hand-picked for their gun hands."

"Maybe my idea of bringing Mattie here wasn't such a good idea. If Bradley finds out she saw his men kill her parents, even a crooked constable would have a hard time looking the other way."

"Don't you worry about him hearing it from me or Vera. I'll not let a word slip. And you're right. Her life wouldn't be worth a plug nickel if word got out. What do you figure to do with her?"

"I was hoping the preacher and his wife might take her in for awhile, at least until I can find out for sure that Bradley is behind all these raids on the local ranches. Maybe I can convince a marshal to take a closer look."

Johnson sat studying the street. When he tried to stand, I gave him a lift. He stuck his crutch under his arm and started to hobble toward where his wife awaited him in the buckboard. He turned back to me with a look of defeat on his face.

"I admire your good intentions, young man, but you're just battin' at flies. No good can come of it. These are very bad people in this town. Watch your back at all times."

"I will, sir. What will you do now?"

"Got no other place to go. We'll just have to try rebuilding what we can. Maybe we can salvage something."

"It appeared the barn and a shed were still sound."

"Thank the Lord. That's a start. We'll stay in town for a couple days, then I hope we can go back home."

"After I get Mattie settled, I'll try to ride out your way, maybe give a hand, if that's all right." Yet I didn't know what my future held any more than Johnson did his.

"You'd be welcome, son. Just don't come draggin' any of Bradley's hooligans along behind you. I still got my shotgun and I know how to use it. I didn't lose my leg fallin' out of a tree, you know." He winked at me as he went to give his wife the bad news.

Chapter 9

It was heartbreaking to watch as Mr. Johnson broke the news to his wife. She buried her face in his chest and cried bitterly. I couldn't blame her. I kind of felt like shedding a couple of tears for them, too. But as I looked to Mattie, I was surprised at what I saw in her face. It was as if all the horrible things she'd witnessed and suffered from over the past few weeks had done something to her soul, emptied it of sorrow, replacing it with quiet, but perceptible, desire for vengeance. Too young, I thought, way too young to be plotting the demise of a few evil characters instead of embracing the joys that come with being young.

Vengeance is mine, sayeth the Lord. Those words chased around inside my head over and over like a wild mustang in a box canyon. It was one of the most powerful passages I remember my ma reading to me when I was Mattie's age. I broke that rule a couple of years back, when I was just twice Mattie's age, and I wasn't proud of it. I've struggled with the consequences of taking a life ever since. But being haunted by those dark thoughts at twelve, well, I couldn't get a handle on that. I felt an immediate need to get Mattie to a safe place where she was out of range of all the devilry being perpetrated by someone right here in Bradleyville. I was beginning to see her security as my job, since no one else seemed to be volunteering, and the law hereabouts didn't appear to have much of an interest in righting the wrongs, either.

We said goodbye to the Johnsons and wandered off to find the church. Joshua had said it sat at the end of the main street, so it didn't seem likely to be too hard to locate. And it wasn't. Just as directed, we found a white clapboard chapel with a cross on the top tucked into a small grove of trees just around the corner at the end of the street. A tall man, with his shirtsleeves rolled up, was sweeping the steps out front. His face was thin, but pleasant, and his nose kinda reminded me of a bent stick. He looked up as we approached.

"Good day to you folks. Welcome to the Bradleyville Church. Won't you come in?" He stopped his sweeping and waved us on by and into the sanctuary.

As much a believer as I was, I had to admit my attendance in church was spotty at best. It's not that I never had an opportunity; it was just something that never seemed all that convenient. After working hard six days a week, I reckon I wanted to catch some extra sleep, as if I could catch up on whatever I'd lost during the week. I never figured goin' to church, in itself, would make me more of a believer. My ma thought differently, however.

The church was brightened by several windows along the sidewalls, and the inside, while small, felt comfortable. I had my doubts about those hard wooden benches, however. The man reached out to shake my hand. I returned the gesture.

"Name's Pike, Jericho Pike. I'm the minister here. And who might you folks be?"

"I'm Rawhide Smith, and this here young lady is Mattie, uh, Jones. I'm here to talk to you about her, if you've a few minutes. The story is rather involved." Mattie looked at me quizzically, but said nothing.

I had to admit, my last minute decision to withhold Mattie's real last name was awkward at best. But if word got out that a Slaughter had survived the attack, her life would be in immediate danger. Jericho Pike looked at me questioningly, then suggested we walk over to the parsonage next door, a two room bungalow. I agreed and we followed him to his house. As we entered, I saw a small woman, with dark hair pulled back into a bun, sitting in a chair darning what appeared to be a rather holey sock, which I assumed belonged to the preacher. I thought of my own socks and how I, too, could use someone watching after my well-worn attire.

"Dear, this is Mr. Rawhide Smith, and his friend, Mattie Jones. My wife, Sarah." "They've come to have a word with me. I wonder if you would mind fetching some cold water for them to drink while I listen to their story?"

"Certainly, dear, I'll—"

"Actually, if it's all the same to you folks, I'd like the missus to hear what I have to say, too. That's because if you agree to my request, it'll involve both of you." He shrugged his shoulders and his wife sat back down across from us.

I began my tale starting with my arrival at Mattie's ranch way up near Fort Stockton to find her pointing a loaded shotgun at me. When I said that, Mattie's face got beat red, and all scrunched up into a puzzled frown. If I said she came from a considerable distance off, there'd be little to tie her to the Slaughter place. Once begun, I had to stick to my story, as big a fib as it was. I told myself a small lie was justified if something good came out of it.

Then I told them all about her having to bury her own

parents and her brother, and how she'd seen the killers from where she had been hiding in the bushes. I told them how I'd decided it would be wrong to leave her alone and was finally able to convince her to accompany me to wherever we could find someone willing to help look after her for a spell. I could see the preacher's wife perk up at that suggestion. She must have been way ahead of me.

When I got to our riding into an attack on the Brewster place by some renegades, Sarah Pike was sheet white and her eyes were wide with shock.

"How are the Brewsters? Will they be all right?" Pike asked.

"I can't say. Every day they stay there might be the day those rattlers return to finish the job. I left with Mattie because until the law finds out who's behind these raids. I couldn't leave her behind to face that possibility."

Pike nodded his understanding of my decision. Sarah clasped her hands to her chest, occasionally dabbing at her eyes with a dainty white handkerchief. I continued with what we'd found when we got to the Johnson spread. The Pikes knew Albert and Vera Johnson because they were members of the church. This news was particularly devastating to them. Pike looked at the floor, shaking his head.

"What can we do to help, Mr. Rawhide?" he asked.

"I was hoping you could take Mattie in for awhile. I need to do some lookin' around, ask a few questions, maybe get on with the Bradley outfit."

"Why the Bradley Ranch?"

"Because I've heard the men responsible for these raids might be two brothers named Venable. I hear they work for Bradley. Hard to imagine they could get away with these foul deeds without Bradley's knowledge."

"Hmm," he frowned and shook his head, "Mr. Bradley

has been a supporter of the church. I can't imagine him doing anything like that which you've described. I'm quite certain you're mistaken."

"Reckon I'll have to give him the benefit of the doubt until I know different. Know where I can find him?"

"Well, I believe he has an office back of the Big Eagle Saloon, which he owns," Pike said.

"You say that like you don't approve."

"Can't say that I do, but without him, this town wouldn't have grown enough to have a church. He put up the money to build it. So, I'm beholding to him for that. I just try to overlook him being a saloon owner."

"Mr. Rawhide, I don't know what my husband is thinking on the subject, but I would be delighted to have this lovely young lady in our home for as long as needs be," Sarah said. The hopeful smile on her face wasn't lost on her husband.

"Of course. No man of God could turn away a child in need. You can count on us," He echoed.

Pleased with the Pike's generosity, I was free to find the source of all the trouble being suffered by the small ranchers. Before shaking Pike's hand, I asked him to keep Mattie's circumstances quiet. I could see plenty of danger to her if the Venables put it together that there'd been a witness who could identify them as murderers. He seemed to understand.

I gave Mattie a big hug and promised her I wouldn't be far away if she needed anything. She tearfully hugged me back, clinging to my vest. When we parted, I knew she would be on my mind constantly, and a big part of my quest would be to bring her the justice she deserved.

As I sauntered through the door to the Big Eagle Saloon, the smoke was so thick I had to wave my hand in front of my face to clear a path to the bar. The bartender asked what I'd have and I asked for a cold beer. He laughed, as did two other fellows also leaning in the bar, their boots occupying the brass foot rail.

"What's so funny? The sign outside says 'cold beer' and that's what appeals to me. Can I get one or not?"

"It's obvious you're new in town or you'd know the closest thing we got to cold beer is a picture some fella drawed in a magazine." The bartender turned to point at a page that had been torn from some eastern magazine with an engraved drawing that showed a man smiling as he held up a foamy glass, saying something about it being the coldest drink north of the Mason-Dixon Line. The magazine, with its yellowed pages, appeared to be about ten years old.

"How long you had that up there?" I asked.

"'Bout as long as Bradleyville's been here, I reckon. Don't get many recent magazines here from back east, and we don't get no cold beer, neither," he added, still chuckling at my expense. "And that sign out front's older than you are, son. Came from somewhere in Missouri."

"Okay, I get the joke. I reckon I'll just have a whiskey."

He poured a glass and scooted it in front of me. "That'll be ten cents."

I tossed a coin on the bar and turned to watch the activities, at least what I could make out through the haze. I took tiny sips of the brownish liquid to keep it from burning my throat all the way to my boots. Pretty soon two men that looked real familiar came through the doors, laughing and rough housing each other as they sidled up to the bar.

"A shot of that high-falutin' whiskey, and serve it up quick, Ollie," said one of them. The way he walked, his general pushy manner, suggested he thought very highly of himself. It didn't take long to find out I was right.

From the time they came in, the one doing all the talking was busy looking important, while the other was looking at me. It appeared likely I was about to find out why as he stepped toward me.

"You look familiar. I can't place where it might have been, but I swear I've seen you before. You from around here?" he asked.

"No. I'm from about a hundred miles east. Small town. Didn't get around much. Then one day, I thought I'd go out and see the world. Saddled my horse, pointed her west, and here I am." I stopped only for another throat burning sip of whiskey. I recognized them all right.

The man squinted as he seemed to be looking me up and down. His partner stopped all his blabbering when he noticed I'd suddenly become the center of attention for his companion.

"This fella say somethin' to get you riled, Joey ?" he asked.

"Naw. It's just that he looks real familiar, that's all." The man called Joey turned back and took up his whiskey and downed it in one swig with nary a twitch. I had to admire his fortitude.

But now, his partner, the braggy one, turned his attention to me.

"You new to these parts?"

"Yep. I just rode in. I'm lookin' for work. Know of anybody hiring?"

The man stuck out his hand and said, "Howdy. My name's Venable, Willy Venable, and this is my brother, Joey. What did you say your name was?"

"I'm called Rawhide Smith. From east Texas. Glad to meet'cha." The chill that ran through me at the name Venable almost made me sick. A bitterness rose in me like bile and I had to force myself to appear even mildly amiable. But smile I did, and then we settled into a conversation about job opportunities.

"What kind of work you figure you're best cut out for?"

"Well, I'm good with horses, and I've ridden my share of drives, all the way to Abilene. So, I reckon I'd best stick with what I know best, horses and cattle."

"Sounds like good advice, Rawhide. That Colt of yours, though, looks like it ain't collectin' dust, either," said Willy.

"I take it out for a walk, now and again. Just to keep it from stiffinin' up on me."

Willy grinned and nodded. I suppose right about then he put me in the category of gunslinger, even though I was no more a gunslinger than I was a bank president. But Bradleyville felt like a town where the tough survived, and the weak didn't. This was no time to appear weak. What could it hurt to put on a little show? I figured sooner or later I'd have to brace one of these two, or both, and an edge wouldn't hurt nothing. If they figured me for a gunslinger, all the better for giving me that little edge. I've seen men backed down by no more than a reputation. Bat Masterson built a fearsome reputation on that very thing. Not that he was a fake or anything, just that he got out of more fights by virtue of what people thought he'd done, than what he actually had. Lots of gunfighters were that way. The bigger the reputation, the fewer the challenges, and the longer the life.

"Tell you what, Smith, you wait here and I'll see if Mister Emmett Bradley is interested in hiring any new men," said Willy, as he moved away from the bar and into a closed room near the back. He went inside, while his brother, Joey, the bigger of the two, continued to keep an eye on me, probably still trying to figure out where he'd seen me before. I wasn't going to let on that it had been while sighting down the barrel of a Winchester. His hand never left the butt of his Remington six-shooter. He kept on eyeing me as he sipped whiskey with his left hand. Maybe the time was right to strike up a conversation with the suspicious killer.

"So, Joey, tell me about this fella Bradley." I was careful to keep both hands on the bar, except when taking a drink, that is.

"Nothin' to tell. He owns it all."

"All of it? How can one man own everything?"

"Far as the eye can see, and then some. And if I was you, I wouldn't question it. It ain't healthy, if you catch my drift."

"What about those small ranches I saw as I was riding in?"

His hand twitched just a smidgen when my words sank in.

"If you're smart, you won't pay them no mind. In a month or so, there won't be any small ranches left."

Just then Willy Venable came back in and stood at the bar beside his brother. He looked at me with serious, intimidating eyes.

"Bradley says to come on back. Oh, he said you was to give me your gun before you go."

I slowly drew my Colt and handed it to Joey who was standing the closest. "Take good care of 'er while I'm gone." I cocked my finger and pointed it at Joey. I could have sworn he winced just a little.

Chapter 10

I knocked before entering the door at the back of the saloon. A gravelly voice told me to come in. I complied, ever bent on pleasing folks. A heavyset man sat at a desk with several papers spread out across it. His shirt was an expensive one, but it was dirty and rumpled as if he hadn't bothered to take it off for some time. A revolver lay on top of some papers where he could get to it in a hurry if need be. Since I wasn't armed, he was safe. I wasn't so sure I was, however. I knew from the first words out of his chewing-tobacco stained mouth, I wasn't going to like this fella.

"First off, what the hell's your name?"

"Rawhide Smith."

"Hmm. What kind of name is that?"

I was at a loss for an answer that wouldn't sound like a smart aleck, so I shrugged and kept my mouth shut.

"Well, don't make any difference, anyway. You any good with a gun?"

"Good as any, I reckon."

"Ever plug a man?"
"Uh-huh."
"How many?"
"I'm lookin' for a job, Mister Bradley, not signing up for a firing squad. It ain't important, at least not to me."

Bradley sat back in his swivel chair and narrowed his eyes. A sinister smile crossed his thin lips. He didn't like my answer. I didn't blame him, but I had to be careful what I said and how I said it. If I sounded like a young colt scared to leave his mama, I might as well keep on riding. And if I came off looking like some bragging gunslinger, I'd be a target before I got back to where I'd tied Chigger.

He looked at his gun, then at me.

"You'd like to make a play for this peacemaker, wouldn't you, sonny? Maybe blow my head clean off? Am I right? Probably think it'd make you a big man in the territory." His eyes went from me to the gun, then back.

"Mister Bradley, I ain't thinkin' any such thing. I'm lookin' for employment, not lookin' for a fight. A man's got to eat, and right now, that's my main priority. I got no beef with you or anyone else around here." I crossed by arms and hoped he didn't notice my hesitation at such a flagrant lie. I had plenty of anger against those two murdering scoundrels out front sucking up cheap whiskey and sounding off like they were the cocks of the walk. And I was rapidly coming to dislike this pompous toad almost as much.

"Fair 'nough. You got brass, I'll give you that. Pay's thirty a month, and board. Willy will see to it you get settled. He's in charge, so you better get used to doing whatever he says. If that don't suit you, beat it. If it does, you may take your leave and let me get back to business." At that he pulled his revolver off the table and stuck it in his belt. He picked up a deck of cards and was shuffling it when I walked out of the room. I reckoned that was the business he spoke of.

"Well, well, it appears he put you on the payroll, mister," Joey drawled, as he drew my Colt from his belt and handed it back to me, then turned to go back to his drinking.

"How did he know that?" I looked at Willy.

"You're still alive, that's how," Willy said with a sadistic grin. He gulped his whiskey and motioned for me to follow him outside. I trailed after him like a well-trained puppy. Joey stayed inside the saloon as Willy and I mounted up and headed down the wide, rutted street towards the north end of town, then we turned west. Over the hazy purple mountains in the distance I could see storm clouds building. I hoped we wouldn't be going far or we would be soaked by the time we got there. The road soon petered out and became little more than a deer trail through the waving grass.

"This ain't the main road to our spread. It's a shortcut to where you'll be bunkin'. You'll get used to it after you've gone over it a few times. We like it 'cause it's tough to track a man through," Willy said.

"You get lots of folks wantin' to track you?"

"Never you mind. It's just safer, that's all I'm saying."

I decided it was time to shut up and listen instead of asking more questions. Besides, I figure he kinda answered me, anyway, with his response.

When we came to a series of low hills, we wound through them until we came to a ridge that looked out over a wide, verdant valley filled with longhorns, thousands of them. We were headed for a lone cabin in a stand of mesquite and cottonwood nestled among the many smaller hills. One horse was tied out front. We dismounted and Willy handed me his horse's reins, jerking his thumb to indicate I was to walk them to the corral and turn them loose inside. It was too early to get sensitive about being told what to do by this rattler, so I shrugged and did as I was told. Ever the good hand, that's me.

The cabin wasn't well built, rickety by most any standards, and obviously not where Emmett Bradley himself hung his hat. This place was purely for the hired help. That fit me to a *T.*

When I returned from putting the animals in the corral, I opened the door to the one-room cabin, and shuffled inside, I saw Willy leaning over a table talking to some rough looking yahoo in a whisper. I figured it had to do with me, and probably was some sort of instruction about keeping an eye on the new guy, making sure I could be trusted. Made sense, because if they knew why I was really there, they'd know right off I couldn't be trusted, at least not to keep whatever I learned to myself. I figured to be a regular blabbermouth when it came to spilling the beans to some U. S. Marshal. And I hoped to come across one of those as soon as possible.

Willy saw me watching and pointed to a bunk where I was to put my bedroll and stuff. I was glad I had brought along my own blanket because the one on the bed looked like it had been used to clean the chimney. A square table sat in the center of the room, and a potbellied stove sat nearby with a short stack of wood piled next to it. I sat on the edge of my bunk. When Willy was through whispering to his buddy, he looked over at me as he went out.

"Get a good night's sleep, Smith. Tomorrow we visit a few of the smaller ranches around here. They're popping up like fleas on a dog. We need to make sure they don't get too settled in." The door closed behind him.

"Where's he goin'?" I asked.

"Ain't none of our business. But I hear he's got himself a lady friend on one of them ranches he was talkin' about," said the man. "By the way, my name's Jake Pardee." He stood and stuck out his hand, callused from working as a cowhand, not a gun hand.

"Good to meet you, Jake. I'm called Rawhide. You been workin' for this outfit long?"

"Ever since I got out of prison."

Jake seemed to be a reasonably decent sort, but definitely on the quiet side. Which meant he might be a difficult man to get answers from. Since he worked with the Venable brothers, it seemed likely he knew what they were up to, and why. It was important to find out the reason for their crusade to eliminate the small ranches, and whether they were doing it with Bradley's blessing. After meeting the big boss, himself, I was guessing very little went on without his knowledge and consent. But I couldn't condemn a man just because he has a reputation for being tough.

I decided to leave Jake alone for awhile and went outside to roll a smoke. I sat on the one step up to the porch, pulled a bag of tobacco from my shirt pocket, and began tapping it into a half-folded paper I drawn from the same place. I licked a line along the edge so it would stick together, then twisted the ends. It didn't turn out as slick as those new packaged cigarettes a man can buy in a store now, but not bad for a hand-rolled smoke. I struck a Lucifer and touched it to the end.

The wind had abated and brief rain showers that had gone through only an hour or so before had left the air clear and clean smelling. Bees were busy extracting pollen from the clover flowers that made a thin carpet alongside and in back of the cabin. A patch of butterfly weed peeked around the back of the cabin. Out front, nothing but rocky dirt flourished. My thoughts turned to Mattie. Was she doing okay at the preacher's house? And why was I worried? Other than the fact that she reminded me a little of myself when I was her age, we had no formal ties, not like family, anyway. But a strong impression was wheedling its way into my soul.

Somehow, Mattie Slaughter was beginning to feel very much like family. I wasn't certain what to do about it, but it felt good, rather like having a kid sister. And any brother worth his salt takes care of his little sister. No matter what.

Just then the door opened behind me and Jake came out.

"Let's get a move on, mister. We got to round up a few head of beeves over on the west quarter and move them to some new land that just opened up."

Jake lit a match to the tip of a smoke he'd just rolled, took a couple of puffs, then tossed it in the dirt and ground it out with his boot. He motioned for me to follow him. He saddled up and led the way down through the hills toward a narrow canyon with a burbling creek that meandered through the center. It had been only a slight rain shower earlier and the water was a little muddy from run-off. Calm waters now, but it would be no place to be during a rainstorm, unless you didn't mind being washed downstream like a leaf.

We rode for about an hour until the canyon walls gave way to foothills and then opened into a wide expanse of empty grazing land, empty that is except for several thousand head of bawling longhorns. I wondered if Jake was figuring on just the two of us moving all that livestock. Fortunately he answered that before I could even ask.

"We'll be cutting out about forty head and moving them through that pass off to the north." He pointed to a narrow split in the hills about two miles away.

"How come we gotta move 'em? They look pretty satisfied right where they are."

"I don't ask questions. I do as I'm told. You'd be well advised to do the same unless you want a bullet for breakfast. That's how things seem to be done around here."

I suspect I swallowed hard at the revelation that this bunch treated each other pretty much the same way they treated the surrounding ranchers. I didn't see this as long-term employment.

"How long have you been with this outfit, Jake?"

"Long enough to know how to keep my business to myself." He yanked his reins hard to the right and I followed him in-trail down a shallow cut and toward a bunch of contented longhorns, munching lazily on the scrubby grass of the valley. They didn't look like they wanted to take a trip any more than I did.

"We'll cut out this bunch here by the mesquite. You take the drag."

I grabbed my rope and started in behind the bunch of longhorns he'd selected, slapping my leg with the rope and whistling to get them moving. Slowly, they began drifting away from the good grass on which they'd been grazing, accepting the inevitable move, although not without bawling their objections. But the whole thing struck me as a puzzle, right off. None of these beeves had been branded. Not one. Why would a man who seemed so protective of his stock fail to do the one thing all cattlemen do: brand them while they're still calves.

"How far are we going? Do we need to stop at the creek to get them watered up for a long drive?" I asked, keeping my questions about whose herd this might really be to myself.

"Don't you worry none about that. I'll be decidin' on where to stop. You just keep pushin' 'em, and don't let 'em get strung out."

It was becoming increasingly clear that Jake wasn't going to be a reliable source of information about the doings inside the Bradley outfit. He was tight-lipped and cautious with each and every word he let slip out. Men like that generally had learned their behavior the hard way, from painful experience. I figured he'd seen enough of how Bradley and the Venables operated to make him skittish and extremely wary, especially around a stranger.

We got the herd moving and had things well under control when a clap of thunder from an approaching storm made the herd nervous. Jake signaled me to skirt the back of the herd, left to right and back, to keep them bunched up. He rode close to the front, doing a good job of stopping any mavericks from straying off to either side. The storm was upon us within minutes, and the thunder and lightning strikes became more numerous and powerful. Shafts of foul-smelling lightning stabbed the ground, throwing up dirt, followed by crashes of thunder so loud they drowned out the herd's cries. The herd was growing too much to handle.

Then the unthinkable happened. With one bolt of lightning striking the ground no more than fifty feet away, followed by a deafening clap of thunder, the herd broke into a sudden stampede, racing for the mouth of a canyon ahead. Jake was caught on the side and was being squeezed closer to boulders that lined the mouth of the canyon. He was in a bad situation and I saw only one way to prevent his being crushed between the herd and the rocks, likely knocked from his horse and trampled by the panicked longhorns. I kicked Chigger to a run straight for the side of the herd that Jake was on, and began firing my Colt in the air. It worked. The shots proved enough to turn the frightened longhorns away from Jake, but causing them to scatter in the process. As they came face-to-face with the canyon walls and a slew of boulders they stopped their run and began milling around, still nervous, but easier to control.

As I reined-in, Jake came alongside, took off his sweat-stained slouch hat, and began wiping his brow with his kerchief.

"Whew. That was close. Rawhide, I never thought I'd be

in a position to have to thank someone for saving my skin, but I am now. That was quick thinking. I reckon I owe you." He replaced his hat, and turned his horse back to the task at hand. "We better get moving before we get drenched."

"I'll pick up the rear and try to get some of the mavericks back into the bunch. Oh, and Jake, you don't owe me a thing."

Jake nodded with a weak smile and rode off.

Chapter 11

As the storm blew over and continued on to the east, its billowing towers of white cotton reflecting the sun's afternoon light, the cattle calmed and became easier to coax along. We continued along a creek to the east, winding through plenty of good grass and shady, tree-lined stretches beside the cool waters. Off to the north, the grass gave way to sandier soil and a healthy crop of sage.

Jake led the herd to a meadow where they could eat fresh grass and signaled for me to stop pushing them. He then rode back to where I sat atop Chigger, one leg crooked around the pommel. I saw that as a chance to roll a smoke. He interrupted that thought with a better idea.

"Let's camp here for awhile and build a fire. I'm starved. Time for grub."

"Suits me, Jake. I'll start gathering some firewood."

He dismounted and began pulling some packages from his saddlebags. I rode a little farther upstream to a place that had a significant amount of deadfall. Firewood was everywhere. My part was getting easier by the minute.

By the time I had a good fire going, Jake had opened a couple cans of pork and beans and pulled out some bacon. He had the coffee pot full of water, the Arbuckle's added to it. We began assembling the foodstuffs into some sort of a meal, one that would at the very least be filling, if not restaurant quality. The smell of fresh coffee drifted across the fire, making me aware of my being hungrier than I'd realized. Jake forked out some bacon strips and began scooping up beans onto two plates. He handed me one, along with a spoon, and I dug in.

"Say, Jake, you whip up some mighty fine vittles."

All he did was grunt, never looking up from his own consumption of the food at hand, probably not certain whether I was joshing him. When we were finished, I took the plates and cups to the creek and began cleaning them with sand. Jake was mounted and eager to get moving by the time I finished, so I stuck the utensils in my own saddle bags and climbed aboard Chigger. Within minutes we had the herd moving toward its new grazing grounds.

The ground was beginning to look familiar, for what reason I had no idea until I could see from atop some low hills the remains of a ranch house recently burned to the ground. The Johnson's place. I saw no buckboard, which suggested that Albert and Vera had as yet not returned, as Albert had said they hoped for. Perhaps they decided to stay in town for a while longer to figure out their next move, whether to rebuild or move on. Then again, maybe Vera didn't cotton to the idea of taking up residence in a drafty barn. I saw this as an opportunity to play dumb, and hopefully learn if Jake had had any role in the raid on the Johnson place.

"Looks like a fire took someone's home. Wonder whose it is."

Jake stopped, stood up in his stirrups, then said, "I have

no idea. Must have moved on, though, because this is where we're supposed to graze the herd."

"We supposed to stay with the cattle?"

"Naw. We just deliver them, then head back for our next assignment."

"I wonder if anyone was burned up in that place, looks bad. You don't suppose some Indians did it, do you?"

"I haven't seen an Indian in these parts for better'n two years. Probably a lantern got knocked over or the chimney got too hot and caught the roof afire."

"Since we're going back anyway, how about we go down and take a look?" My curiosity over what Jake's reaction would be was gnawing at me. He appeared innocent enough, but I wondered if finding a fresh grave would push him to give up any information he had.

"Can if you want. I don't reckon I care one way or another. Bradley says these small ranchers are eating up the good grazing land and putting the big ranches out of business. I got no real sympathy for any of 'em. All you got to do is listen to the boss to find out how bad it's getting."

His cavalier attitude about the welfare of another human being, while not saying much for his character, was not evidence of his involvement. I decided to ride on down to where I'd buried the body in the Johnson's yard, anyway. Maybe he'd follow, maybe not. But he did. When we got to the burned out house, I pointed to the grave.

"Looks like one of them didn't make it out."

"Well, someone did."

"How do you know?" I asked.

"That body didn't bury itself."

I had to admire his grasp of the obvious. Jake was quicker than I'd given him credit for. And he sounded sincere as to his lack of knowledge of the events leading up to the fire.

Either this made him very good at covering up his participation in the Venable's deeds, or he truly was outside the circle of perpetrators. All of which brought to light another possibility: Maybe Emmett Bradley and the Venables were keeping their attempts to drive off the smaller ranchers to themselves, just in case someone should get mouthy and spout off to a marshal or a ranger. Too many people with knowledge of a plan this evil could make it hard to keep word from getting out. Pretty smart, if that was the case.

"Wonder if this was a man or a woman?" I looked down at the grave.

"I 'spect it was a woman."

"Why do you say that?"

"This ground's too blamed hard and rocky for a woman to get a shovel into it. Takes some heft to dig a hole as deep as that likely is." He pulled tobacco and papers from his breast pocket. As he rolled a smoke I was beginning to figure he really *was* just a hired hand with no knowledge of what his employer was up to.

Still, I was no closer to what was going on than I had been when I signed on with the Bradley outfit. Gathering enough evidence against the Venable brothers and Emmett Bradley to present to a marshal seemed as elusive as an owl in daylight.

We mounted up and headed back to the line shack, I began thinking about Mattie and how she was getting along with the preacher and his wife. Maybe by the time I saw her again, she wouldn't have quite so many questions concerning the Bible, and we'd be able to talk about things easier.

About that time, Jake pulled up and pointed to some riders coming toward us in a dusty hurry. I didn't recognize them, and Jake obviously didn't either. He seemed to be edgy at their approach. About a mile further down the road, we met.

They reined in, blocking our path. They didn't look happy to see us. We both kept our hands away from our guns.

"Who are you boys?" The leader was a stocky fellow with a drooping mustache and dark, narrow eyes. He crossed his hands on the pommel and leaned forward.

"Just a couple of cowboys from the Bradley spread," Jake said.

"Bradleyville?"

"Yep," said Jake.

"Well, that's where we're headed. What say you ride with us. That way we can check out your story with the constable."

"What story would that be?" I asked.

"That you're employed by Emmett Bradley and not the two rattlers we been doggin' for four days. That's what story."

"Who are these fellas you say you're trackin'?"

"Don't have any names, just a fresh trail. They killed the County Sheriff over in Staub."

"You fellas deputies?"

"Nope. We're what you might call 'volunteers.'"

Great, I thought. *We're riding back to town with a bunch of vigilantes. That is if we get back alive.*

I didn't like being herded back to Bradleyville like someone just grabbed for rustling. The kind of trash that usually made up gangs of vigilantes were seldom any better than those they rode down and often hanged without benefit of trial. I looked over at Jake. By the look on his face, he was likely thinking the same as I was. The vigilantes rode in silence. It would have been easy for them to stop at the nearest tree and string us up on principle. Vigilantes have few scruples when they are on a hunt. This bunch didn't look like a few law-abiding citizens just out to right a wrong. They were hard-bitten and silent.

When Bradleyville came into sight, we both let out a

sigh of relief. It would be too risky to try hanging us this close to town. We all rode down the main street, pulling up in front of the Big Eagle Saloon. Jake had told the men where Bradley could be found. The stocky man dismounted and strode into the saloon. After a couple of minutes, Emmett Bradley came out with the man.

"Now what's the problem, gentlemen?"

"We're on the lookout for a couple of men who shot down our sheriff. We'd just like you to back up their story that they work for you."

Emmett's eyes narrowed and his expression turned sour. "These are two of my men, all right. They were deliverin' a herd of beef up county. What gives you the right to come haulin' them in like a couple of steers for branding?"

As Emmett's anger grew, the Venable brothers sauntered out into the street, their hands on their six-shooters. Emmett also had his hand on the Colt I'd seen on his desk when I asked for the job.

The riders grew nervous at seeing two obvious gunmen facing them, feet apart as if fixing for a showdown. The leader decided it was time to fold his tent. He touched the brim of his hat in a salute, and wheeled his horse around.

"Our mistake, Mister Bradley. We won't bother you further." They started to ride off when Willy Venable called out.

"Hold up there, mister."

The stocky man pulled up and twisted around in his saddle. "Yes."

"What makes you think we're through with *you*? You can't go around accusin' a man of somethin' without proof. We got laws."

"I said I was sorry, mister. Now that's the end of it." The group again began to ride off. Willy wasn't through, not by a long shot. He fired his Colt into the ground near the lead horseman. The man grabbed for his own six-shooter, but Willy was ready for him. He was aiming right at the man's head. The man stopped his draw after seeing it was pointless, and that he would lose. He drew his hand away from his sidearm and glared at Willy.

"That's a warnin' not to come this way again. The next time, well, I don't reckon I have to draw you no picture. Now git!"

Willy was grinning from ear-to-ear as the men spurred their horses to a gallop and disappeared around the hill at the east edge of town.

"You two git back to what you were doin' before those hot heads drug you in here," Willy said, as he and his brother and Bradley all turned to go inside the saloon. Jake and I looked at each other and started our ride back to the line shack.

I unsaddled both our horses and put them in the corral. When I entered the door to the shack, Jake was already at the table laying out a hand of poker. I took a seat across from him.

"I'm busted clear down to my socks, Jake. Got no money to gamble away. Sorry."

"That's all right, we'll play for matchsticks. That's what I usually do. None of the others ever have any cash, either. Cut the pasteboards."

"What do you figure that set-to in town was all about?" I picked up my first four cards.

"Don't know, don't care. Willy took care of it, and I don't figure that bunch will hang around these parts long enough to stir up any more trouble."

"They said their County Sheriff was shot down. I didn't

even know there was a County Sheriff here. What town is there of a size to house a sheriff's office?"

"Just Traub. Ain't much more than a place to bed your horse down for the night, and maybe get a belly full of hash from Maude Porter."

"Maude Porter?"

"She's got herself a stage depot, boarding house, and restaurant, all in one falling down adobe hut. I hear tell that years ago it was a place where buffalo shooters gathered to plan their next take down."

"Take down?"

"Sure. You couldn't call what them fellas did as hunting. They would sit out there on a rise until a herd came by, then they'd begin a'shootin', take 'em down as fast as they could reload. Barrels of them rifles could get red hot. Sometimes there'd be two, three hundred carcasses lying out there in the sun, stripped of their hides and left to rot. Pitiful sight, it was."

I thought about that for a moment, unable to understand why men would get caught up in such wanton waste. I remember a time when there existed a market back east for buffalo hides, but that seemed almost a lifetime ago, and the market had dried up since then. I also remembered some talk of the government sanctioning such kills as a way to bring the Indians under control, the theory being that if you could control the Indian's food supply, you could control the Indians. Close as I remember, all it did was to make things worse for everyone.

"Traub don't sound near as big as Bradleyville. How come *it* ain't where the sheriff hangs his hat?"

"The way I hear it, Bradley didn't want an elected sheriff here. He wanted the town to have a constable that he appointed, and nothing more."

"Sound's like the county commissioners would have a say in it."

"The county commissioners don't have the Venables."

It all made sense when put that way. I decided to change the subject.

"Where'd you come from, Jake? You live here all your life?"

"Naw. I come from Kansas. When railroads started poppin' up all over, ranchers didn't have to drive their herds so far to get to market. So, work was getting' scarce. I came down here to where most of the beef was bein' raised. Got on with this crew 'bout a year back."

"What do you think of the Venable brothers?"

"Not much, but I wouldn't want that to get out. They kinda got their own peculiar ways about 'em. You seen a bit of that today, the way Willy pushed them fellas harder'n he needed to."

"Yeah. I reckon he did at that. I wonder why?"

"If I was you, I wouldn't wonder too loud. Them boys don't like questions. I've seen 'em beat a man half to death for suggestin' there might be a card or two missin' from the deck. When he recovered enough to travel, he drew his pay and skedaddled outta here faster'n a jackrabbit with a coyote on his tail."

"Was he right?"

"I wasn't there. Don't know. But I reckon it wouldn't be the first time Willy has stepped over the line."

"He wouldn't go so far as to kill a man, would he?"

Jake didn't say another word, just folded his hand, and stepped outside for a final smoke before hitting his bunk. I watched him for a minute to see if he'd chew on that for awhile, then give me an answer. He didn't. I decided to let it drop. I already knew the answer, anyway.

Chapter 12

The next morning Jake was already up making coffee. The air was clean from the previous day's rain, but it was going to be another scorcher. I had no idea what we'd be called on to do, but hoped it wouldn't entail sitting atop Chigger in the blazing sun. But it was to be a day of surprises. The first one was riding up just as we drank our coffee.

"Jake, get your lazy butt out here," Willy shouted. "And bring that Rawhide fella with you." We both went outside to meet the gruff-voiced foreman.

"You two are going down to Black Canyon to pick up some horses. There'll be a couple of riders from the Vega spread to turn them over to you. Bring 'em up here and corral 'em till I tell you what to do with 'em. Understand?"

"Yep. How many we expectin'?" Jake said.

"About twenty-five head, all broke and ready."

"We could sure use some help. Anyone available?"

"Nope. I'd have sent Rivera, but that didn't work out. Had to let him go a couple days ago. Learned a good lesson before he left, though. Don't try pullin' an ace outta your boot while I'm in the game." With that, Willy Venable rode off in a cloud of dust.

Jake looked at me and shook his head. "Rivera never cheated at cards in his life," he muttered, returning to the shack to pick up his gear. I followed.

"Who is this Rivera? He work here long?"

"Not long. Maybe two months, something like that. Man of integrity. Maybe too much integrity. Let's get moving."

"Just out of curiosity, what did this Rivera fella look like? I think I know a man of that name."

"Short, like all them Mex's, with a scar across his cheek where I heard he'd been flayed open by a whiskey bottle. Story was he'd gotten into it some years back with a jealous suitor for the affections of a woman who worked the saloons regular. Rivera said he'd never even met the woman, but the other man wasn't taking his word for it."

"What happened to the other fella?"

"Folks said the sheriff ended up shooting him. Turns out the sheriff had been the one all tangled up with that soiled dove all along." Jake just grinned.

Jake's description of the man named Rivera didn't ring any bells, but there had been three riders at the Johnson place the day it burned. I wondered if this Rivera had been the third man. I was still pondering that question as we rode out of sight of the line shack.

The location of the place we were to meet up with the drovers with the horses turned out to be a hard two-day's ride south, almost to the border. I couldn't figure why they didn't just bring them up to the Bradley ranch themselves. This thought I kept to myself, however. Jake was a better source of information as long as I didn't ask too many questions, or appear too curious about the Bradley organization.

The second night, we camped beside a nearly dry creek that meandered through a sea of sagebrush and scrubby patches of grama grass into a seemingly impassable canyon blocked by boulders and smaller rocks piled high. It looked as if they'd been dynamited down from the rim on purpose, maybe to close the route to someone or something. It didn't look at all like a natural occurrence, not even an earthquake or severe storm. We were miles from any town, and had seen only two ranches since leaving Bradley land. That, too, seemed strange to me. Why travel such a difficult route to pick up a few horses?

Jake had said little as we rode, giving me a chance to think about Mattie and how she was adjusting to living with the preacher and his wife. Her reluctance to see me leave brought a sadness that even I struggled to fully understand. I'd been so long without sharing my life with anyone that it felt unnatural to have feelings for a stranger I'd met only a few days earlier. Yet, still, it was undeniable that my heart felt heavy from her absence. Her complete innocence was refreshing in a world so full of danger and deceit.

The next morning, I was awakened just before dawn by gunshots. I called to Jake, but he was nowhere to be found. His blankets and saddle were still there, as was his horse, but no Jake. I strapped on my gun belt, struggled into my boots and began my search for him. As I slipped and slid down a hill strewn with sand and gravel, I heard two more shots ring out, echoing off the canyon walls in the distance. There, at the bottom of the hill, the creek flowed into a thick stand of trees, mostly cottonwood and willows. That seemed to be from where the shooting was coming. And that's where I found Jake hunched down behind some fallen timbers, trading shots with what looked to be three men with rifles downstream behind an outcropping of boulders.

I dove for cover as bullets chinked the trees around me. I stayed low and tried crawling toward where Jake was pinned down. I could get no closer than a few yards, but at least I could talk to him, and figure out what to do next.

"Who in tarnation are those hombres, Jake?" I shouted.

"Don't know. When I came down for some water they were over there across the stream holding their guns on three Mexican fellas. May have been the rider's from the Vega Ranch we were supposed to meet near here."

"Where are the horses they were supposed to be bringing?"

"Probably somewhere down that draw yonder. I thought I heard horses from that direction when I first got here. Then that bunch started throwing lead my way."

They kept us down by firing shots our way with enough regularity to keep us where we were. We weren't sitting there picking ticks out of our hair, either. Fully prepared to defend myself, I sent the occasional slug their way, knowing I had no chance of hitting anything at that distance with a revolver. We did, however, present enough of a threat that they probably wouldn't try rushing us, since Jake had had the good sense to grab his rifle on the way. I kicked myself for not doing the same. We were fairly secure for the time being. But bullets ricocheting off rocks always presented another problem, and if you got hit by a flattened piece of lead, it was bound to cause serious damage. So, rather than try for the larger rocks nearby, we chose to stay in the trees, letting them absorb whatever shots came our way.

The whole incident lasted for about an hour. Then, almost as quickly as it began, the shots ceased coming and we were once again greeted by the serene quiet of nature when left alone, free of man and his weaponry. We waited a respectable time before venturing out to discover what they were doing there in the first place. We didn't have to go far to make a grizzly discovery. Three dead Mexicans lay near the creek. Tracks of about thirty or so unshod horses showed they had been driven to the creek to water, then they were driven back the same way they had come, although by different riders.

"Who do you suppose took the horses?" I assumed the missing horses were those we were supposed to drive back to the Bradley ranch.

"I don't know. But these three *are* from the Vega spread. I've seen them before. And I know that Mr. Bradley ain't goin' to be happy about this, no sir." Jake stood over the dead men, then motioned me to follow him back to where we'd made camp to get our own horses. "I dread having to tell him. Let's ride."

For some reason, I did, too.

Even though I'd only met the man once, I was as certain as Jake was about what Bradley's response would be to the events surrounding the loss of the horses. I wasn't disappointed, as we walked into the Big Eagle Saloon two days later to find Bradley playing cards with Willy and Joey Venable, and a man I hadn't seen before. The man was hard looking, with graying stubble and dark, deep-set eyes. When we walked up to the table, Willy looked up at Jake and said, "What did you do with the horses? Didn't expect you back until morning."

"We don't have them, Mr. Venable. They were stolen out from under us. Three Vega wranglers are dead, too."

"What!" shouted Bradley as he jumped up, and slammed his cards onto the table. Money went flying as his face turned red as fire. "How could this have happened? Who did it?"

"We were camped up in the pass for the night. Just before dawn I heard echoes of gunshots coming from the valley. When I went to investigate, someone started throwing lead at me. Rawhide came down to where I was holed up and the two of us returned fire, but we were so far away, I doubt we did any good. Those Vega men were probably dead from the first shots I heard, ambushed in their sleep," said Jake, nervously.

"You look to see which way they went?" Willy asked.

"Tracks led south. Back toward the border."

Bradley sat back down, leaned on the table and began stroking his chin as if in deep thought. He looked over at Willy, nodded, and got back up. He went into his office at the back of the saloon and closed the door. Willy motioned for his brother and the two of them left together. Everyone else in the saloon went back to whatever they were doing when we came in, leaving us standing there, feeling like orphans. The other man at the table started shuffling cards, but said nothing. Jake finally shrugged, said he was going to get a whiskey to settle his nerves, and that he'd probably be heading back to the line shack in about an hour. Told them I'd pass on the drink and wandered out to find Mattie, since I hadn't seen her for a nearly a week.

I walked down the main street and turned the corner at the end. There, sitting on the porch of the little house next to the church were Mattie and Sarah Pike, rocking and giggling like a couple of schoolgirls. Mattie seemed happy, but when she saw me round the corner, she jumped up and came running.

"Mister Rawhide! You've come back."

"Just for a little visit, girl. I have to get back to my job soon, but I wanted to see you first. Couldn't leave town without saying hello to my favorite young lady, now could I?"

"Am I really? I mean, really your favorite?"

"Of course, who else could I mean?"

Mattie broke out in a wide grin. "You must come sit and tell me everything you've been doing, Mister Rawhide."

Sarah Pike smiled, then got up and went inside. She came back after a few minutes with two glasses and a pitcher.

"Why don't you two have your talk over a glass of lemonade? I'll bet you're parched after your ride from the ranch, Mr. Smith." She poured the glasses full and handed us each one, then sat back on her rocker.

"Mighty thoughtful of you, ma'am."

"Yeah, Mrs. Pike, thanks," Mattie said quickly, just to let me know she'd been working on her manners.

"Well, Mattie, I've been working at a ranch, nothing very exciting."

"I'm sorry your work isn't exciting, but Mrs. Pike has been reading some very exciting stories to me. Did you know about a really strong man who pulled down a whole building?"

"You mean Sampson. Yeah, I knew about him."

"Boy, that must have been a sight. Oh, and what about that Moses fella when he made a road right through the middle of the sea? Didn't even get wet. You ever hear of such a thing?"

I had to chuckle over her exuberance at relating those Bible stories. All at once I knew I'd made the right choice in bringing Mattie to these good people.

My visit was cut short, however, as I was rudely brought back to the realities of my job. Jake was out front of the saloon hollering for me to get mounted for a ride. I said my goodbyes and promised to come back very soon. I told Mattie I'd be looking forward to hearing more stories. I began missing her even before Jake and I had ridden out of town.

* * *

When we reined in at the line shack, there were two other riders waiting for us. One of them was the sour faced man who had been playing cards with Bradley and the Venables. The other man looked just as rough. I had a bad feeling in the pit of my stomach. I had no idea what these men had in mind, but I was already certain I wasn't going to like it. We dismounted. They followed us into the line shack.

"Who's the new guy, Jake?" asked the man from the card game.

"Name's Rawhide Smith. Good man to have around. Rawhide, this here's Snake Benson, and the other one is his partner, Amarillo."

"Amarillo what?" I asked, probably too quickly.

"Just Amarillo. You don't need to know more'n that, sonny," Snake said. I just nodded and took a seat on the edge of my bunk. The others gathered around the table. Snake pulled out a piece of paper that had been rolled up and stuck inside his vest. He spread it out on the table and leaned on it to keep it from curling back to its original shape.

"Jake, Bradley wants us to go after those horses, all the way into Mexico if need be. We can't let a bunch of cutthroat Mex's spoil our play."

Jake stared at the map, stroking his chin, and curling his mouth as if in a question mark.

"That where you think they took the stock?" Jake asked, pointing to a place on the map that had been marked with an *X.*"

"Uh-huh. Leastways, that's where Willy figures they must have taken them. You got any different ideas, take 'em up with him. You two get ready to ride. We leave in an hour, right after we get some grub."

I got up from my bunk and walked over to where Jake was still studying the crude map. I didn't say anything, but it was clear to me that Jake had his reservations. It really didn't matter, though, as it was quite clear that these men carried the message straight from Bradley, and there would be no room for disagreement. We looked at each other for a moment before Jake walked away to add more wood in the stove to cook beans and bacon.

After we had eaten and cleaned up, Snake said to gather all the guns and ammunition we could because he was expecting plenty of resistance to our taking back the horses. As we were getting ready to mount up, I looked over at Jake and whispered, "Who are these fellas we're going after?"

"I got a bad feelin' it might be the owners."

Chapter 13

The realization that I was about to take part in rustling a bunch of horses didn't sit well. I couldn't believe I'd allowed myself to get caught up in all this. My original plan was just to gather evidence against Bradley and the Venables for murder, rustling and house burning, plus anything else I could dig up along the way. I never imagined I'd end up becoming part of the evil I'd hoped to end. I didn't like the feeling, either.

I had also begun to believe that Jake Pardee was, like me, simply another cowboy who needed a job and got caught up in the thievery of the Bradley bunch. But questions began to muddle my thinking concerning this seemingly decent man. It was obvious he knew more about Bradley's operation than that of an innocent bystander. Much more. And now I was slowly being drawn into a dangerous game, one that could certainly end up raining death down upon some soul, innocent or not. It wasn't my place to be making judgments about who should be held accountable for stealing some horses. But here I was, apparently committed to participate in a ride for retribution, and beginning to suspect it an undeserved one.

As I rode along, bringing up the rear of the single-file column, woolgathering about my part in all this, I was quite suddenly aware that I *was* making judgments. After all, wasn't I making a judgment by searching for evidence that would help prosecute the Venables for the terrible crimes I'd already witnessed? And now it was beginning to look like Bradley's operation stretched far beyond just pushing some small ranchers off their properties.

"Jake, you take the point. Get us back to where you say the Vegas were shot and the horses stolen." Snake's orders brought me out of my own interior conflicts.

Jake spurred his horse into the lead. We rode for a day and a half before coming close to where we had camped the night before. As we pulled up in the trees, the remains of our fire were clearly visible. Jake got down and kicked at the unburned sticks.

"This is where we camped, Snake. I heard the shots coming from down the hill over there." Jake pointed in the direction we'd followed to find out who had been shooting. We all walked to where we were forced to take cover, pinned down by their rifles.

Snake bent down, looked at Amarillo, then started on down the hill to where we'd found the bodies of the Vega men. Three fresh graves marked the spot.

Snake stood up. "It looks like the tracks go south from here. Probably fifteen or twenty horses, all of 'em unshod. That looks like what we came for. Let's get mounted and go after them, boys."

At least our story was confirmed. I had the feeling there had been a seed of doubt in Bradley's mind about whether

Saving Mattie

we might have somehow been involved in the shooting and taking of the horses. When greedy, dishonest men feel wronged, they often accuse those around them. Being adjudged truthful by owlhoots like Snake and Amarillo didn't make me feel any better.

Snake was pushing us hard to make up time. The trail we were following took us along mostly dry creek beds and through occasional wooded stretches that fell away to rocky gulches and sagebrush vistas. It quickly became clear that men who knew what they were about were herding the horses back to where they had come from. Mexican vaqueros were known to be great horsemen, and this bunch was no different. When we came to where they had crossed the Rio Grande, they had been careful to pick a spot so shallow that they wouldn't be held up trying to make a difficult crossing. That should have been a clue as to with whom we were dealing. They knew we'd be following and the sooner they got safely below the border the better.

But Snake didn't seem to be heeding any rules of caution. He let it be known from the beginning that he intended to get the horses back by force, if necessary, and at any cost. It showed in his eyes, dark foreboding eyes that were devoid of emotion. He wouldn't be denied. I felt as though I was being swept along in the wake of a cyclone. A killer. We splashed into the river and proceeded across to Mexico, dangerous in good times, deadly in bad. This could prove to be one of those bad times.

As we topped a ridge that looked out over a thousand acres of flat, scrubby desert right in the middle of rugged, high mountain ranges, we saw them. Four riders slowly pushing a small bunch of horses, leading south from the river, headed toward what appeared to be a box canyon, and they didn't seem to be in any particular hurry. It was a perfect place to corral the herd and keep them out of the hands of any who might be foolish enough to try taking them back. A dangerous place, too, for four gringos unfamiliar with the territory. Snake reined in.

"Okay, boys, let's get to doing our job."

"What's your plan, Snake?" Amarillo asked.

"We ride in there and take back our property. That's all there is to it."

"Seems risky, to me," said Amarillo. "They can hold off a regiment in that box canyon. How do you figure to get in there in one piece?"

"Amarillo, are you startin' to crow foot on me?"

"No, Snake, but I *am* lookin' out for my own skin. And I don't intend to get it shot full of holes. I say we figure a real plan before we go lookin' for the kind of trouble we're bound to find."

As the two argued between themselves, Jake looked at me with a worried frown. He didn't say anything, but I could tell by his expression that he didn't feel any better about our predicament than I did. But we both knew we weren't likely to get any choice in the matter.

Snake suddenly jumped off his horse, pulled a pair of field glasses out of his saddlebags, and walked to the edge of the ridgeline. He seemed to be studying the land between our location and the canyon. He turned from side to side, finally coming to rest on what appeared to be a fairly well protected dry creek bed that ran very close to the canyon. I could almost read his mind. He was planning to stay low until we got close enough for a surprise attack, then we smother them with rifle fire, pretty much what they had done to the three men Jake and I had buried.

Sure enough, when Snake got through panning the valley with his glass, he stooped down, picked up a stick, and proceeded to draw in the sand the very plan I figured he would.

"Any questions, gents?"

No one said a word.

"Then mount up, and make sure your rifles are fully loaded. We're goin' down there and pick ourselves off some Mex's."

"Wonder why those hombres stole Bradley's horses in the first place, Snake?"

"Don't you worry none about it, sonny. It ain't anything you need to bother yourself with."

"Well, it sure looks suspicious, sorta like they might have been stolen in the first place, and these boys were just takin' back what they figured was theirs."

As soon as it came out, I knew I should have kept my mouth shut.

Snake whirled around, gun in hand, and pointed straight at my head.

"Don't make me tell you again, sonny. It ain't none of your business. Do as you're told and you may get out of this alive. That is, if I'm feelin' generous."

There was little I could do but swallow hard, as I stared down the barrel of Snake's revolver. I nodded my understanding as he lowered his weapon and slid it back into his holster.

"Now, no more thinkin' on the part of any of you, hombres. Understand? Now let's ride."

And ride we did, single file down below the ridgeline using a deer path all the way to the bottom. Once down on level ground again, we picked up the creek bed that Snake had planned to follow. The trouble was, the sun was getting low, and the shadows were growing longer. We'd be easy to spot wherever the creek embankment was low or non-existent, our progress magnified by the lengthening shadows of horse and rider.

Darkness would be upon us well before we reached a point at which we could engage the men in the canyon. Snake realized that, too, and called a halt.

"We'll stop here and put up a dry camp for the night. Get a start early, before dawn. Maybe we can surprise those Mexicans just like they did the Vega riders."

We all dismounted, unsaddled our mounts and led them to the creek to drink from the occasional puddle left from the last rains. The creek had all but dried up for any meaningful flow, but deep holes dredged out during spring storms held water for a considerable time afterwards, saving many a traveler during the dry season.

I dropped my saddle over a fallen log to keep it out of the sandy dirt, took off my hat, and dropped down on my haunches to splash water over my face. The water was warm. I wiped my face on my shirtsleeve and went over to where the others were either stretched out on the ground or trying to roll a smoke. Jake sat a ways away from the others almost as if he considered them carriers of a plague, or something. Snake and Amarillo weren't natural-born socializers, the type to instill in others good feelings about themselves. I dropped to the ground next to Jake. He was staring at the ground and didn't look up at my approach.

"Got any tobacco?" he finally said.

"Sure, help yourself," I offered, handing him my pouch of rough-cut.

It was clear Jake wasn't in the mood for conversation, so I didn't try to engage him. I hadn't quite made up my mind about him, anyway. He seemed a good sort at times, and at other times, well, he appeared willing to go along with whatever was asked of him, not making a judgment as to its legality or morality.

I've always prided myself on intending to do the right

thing. This situation seemed to put me smack in the middle of a quandary. I didn't think this whole situation smelled right, not even slightly. Sure, it appeared those fellows in the canyon stole the horses that were intended for the Bradley ranch, and shot down three men in the process, but had the horses been stolen from someone else in the first place? I don't like finding myself in the middle of something I don't know all the facts about and don't have any control over. This time I just might have crossed the line and allowed myself to become a part of something that many consider a hanging offense. Fighting an enemy you can see is one thing, fighting an enemy within is a whole different story. And it wasn't really a comfort to know I meant well in everything I did, because a man can mean well and still get sent to prison, or worse.

It wasn't long before all four of us had drifted off and were doubtless snoring in a kind of crude orchestral unison.

Just as false dawn lightened the sky in the east, I opened one eye at the sound of someone moving around the camp. I looked over at Jake, who was still asleep. On the other side of him, I saw the still unmoving forms of Snake and Amarillo, both rolled up in their blankets. I slowly opened one eye, and tried to identify where the sound was coming from. I slowly eased my hand down to my Colt, preparing to move into action if the need should arise. Just then Snake must have heard the same sound, for he sat up abruptly, blinked, and tried to throw off his blanket and get to his gun. He was too late. A rifle butt, wielded like a club, crashed down on his head, and he slumped back, sporting a bloody gash in his forehead.

Rather than make the same mistake, I slowly opened both eyes, intent on making no hasty movement. I saw a Mexican in a wide sombrero looking down at the man he'd just bludgeoned. He had a satisfied smile on his face as he kicked Snake to make sure he was unconscious. He looked over at me, saw I was awake, put a finger to his lips, and then motioned for me to sit up. I complied, moving my hand away from my Colt. There would be no point in exhibiting any bravado at that juncture. He had the drop on us all, and I wasn't in the mood to be his next casualty.

The Mexican kicked the feet of Amarillo and Jake, They both moved groggily, rubbing at their eyes. Amarillo muttered some oath exhibiting his displeasure at being rousted so early. Jake eased up on one elbow, opened his eyes, and tried to speak. The Mexican shushed him, motioning for us all to stand, drop our gun belts, and move to where our horses had been hobbled.

Señors, it appears you have wandered into my country. My compadres don't like uninvited visitors," the Mexican said. "Now, you will tell me what you are doing here."

Snake had regained consciousness, but was clearly not able to speak coherently. Amarillo tried to assuage the Mexican's anxiety over our presence. Amarillo's inexperience at cross-border diplomacy was quickly evident.

"Who the hell are you to ask, greaser?"

The Mexican wasted no time in letting Amarillo know his answer was unacceptable. He jammed his rifle butt in Amarillo's stomach, causing the air to go out of him as he doubled over with a scream of pain.

"Would either of you gentlemen care to answer my question?" He looked at Jake and Me.

Jake didn't seem ready to come up with an explanation, so it looked as if it was up to me, the butterflies in my stomach, notwithstanding.

I pointed in the direction of the box canyon. "We were

Saving Mattie

following a herd of horses that were stolen on Texas soil. The men that did it murdered three of your people. They are over there, holed up in that canyon, yonder."

The Mexican shaded his eyes, straining to see what I was talking about. He shook his head. "Why should I believe you?"

I eased over to Snake's saddlebags and pulled out his field glasses, handing them to the Mexican. He raised them to his eyes. A grin came over his face as he handed the glasses back to me.

'Those men are very bad hombres, señor. Comancheros. To tangle with such men is certain death. You have chosen a terrible way to die. Go back across the border while you still can." The Mexican lowered his rifle and began to walk away.

I started to say something to him as he mounted his horse, but the thought escaped me as I saw about twenty Indians on horseback racing across the barren desert toward the canyon and a probable rendezvous with the comancheros. It occurred to me at that moment that the Mexican might have just saved our lives. I doubted Snake and Amarillo would see it that way, though.

Jake and I got saddled and mounted up after helping the other two to their horses. Jake led the way back toward the Rio Bravo and the safety of American soil.

Chapter 14

Our horses splashed across the river at a shallow point, stopping near the opposite side to drink. As soon as we got to the other bank, Jake looked at Snake with a frown.

"Rawhide, we best head straight for the Bradley spread. Snake, here, don't look so good. I'd say he's busted up inside from the looks of that lump a'growin' on his noggin."

I had to agree. Snake was slumped in his saddle, his eyes were glazed over almost as if he had been clubbed unconscious with his eyes open, and had lost the ability to shut them.

"Lead the way, Jake. I'll bring up the rear. I'll watch our back trail to make sure no one's following us, although I can't imagine why anyone would."

We stopped once again to water the horses at a little creek, but when Jake tried to give Snake a piece of jerky in order to keep his strength up, he was rebuffed by Amarillo who insisted we just leave his partner alone to his misery. Strange fellow, that Amarillo.

It was another two days of steady riding, and with only

one encampment, we reached the boundary of the Bradley ranch. Off in the distance, a two-story, stone house stood atop a hill. The house was imposing with its high windows and four dormers jutting from a steep roof. One of the main floor windows was open and a lace curtain wafted in and out with the breeze. The shutters were nicely painted and the windows free of the grime one invariably finds on a windswept prairie. A wide porch ran the length of the front and wrapped around both sides, too. Bradley had a view of grassy hills, stands of cottonwoods, wide pasturelands, and a burbling creek. All he had to do was walk around his big porch to see it all.

Emmett Bradley came out the wide oak door and stood at the edge of the porch with his hands on his hips. He scowled and chewed on a cigar. His collarless shirt lay unbuttoned halfway down, and his suspenders were twisted as if he'd pulled them up in a hurry. It was quickly apparent that he had no intention of inviting us inside.

"I still don't see any horses. Where the hell are they? And what happened to Snake?"

"We lost the horses to a bunch of Comancheros, and some Comanches that didn't look willing to share their bounty," said Jake.

"And Snake?"

"He got himself busted good by some Mex who snuck into our camp as we were getting up. He rifle-butted Amarillo pretty hard, too. Snake moved a mite hastily for his gun."

"And Amarillo, what happened to him?"

"He maybe shouldn't have called the man a 'greaser.'"

"What was the Mex doin' there in the first place?"

"Didn't say, but he didn't sound all too glad to see us wanderin' around south of the Rio Bravo. He may have been part of what passes for the law down there in Chihuahua. I didn't see any sort of badge, though. I reckon these two could both do with a little medical attention."

"Take 'em both into town. Let the doc take a look at 'em. Get yourself a shot of whiskey, then you two go back to the line shack and wait for me. I'll be there later today. Got business in town with a troublemaker, Albert Johnson."

I looked bewildered at his mention of Mr. Johnson, a man I knew would not likely want anything to do with Bradley, at least not willingly. And I didn't like the tone of Bradley's voice as he mentioned Johnson's name. Jake took the reins to Snake's horse and began leading him back out through the wrought-iron gate on the way back to Bradleyville. Amarillo was able to sit his horse, but he was still groaning, doubled over from the pain inflicted by the Mexican's rifle butt.

Bothered by Bradley's reference to Mr. Johnson as a troublemaker, I spoke little all the way back to town. I'd found myself engaged in deeper thought of late than I usually allowed. And the thoughts I was having were not generally pleasant. More and more I seemed to be wrestling with all the principles of life I'd learned at the knee of a mother who was deeply spiritual, and the practical side of life I'd gotten from a father who was hot of temper, highly pragmatic and quick to judge. With those conflicts within me, I daily walked a narrow line lying somewhere between being a lay preacher and a gunslinger. This was shaping up to be one of those times when the gunslinger side seemed to want to bubble to the surface.

When we rode into town, Jake said he would take Snake and Amarillo to the doc if I wanted to go on and have a drink at the saloon. I agreed to meet him there. Instead of going to the saloon, however, I went to the church to find Mattie. She was not in sight as I went to the front door of the parsonage and knocked. I waited for a minute, then, hearing no sounds coming from inside, I walked on over to the church. The front door was open, so I went inside. Jericho Pike was on a ladder putting up a hand-painted banner across the back wall. He heard my steps and turned with a warm smile.

"Mr. Smith, I'm happy to see you back. Are things going well?" He came down the ladder and extended his hand.

"Well, Parson, I can't say all is as I would prefer it to be, but I'd welcome an opportunity to chat with you, just the same. If you've the time, that is."

"Always have time for a brother with a problem. Sit and tell me what's bothering you."

We both sat in the first wooden pew. For some unknown reason, I felt nervous at confessing the demons that had recently come into my life, namely the Venable brothers and Emmett Bradley. The events concerning Snake and Amarillo came rushing to mind as well. I was torn as to just how much I dared share with him, especially with my limited knowledge of his position in the town's hierarchy. If he'd been brought here by Bradley, there might be some loyalty that extended beyond his church.

"First, I'd like to know what's happening with Mattie. Is she doing okay? Not causing any trouble for you and Mrs. Pike, I hope."

"Why, how could that sweet child cause anyone trouble? She's been a joy and a wonderful companion to Sarah. I must admit I have often failed in my duty to spend as much time with my dear wife as I should. Building a new church has been more time consuming than I'd believed possible."

"Has Mattie told you how she came to be in my care?"

"No, she hasn't. Whenever we ask, she just says you are her uncle and that her parents were gone to Heaven. That's all we've been able to get her to share. Is there something you'd like to tell me?"

I squirmed in my seat, not at all certain how much to tell him, even though it would seem to help if the Pikes knew the horror she'd been through. I began to hem and haw around. Pike quickly picked up on my discomfort, and he gently attempted to make things easier.

"Tell you what, Mr. Smith, why don't we go have a cup of coffee. Churches tend to make people uneasy. I sure do understand that. If you feel like talking, I'm a great listener. What do you say?"

Strangely relieved to be outside, I agreed to accompany him to a small restaurant about a block down the street. I even offered to buy.

He looked across the table at me, awaiting my presumed intentions to share with him more about Mattie's past than he already knew, or thought he knew. Since Mattie had not been exactly forthcoming with him when asked about her past, I struggled with saying anything more. But I also felt it necessary for the Pikes to be aware of those things in Mattie's past that might affect her relationships with others. It was then that I made a decision that I would later regret. I told Pike about the raid on the Slaughter ranch, and why I'd chosen to stretch the truth about who she really was. And why I'd done it.

"Mattie's been through a lot, what with seeing her pa and ma and brother shot down in cold blood as she did. Then, this waif of a girl was forced to dig holes and bury them all. An experience I doubt I would have handled as well."

Pike was almost in tears at the telling. I could tell these facts had touched him deeply.

"Merciful heavens, Mr. Smith, it appears Satan has done a terrible work hereabouts. I am pleased that you have told me Mattie's story, for now we can deal with her darkest fears as they arise," Pike said.

"That's what I'd hoped you would say, Reverend. I've grown quite attached to her in the short time I've known her, and I want the best for her. That's why I asked you and Sarah to keep watch over her for awhile until I can get the men responsible put away."

"Mr. Smith, you can count on us for her complete safety and comfort." He reached across the table to shake my hand.

"I thought I could. Now, if you'll excuse me, I'd best be going back to meet one of the other wranglers and head to the ranch. I'll see you soon, sir." I got up, and left after stopping to pay for our coffees on my way out.

As I walked over to the saloon, I should have felt a great relief from my conversation with the preacher, but I didn't. Something nagged at me, like a tick burrowing in under my skin. Why would I have misgivings? I had been assured nothing would happen to Mattie, and that she would be taken care of, hadn't I? So why this sudden foreboding that had so entrenched itself within me?

Jake came out of the saloon as I approached.

"We gotta get out to the line shack, pronto. There's doings."

"Did you get Snake and Amarillo to the doctor?"

"Yeah. He said Amarillo would be fine after he gets over his bellyache. He ain't busted up inside or anything. Snake's a different story, though. Doc thinks he's in bad shape. There's blood seepin' out his ears, and he can't talk nor nothing. Doc's goin' to keep him down for a spell. That puts Bradley one man short."

"One man short for what?"

"Didn't say, just that he's one man shy for a job that's comin' up."

"So, you talked to Bradley? He came into town?"

"Yep. Just got here. Willy and Joey were with him."

Those three seem tighter than wet leather left out in the sun, I thought. It's almost like they're of one mind. If that proves true, then it was Bradley for sure that called for the raids on the Slaughter place, the Brewster place, and the Johnson's, too. Once proven, I could go to the marshal up in Fort Stockton or the ranger station over in…

"Hey, Rawhide, what's got you bothered? You didn't even hear what I said," Jake grumbled.

"Uh, no. Sorry, Jake. I reckon I was carried off in my thoughts. What'd you say?"

"Said I overheard Willy tell Joey that they were goin' to brace Albert Johnson about something, didn't say what. That looks like Johnson's buckboard in front of the feed store."

"Johnson seems like a harmless man. Why would they want to go after him?"

"Probably because Bradley's got a burr under his saddle over Johnson's refusal to move out and give up his claim."

"Why would he? He's put in a lot of time and effort building the place up. I probably wouldn't want to give all that up just because somebody else wanted me to. Would you?"

Jake didn't respond to that. He shrugged and kept walking toward our horses. Just then Willy and Joey crossed the street to the feed store. Albert Johnson emerged with a sack in one hand. He didn't look up to see the Venables coming up on him, as he tried to negotiate the step with his crutch. Willy grabbed Johnson by the arm and spun him around, causing him to lose his grip on the package. The bag of flour burst on the boardwalk, spreading brown flour all over. Johnson sprawled in the dirt, trying to reach his crutch, which had also gone flying. He looked up at the two men in disbelief.

"What'd you do that for, mister? I never did anything to you."

Vera Johnson came through the door accompanied by the proprietor, Ollie Prentice. He was dragging a box that was obviously too heavy for one man to carry.

Prentice dropped the end of the box and stared angrily at the Venables.

"What's goin' on here, Mr. Venable? This man didn't do anything to you."

Willy shoved Prentice back against the wall. "Stay out of this, old man, unless you want busted up real good," growled Joey. "Go back inside where you belong. And stay out of Bradley business."

I stopped in the street. Jake kept on walking. He called back over his shoulder, "Best stay out of that, Rawhide. It ain't none of our concern."

"Anytime I see two men picking on one old man, and a crippled one at that, it becomes my concern." Made my voice loud enough to be heard by all concerned. I turned and started walking toward the Venables. Joey saw me and stepped off the plank sidewalk, stopping me in the middle of the street. He put a hand in the middle of my chest and halted my progress.

"Jake gave you some good advice, Smith. Like he said, it ain't none of your business."

His hand fell to his sidearm. I could feel the anger rising inside.

About then, a man stepped out of the constable's office just down the street. It was Constable Stub Emory, and he had a deep frown on his face. He walked up to Joey and said, "Joey, why don't you go have a drink. I'll take care of whatever this man's done."

Joey had the good sense to remove his hand from the butt of his revolver and walk over to Willy. The constable turned to face me. "We ain't met, Mister, but I hope you'll take my advice and not get yourself involved in Bradley business, like the man said."

I was fuming. The constable was clearly taking the side of these two bullies without even appearing to find out what the problem was. Jake came over and grabbed me by the arm, pulling me away and toward where our horses were tied to a rail.

"It's like I told you, Rawhide, it ain't healthy getting' all twisted up in whatever devilment those two brothers got in mind. They ain't someone you want to tangle with, believe me. C'mon, we need to ride on outta here while we still got jobs."

I stood a distance away as Willy told Johnson to get out of town and not come back. Albert was helped to his one good leg and given his crutch by the storeowner, and the Johnsons got in their buckboard and left. All I could do was shake my head in disgust.

My interest in my job had about run its course. The very thought that I could actually put in a hard day's effort that in any way might benefit these twisted men turned my stomach. I mounted up and rode out of town with Jake, but that wasn't the end of it for me, not by a long shot.

Chapter 15

We rode about two miles out of town before my anger subsided sufficiently to speak. Jake had made no attempt to start any conversations, either. It was time to put Jake on the spot, to find out which side of the fence he intended to graze on.

"Jake, what'd Albert Johnson do to get on the wrong side of Bradley's fence?"

"You're better off not knowin' Bradley's business. The less you know, the better off you'll be. No sense stirrin' up a hornet's nest unless you just love getting' stung."

"I never ran from a fight in my life. And I'm not afraid of those Venable brothers, either. I just want to know what's goin' on around here. Are you goin' to tell me, or not?"

Jake looked over at me with a frown and shook his head.

"It's your funeral, Rawhide, but don't say I didn't warn you."

"You're off the hook as of right now, Jake. Go on."

He sighed as he began his story. "Bradley doesn't want

the small ranchers getting' a foothold around here for a lot of reasons. Mainly because the more people that settle hereabouts, the more eyes and ears to discover all his crooked activities, and I'll tell you, they are aplenty."

"But there's lots of range out there. He doesn't need it all. Besides, he's already got more longhorns than he has men to watch 'em."

"First of all, those longhorns aren't his, at least he didn't buy them. He has contacts in Chihuahua that steal them and drive across the border. He aims to push those beeves all the way to Fort Worth and sell 'em."

"What does that have to do with the smaller ranchers?"

"Nothing. He just don't want anyone around seein' too much and figuring out what he's up to. If he can get enough money out of selling stolen cattle, he can get a rail spur built off the Southern Pacific line, then he can ship his stolen stock out of here a lot easier and quicker."

"What about those mustangs we were supposed to bring back?"

"Same thing. They're from Chihuahua. He was goin' to move 'em, as soon as he had enough gathered up, and sell 'em to the army up at Fort Stockton."

"But rounding up wild horses isn't illegal."

"It is if you steal them in Mexico and drive them across the border."

"So those horses we were to pick up yesterday were stolen?"

"Yep. And Bradley's real worked up about that, too. Wouldn't surprise me none if he didn't make a raid on the Comanchero hideout. He knows where it is because he's done business with them before."

I had to shake my head. It was all so blatantly illegal. I couldn't see how Bradley was able to operate so openly, yet not get caught and punished.

"Why haven't the rangers come down here and closed Bradley down?"

"That's why he built this town in the middle of nowhere, so close to the border, and why he wants all the settlers out of here. As soon as they catch on to his thievin' ways, they'd demand that either the rangers or the army do something about it. So far, no one seems the wiser, but folks like Albert Johnson, Joshua Brewster, and Mister Slaughter have proven to be darned hard-nosed about leavin' peaceable like. They've all been spoutin' off like they're of one mind, and not real willin' to suffer the demands of a despot like Bradley. All three have rejected Bradley's offer to buy them out, and they been talkin' about callin' in them Buffalo soldiers at Fort Stockton."

"That Constable Emory, he one of Bradley's men?"

"Yep, bought and paid for. You can't look to him for help if you was to run afoul of Bradley or his cutthroats."

"I don't mean any disrespect here, Jake. But I need to know where you stand."

"Why? What difference does it make?"

"I wouldn't want to have to keep lookin' back to make sure I don't get a bullet if I ride out of here."

"I work for the outfit, yes. But I'm no back shooter. I'm just a simple wrangler, that's all. I never took part in any of Bradley's underhanded attempts at scarin' folks off their rightfully owned land. Push comes to shove, and I get called on to plug somebody that's mindin' his own business, well, I reckon I'd have to head for parts unknown myself."

"That's good to know, Jake. I'd rather have you for a friend than an enemy."

Jake squinted at me for a second, then said, "I don't reckon I take your meaning."

"I'm sayin' I'd have to part company with a man who'd shoot a family down in cold blood."

"What are you plannin' on doin' about it?"

We came to a fork in the road. "Whatever I have to. I'll be leavin' you here, Jake. I'd sure be grateful if you'd consider ridin' with me, but if not, well, I wish you good fortune." I reined Chigger to the right and started off down a trail that looked to head into the mountains to the north. I figured to circle around and come back into town from the east and maybe see Mattie once more before I started my campaign to clean up Bradleyville, as foolish as that seemed. I looked over my shoulder to see if Jake was following. He was sitting his horse as if pondering his next move.

Having principles sometimes carries a heavy price and I could see that I was likely riding straight into hell, a place I was determined never to visit.

When I was young, my ma let me know in no uncertain terms that hell wasn't a place I wanted to spend eternity. She scared me plenty, and I've never forgotten those stories about fire and brimstone, folks crying out in agony forever. And yet here I was about to set off on a trail that could easily put me smack in the face of mortal danger. It didn't feel real promising after what I'd heard of the Bradley bunch from Jake.

I heard the pounding of hooves behind me. I turned in the saddle to see Jake riding hard after me.

"Now hold up there, Rawhide. You got to listen to some common sense. I ain't about to stand in your way, pardner, but those boys will shoot you down just for starin' at 'em the wrong way."

"Could be, but I owe somebody. I promised to corral these owlhoots and I mean to do just that. I know you don't understand. And I don't have time to explain, but it's important to me that I keep my word."

"Who'd you give your word to?"

"That's not important. The truth is, the only real thing of value I have in this world is my word. I have to keep it."

That's when I reached into my saddlebag and drew out my battered Bible. He looked at it like it was something he'd never seen before. Come to think of it, he probably hadn't.

"What's that?" He scowled.

"It's the Good Book, Jake, and I live by what's in here. That's why I can't walk away and let these gunslingers take more innocent lives."

"You a lawman?"

"Nope."

"A preacher?"

"Nope."

"Then what's your stake in all this?"

"I'm just a man who believes in living my life the best I know how. And that sometimes means stickin' my nose into other people's business, especially if that business hurts others."

"This time, I'm afraid it could get you hurt, or worse, killed," Jake said.

"A fella can't run away from trouble just because it might be painful. You comin' with me?"

Jake scratched his head and stared at the ground for a full two minutes before answering.

"I wish I could, Rawhide, I really do. But I got no yearnin' to be buried with my boots on."

I wished him well, and went on my way.

Later, I found myself saddened that Jake had chosen to ride away. I hadn't yet formed an opinion about him, whether he was just a man trying to get along in life, or if he had some dark secret that kept him locked into the crooked doings of Bradleyville and its leading citizen. There are too many things that can drive a man to hide within himself. Trusting others may have been impossible for such a man. I didn't really know him, yet I felt some inherent goodness. Still, I hoped I wouldn't have to come up against him and his gun sometime in the future. Having the slightest hesitation about drawing down on a man can get you killed.

I continued into the mountains to the north, into a cut that led through some of the most rugged country around. The barren cliffs had sparse vegetation, only the occasional pinion tree jutting from the crags above me. The trail, narrow and seldom traveled, led me deeper and higher into the mountains. The sun was sinking lower, and I knew I'd better make camp soon or I'd be trying to negotiate the winding trail with its steep drop-offs in the dark. I came to a low mesa that seemed to afford some protection from the ever-present dangers a man might experience being alone in the high desert, and chose a place with sufficient grass that Chigger could satisfy his appetite. I, on the other hand, would have to survive on what little jerky I had in my saddlebags, and perhaps some coffee, providing I could find water other than that I had occasionally seen in a stagnant pool. Although I had my Winchester rifle in a saddle scabbard, I had few illusions about any prospects of a plump deer wandering into camp begging to become dinner. And what little water I'd seen appeared unfit even for a self-respecting fish. Fortunately, I did have a nearly full canteen.

As I settled down in my blankets with a small fire warming my coffee, which I'd combined with canteen water and brewed up in an old tin can saved for just such an occasion, I was aware of the night sounds that I'd always found comforting. The howls of coyotes, owls taking flight to search out their prey, and the flickering presence of bats changing direction like ricocheting bullets, offered the evening's entertainment. A thin ribbon of smoke wafted lazily upwards from my fire, giving off a delightful aroma from the mixture of dead branches from nearby juniper and pinion. As I began

Saving Mattie 135

to relax, my thoughts drifted away from the Bradley bunch and to Mattie. I began to wonder if she might not be better off with the preacher and his wife than with an often out of work cowboy such as me, and how she would take it if I suggested it. I really didn't want to give her the impression I'd rather not have a twelve-year-old tagging along, but she might take it that way. I had learned from being around her what little time we'd had together that males and females don't always hear things the same way. I slipped off to sleep tangled up in those thoughts.

The morning came soft and warm, and I took my time crawling out from under my blankets. I rose and stretched, moving my arms about to shed the stiffness that comes with sleeping on the ground. As I looked off in the distance, I thought I saw something that seemed a little suspicious. Back along the trail I just traversed, there was a single man on horseback, stopping occasionally to look down, then continue on, directly toward my present location. It occurred to me that I might have been followed. But why? Had Bradley been so incensed by my leaving that he'd send someone out to get me? Or shoot me? Perhaps he was afraid of what I might spill to some ranger I came across about his nefarious deeds. On the other hand, did he even know I was gone?

I saddled Chigger, broke camp, and rather than ride back down the trail off the mesa, I led my horse slowly, keeping my eye on the approaching rider. When he had gotten close enough for comfort, I sought out a cut in the cliffs that would offer good cover, a place to wait until he rode by. Then I figured to make a run for it toward a barely discernable trail I'd seen about two miles back. I hoped it would carry me well into the more rugged parts of the range, and I hoped to elude my pursuer by some clever tactics I'd learned years ago from an old Indian.

Chigger was as sure-footed as any horse I'd ever ridden, but the going was still treacherous. Taking it slow would keep my horse from injury, and me the same. Deadly sharp cactus, jagged rocks, snakes, and hidden prairie dog holes were only a few of the dangers that faced the unwary. I didn't intend to become a victim of my own inattention or carelessness. We pulled up behind some boulders, out of sight of the trail, and waited.

The sound of hooves on rock came closer, heralding the rider's approach. He looked to be coming close enough to afford me a look at whoever was following my trail. At least that's what I hoped for. As the rider passed unaware of Chigger, and me, I got a good look at him, but it wasn't any of the Bradley outfit I'd seen before. I figured to be cautious anyway, and not reveal our hiding place. While my curiosity was killing me, I couldn't be certain of his intent. Better safe than sorry, I reckoned. After waiting a decent time, Chigger and I continued on our way, with plenty of stops to check our back trail. I saw nothing that would alarm me, so we increased our pace. I was anxious to get back to Bradleyville and Mattie Slaughter.

As the trail took us up Bradford's Pass, we came to an overlook that opened onto a wonderful view of the valley below, Bradleyville, and the road east where the Slaughter ranch had been. I sat there thinking what a beautiful sight spread out below me, and how it was a shame someone like Bradley and the Venables could take that beauty and turn it into something evil.

Lost for the moment in woolgathering, I failed to hear the sound of an approaching rider. When I finally snapped out of it, I spun around to come face-to-face with the man who had been following me. He made no move for his gun, so I didn't either. He was a craggy-faced man with a droopy mustache and black eyes that could burn a hole in a blanket. He was tall and rangy, and his face showed he'd faced some bad times but obviously came out the winner. Just what he'd won I dared not think. We sat staring at each other for a moment before I broke the silence.

"Howdy, stranger," I said. "Didn't hear you ride up."

"Didn't mean for you to," His voice sounded deep and raspy.

"You wouldn't happen to have been followin' this poor cowboy's trail, would you?" I leaned back in my saddle, and crossed my hands on the pommel.

"Could be. You the fella they call Rawhide Smith?"

"Could be. Why do you ask?"

"I'm told you might be able to help me answer some questions."

"What questions would that be? And before I answer anything, I'm powerful interested in just who you might be, stranger."

"Someone whose side you want to be on." His eyes narrowed as he stared at me, clearly awaiting my next words.

This hard-looking man was full of mystery. I sensed he wasn't going to be too free with whatever information I might want, but I needed to reach a sense of trust, tried to see behind those dark eyes. Chigger snorted and shook he head. I suppose that was her way of saying let's get on with it. She was right, if that's what she wanted to get across to me, for I was not going to win this stalemate. We stared. Two men sitting on a mountain pass, each waiting for the other to move the conversation to a point where one of us got what he wanted was no way to spend what was rapidly becoming another blistering Texas day. I realized that my natural stubbornness was getting me nowhere, and that's when I saw it, a splash of sunlight glinting off the tip of something almost completely hidden by the tall man's vest. He saw my eyes dart to that place. His hand slowly pulled back the vest to reveal a silver badge, the badge of a U. S. Deputy Marshal.

Chapter 16

The tension between us grew sufficiently that my hand almost imperceptibly, and quite unconsciously, eased toward my Colt. All of a sudden, when I saw that piece of slightly tarnished metal, I felt at ease. With a sigh of relief that I wasn't about to have to engage in a shootout with one of Bradley's many faceless owlhoots, I slumped in my saddle and interlaced my fingers on the pommel.

"I'd kinda like to know exactly who I'm addressing, marshal, if you wouldn't mind."

"Don't mind. Name's Brewster, Moses Brewster."

"Brewster, eh? You by chance related to Joshua Brewster? He's got a little spread about ten miles east of town."

"Joshua's my older brother. He and Anna bought that place a while back, and ain't had much luck with it."

"I know. I helped 'em drive off a couple of varmints with a mind to dislodge them from their holdings with or without consent."

"Sounds like you'd be the Rawhide Smith Joshua told me about. If so, you're just the fellow I had hoped I was tracking."

"I am called Rawhide. And why would you be trackin' me? I've done nothin' to have the law interested in my doin's. Have I?"

"Nope. I was intendin' on lookin' you up for another reason. I stopped in town to have a talk with the constable. He mentioned you might be workin' for Bradley. That didn't seem to line up with what I'd been told about you by Joshua, so I had to come lookin' for you to see for myself."

"Well, I had a reason to hire on with his outfit, but I'm not workin' for him anymore. Let's just say we don't exactly see things from the same perspective."

"That's good."

"Then what is it you want with me?"

"From the letter I received from Joshua about a month back, there's been some attempts to run him and others off their ranches."

"Yep. That's the way I see it. Bradley looks like the one behind all the shenanigans. I can't prove it beyond a doubt, but—"

"But you got a good solid notion about him, right?"

"Right."

"What was your aim in hirin' on with the Bradley bunch?"

"It's a long story."

"I got time," Moses said, as he pulled a package of papers from his pocket along with a bag of tobacco. He began rolling a smoke. He held out the bag to me. "You like one?"

"No, thanks. Got my own. Well, I reckon it all started when I met Mattie Slaughter for the first time."

"Mattie Slaughter?"

"Yep. She's a twelve-year-old little lady with a likin' for cut-down scatterguns. Came close the ventilating my hide."

"Go on," he said, taking a deep draw on his cigarette.

I told him about her seeing her folks killed by two men she identified as the Venable brothers, both of whom work for Bradley. I told him how she'd been forced to bury her own kin, and her hardly big enough to stomp the shovel into the ground. Then they came back and burned the place to the ground while we were out trying to gather enough food to stave off imminent starvation. Then I told him about coming upon the attack on the Brewster place, and how we had them in a crossfire, and they rode out at a good clip. I told about sticking around awhile, at least long enough to make sure those raiders wouldn't be sneaking back soon. But since I wanted to get Mattie to someplace safer than a small ranch where another attack was inevitable, I figured to go to town and get on with Bradley, maybe find enough evidence that he was behind these attacks to put him out of business. He nodded as I rambled on for over half an hour.

"When we rode past the Johnson place, we found a man shot dead. I buried him. I was able to get the preacher and his wife to take Mattie under their wing for a while. I landed a job as a wrangler with Bradley. But circumstances forced me to reconsider. Even while trying to get evidence against him, I couldn't be a part of his bunch of cutthroats any longer."

"That's quite a story, Rawhide. Pretty close to what Joshua related."

"Well, I'm glad you're here, now, and I can take Mattie and leave. I reckon Bradley won't try anything with a marshal breathin' down his neck."

"I'm afraid it isn't quite that easy. You see I'm way out of my jurisdiction. I'm workin' for Judge Isaac Parker up in Fort Smith, runnin' down outlaws in the Territories. I don't have the authority to arrest a vagrant down here."

My hopes for an easy solution to the Bradleyville problem

had just gone up in Marshal Brewster's cigarette smoke. I sat staring at the ground for a moment, wanting to ask what he was doing here if he couldn't help, but I didn't say it. Nothing could be gained by dragging him into my anger.

"I understand what you're probably thinkin', son, but it can't be helped. Laws have to be followed if we're ever goin' to have a country worth livin' in. I'm sure you understand that."

"Yep, reckon I do. But that don't help none with the need to string up Bradley and the Venables for murder and cattle rustlin' and–"

"And a lot of other grievous offenses, I'm certain."

"If what you're tellin' me is you can't do a blamed thing about the crimes bein' committed around, includin' those to your own kin, then what are we doin' wastin' our time palavering?"

"I didn't say there wasn't anything I could do, just not what you are lookin' for."

"I don't think I grasp your meaning, marshal."

"I got some time off comin' to me. I can hang around, keep an eye out for shady dealin's, and cover your back while you continue to dig up that evidence you been talkin' about."

"You got the badge, and you can't do anything. I got no badge, but you expect me to stick my fool neck in the noose. No thank you. I'm goin' to get Mattie and skedaddle outta this viper pit. See you around, Marshal." I wheeled Chigger around to take the trail down to Bradleyville.

"Now hold on, son, don't go stampedin' on me. I don't aim for you to make yourself a target. But we got to work together on this thing, and you're in a better position to get the goods on Bradley than I am. You're already in with the man."

"Not any more, I ain't. I quit, remember?"

"Well then, maybe you oughta find a way to un-quit."

I'm certain it must have been the look of incredulity on my face that made him burst out laughing. I had failed to find the humor and I certainly wasn't feeling as cheerful as Marshal Moses Brewster seemed to be as I rode away from him toward town. My head was awash with how I might get back in Bradley's good graces so as to continue my quest to get enough on the man to get him strung up from the nearest tree. Since Jake was the only one who knew of my intentions, maybe he hadn't passed that information on, at least not yet. I could only hope.

I rode into town with considerable trepidation. I felt like every owlhoot within a mile of any direction was looking at me like I was a target hung on a tree, and just asking to get plugged. The hair on the back of my neck felt like it was standing straight out. I would have bet a dollar on it. As I reined Chigger in front of the saloon, I saw Jake come through the doors. He was alone. He walked up to me with a quizzical look on his unshaven face. He looked around before speaking.

"Rawhide, what are you doin' here? I thought you said you were quitting."

"Have you told anyone of our conversation, Jake?"

"No. I came in, had me a couple beers, and now I'm headed back to the line shack. Why?"

"I got to thinkin' about what you said, and maybe you were right. I need the work, anyway."

"Now you're talkin', Rawhide. Good to have you back. Like I said, you don't have to worry none, 'cause I didn't spill the beans to no one." He stuck out his callused hand. I took it in a hearty shake.

"Listen, Jake, I got a couple things to do first, then I'll meet you at the shack. That okay?"

"Sure. Take your time. Nothin's doin' right now, anyway. See you later."

He gave a little salute as he mounted up and spun his horse around. I waited until he was out of sight before heading for the preacher's place. I wanted to see Mattie before leaving town again, assure her I was all right, and make sure she was, as well.

I was about halfway down the street when I saw Willy and Joey riding in with Albert Johnson. Albert looked as if he'd been dragged behind a wagon for about a mile. The Venables dismounted in front of the constable's office. Joey pulled Albert from the back of a workhorse. He was in no shape to dismount on his own. His good leg was wobbly and he came down like a man with a leg made of straw, as he crumpled to the dirt. His hands were tied behind his back, and his face was badly bruised. Blood had trickled from the corner of his mouth. I tried to get as close as possible without being noticed by either Willy or Joey. Joey dragged the man into the constable's office.

I slipped off toward a short alley that ran between the constable's jailhouse and the dry goods store. I hoped that a window I'd noticed earlier on the side might let me get close enough to hear what was going on inside, at least, that's what I was counting on. I slipped between the buildings and eased as close as I dared to the window, which by luck was slightly open in an attempt to get some sort of cross draft to bring the jail building some relief from the dizzying heat. Taking care with each step to avoid stumbling over the collection of trash, empty tin cans, and splintered boxes that littered the alley, I slipped up to the window just in time to hear Albert protesting his being beaten by two of Bradley's men.

"These rattlers got no business comin' onto my land makin' claims that aren't true. Layin' hands on me and my missus. They got no business, at all, you hear me, Emory?"

"Yeah, I hear you, Albert. Matter of fact, I figure

everybody within a block can hear you. Now what's this all about, Willy?" said the constable.

"He's been caught red-handed with rustled cattle, our cattle, with our brand in plain sight. Seen 'em with my own eyes. Our brands on every last one of 'em."

"This is a serious charge, Albert. What have you got to say for yourself?"

"I didn't steal any cattle, and these varmints know damned well I didn't. When we got back from town day before yesterday, I noticed a small herd down in the draw, near the fence line. I never saw them before in my life. They weren't there when we came to town. And that's the gospel truth."

Constable Emory was stroking his chin when I peeked in. He looked as if he were mulling over the truthfulness of the charges aimed at Albert by the Venable brothers. I knew what they were accusing him of wasn't true, and what little I knew about the man didn't include anything illegal. But somewhere in the far reaches of my mind, a bad feeling was coming to the surface. But I needed to talk to Jake before opening my mouth. I watched for a few minutes more. Then the constable said Albert would have to stay in the lockup for a few days until a judge could be summoned for a trial. I heard the steel door slam and the key turn. Albert was still protesting as I hurried off to find Chigger and track down Jake.

As I reached the mare, I saw Willy and Joey come out of the jail and cross the street to the saloon. They were grinning like they'd just raked-in the biggest poker pot ever seen. Joey slapped Willy on the back.

"That old fool will still be blabberin' when they string him up. That was about the easiest set-up we ever pulled. Bradley will be eager to hear this one," Joey laughed. The two were in a joyous mood having just falsely accused an innocent man of a hanging offense.

I climbed aboard Chigger and spurred her to a run. The sooner I found Jake, the sooner I could get to freeing Albert Johnson from jail. At least, that was my aim. The first thing I had to do was convince Jake to do the right thing and back my play. If he didn't, I could be in more trouble than I could handle. As I rode, my mind thought back on what David must have been thinking and feeling when he was sent out to battle the giant, Goliath. Was he full of confidence, or was he scared stiff? I would have bet on the latter. But he had faith, and that was exactly what I knew I had to have if I was to accomplish my goal of helping some innocent settlers get free of Bradley's men, and whisk Mattie off to someplace where she would grow up free of the kind of malevolence that seemed to permeate this town. Astride a galloping horse seemed a strange place to pray, but that was as good an alternative as any, at the time. So I did.

I could hear gunfire coming from the saloon and the street out front. Bradley's men were already celebrating another victory of evil over good. I urged Chigger to a faster pace.

Chapter 17

I reined Chigger in front of the line shack. Jake's horse was grazing off to the side, hobbled so she wouldn't wander off too far. His saddle had been dropped over the hitching rail that ran the width of the cabin. It had obviously been built in expectation of several riders gathering there at one time. There was no barn, just a rough corral and a stand of trees on the side of the hill about fifty yards away. A well sat in the middle of the yard. It was covered with several boards. A bucket rope was tied to the stump of a long dead tree right next to the well opening. Jake came out the door as I was dismounting.

"What took you so long? I thought you were coming right away."

"Yeah, well something happened to slow my progress. You remember those cattle we delivered the other day east of here? About forty head? None of them had any brands. I remember because I thought that was strange to be moving horses so close to someone else's ranch without brands."

"Yeah, I remember. What about them?"

"As I was about to leave town, Willy and Joey brought Albert Johnson into town. They'd beat him up pretty good, accusing him of having the Bradley brand on a bunch of cattle on his property. Emory stuck him in jail until a judge comes to town."

"Uh-huh. What's this have to do with us?"

"I think some of Bradley's men branded those longhorns after we left 'em. It was a setup to make Johnson look like a rustler."

"Now why'd Bradley go to all that trouble? Naw, the old man probably did rustle that stock."

"Well, I'm riding out there to see what happened to those beeves we delivered. I can identify a couple of them by sight. I'll know soon enough. You want to ride along?"

"I, uh, don't think that would be such a good idea, pardner. Bradley don't like it when his men start thinkin' for themselves. I'd better hang around here."

"Suit yourself, but I can't sit around while some owlhoots railroad a decent man into the gallows." I made sure he caught the annoyance in my voice. He didn't respond except to turn and go back inside.

Jake's reluctance to look into the matter bothered me more than a little. I had begun to think he was a decent man, largely ignorant of the worst of Bradley's doings, and that when he saw the truth, he'd come around. Besides, I knew I'd need some help before long if I turned up what I thought I would. I climbed on Chigger's back, wheeled around and urged her to a trot toward the range where we'd last seen that bunch of unbranded longhorns.

I came upon the Johnson ranch from the west end, down from some low hills that ambled around like knobs on an old hickory. I could see the burned out ranch house in the distance, and the barn and ramshackle shed. Before I got to looking

Saving Mattie

around for the cattle, I figured it wouldn't hurt to go have a talk with Vera Johnson. She was standing in the wide doorway of the barn as I rode up. She had tears in her eyes. Her face showed red marks, signs of having been slapped. One eye had already started to discolor. She watched me, startled as I approached. She turned and ran inside, then returned quickly with a rifle.

"Don't you come no closer or I'll plug you. Bradley men ain't welcome on Johnson land."

"I, uh, don't mean you any harm, Missus Johnson. I just heard about your husband and I wanted to see if there was anything I could do to help. I'm Rawhide Smith. You remember me from town, when I came in with Mattie Slaughter, don't you?"

She slowly lowered the rifle, a Henry model, probably from Civil War times. She shaded her eyes from the glare with her other hand.

"Oh, yeah, I reckon I do recognize you. Well, step down and say your piece, Mister Rawhide.

I got down and walked to her. Her face red from her being roughed up, and although the skin was beginning to turn various colors, there was no sign of blood. It took some very brave men to hit an old woman. My anger grew like a fire in a woodpile.

"I heard what the Venables said about Albert. I know it ain't true. But how can I prove it?"

"That bunch of vipers has to be stopped before they kill every living soul in this valley, Mister Rawhide. Something's got to be done."

"I was thinkin' of ridin' out to where they say they found the longhorns that Albert was supposed to have stolen. Do you know where that is?"

She took a couple of steps out into the open, turned and

pointed to a stand of trees off to the west. That would correspond to the approximate area where we moved those few head of cattle of Bradley's just days before.

"If I have your permission, I'll ride on over there and take a look. Maybe I can find something that will help Albert."

She nodded her acceptance of my offer. I tipped my hat as I rode off, uncertain of exactly what I could do even if I did find something that incriminated the Venables.

As I came to a split in the hills, I looked down on the herd that Willy had used as his proof of Albert's thieving ways. I rode in amongst them, instantly recognizing three or four of them by broken horns or splotches of unusual coloring as the ones we'd driven onto this land. Off to the west a little farther, near a creek, were the remains of a fire and all the signs of recent branding. The Bradley bunch had come onto Johnson's land, branded their own cattle, then accused someone of stealing them. But it made no sense. Why move a whole herd of beeves onto someone else's land, then stick the fire to them? I sat there for several minutes trying to figure that one out. I couldn't for the life of me get a handle on the whys and wherefores of that Bradley bunch. Nothing they did made a lick of sense. Of course, I had failed to take into account that a man has to think like a snake to actually get down and slither like one. That's exactly where I found myself, unable to think like Bradley or his hired devils. That would have to change if I was to bring that bunch to its knees.

I got down and started sifting around for something, anything to prove the Venables had been a part of branding those cattle before riding in and beating Johnson and his wife, and accusing them of rustling. As I was about to give up and leave, I saw it, glinting in the sun, a watch fob. It was silver and had a distinctive engraving of a man's initials intertwined. It must have fallen off while the man was wrestling with the branding iron. I was certain the owner would take a great joy in getting it back, just as soon as I saw the right time to make the presentation. Yep, Willy Venable would get his keepsake returned to him. In spades.

I stopped back by the Johnson barn before going back to the line shack. There I tried to comfort Vera Johnson with the news that I thought I could prove the Venable brothers were behind the whole scheme to get she and her husband shoved off their property. She was skeptical that anything could be done. "The whole town is corrupt. An honest person hasn't a prayer," she said sobbing. "And heaven knows I been doin' lots of praying. You best watch yourself, or you'll get a bullet for your trouble. You seem a decent man, and I wouldn't like to see something bad happen to you, too."

Having had very little experience consoling despondent women, I took my leave with what few words of encouragement I could muster, and rode off. Should I go to town or to the line shack and make one more attempt at getting Jake to join me in my quest to right a serious wrong? Maybe if I showed him the watch fob he would see how rotten the bunch was that he chose to give his allegiance to. It was a long shot, but worth a try.

I arrived at the line shack just before dark. Jake wasn't alone. Two men I had never met were inside. All three of them were sharing a bottle of whiskey and laughing, hysterically. When I opened the door, Jake was all smiles. The others grew quiet. Jake stood up, shakily, and motioned me to join in the festivities. The place smelled like a saloon.

"Well, well, look what the wolves chased in, it's my good friend, Rawhide Smith. Come on over and have a drink, good friend. Say, where you been?"

He knew good and well where I'd gone; why was he trying to put me on the spot? And who were these other two saddle bums?

"Thanks, Jake, but I'm tired. Think I'll turn in. You go ahead and have yourselves a good time, though. It won't bother me none." I waved him off and sank onto my bunk, thinking that would be the last I'd hear of it, but I was wrong. One of the other men struggled up from the table and came over to me, grabbed my arm and pulled me up, then led me to the table and shoved me into a chair. He was weaving so badly, I wasn't sure he could find his own seat again.

"That's more like it, now everybody's included. It ain't a party if there's a holdout. By the way, my name's Holden. This here's my buddy, Greer. Have a drink, Mister Rawhide." He shoved the bottle toward me. I raised it to my mouth and pretended to take a gulp. Just the touch of the foul tasting liquid on my tongue made me glad I'd never become a drunk. I handed the bottle back with a thanks.

"So, Mister Holden, what do you and Greer do around here?"

Holden looked at me with surprise, then a grin crept across his lips.

"Why we stamp that ol' flamin' iron on stock horses, cattle, anything that'll stand still long enough to burn Bradley's sign on 'em." Then he and Greer both burst out laughing. Jake's expression was hard to decipher. His mouth was set as if he'd just bitten into a persimmon, and his eyes were dark, brooding. Had he known all along that these two were likely to have been with Willy branding the cattle we'd moved to Johnson's land? And if so, where did he stand on the issue?

"Maybe Rawhide's right, maybe we better call it a night. I'm a mite weary, myself. You two can take the back bunks." He motioned toward the bunks at the far corner of the shack. He got up from the table, stretched, and went over to his own bunk and dropped onto it. That was my opportunity to do the same, but something was holding me there for another minute at least.

"Holden, you didn't brand some beeves just east of here a day or so ago, did you?"

"Why, sure. We do all of Bradley's brandin', didn't I tell you?"

"Was Willy Venable with you?"

"Yep. Willy and us, we're the best crew he has. What makes you ask?"

"Nothin', nothin' at all."

Holden's eyes were drooping and he was having a time of it just trying to keep from falling on the floor. He was too drunk to bother following up on why I seemed so curious about Willy. Greer tried to help him to his feet, but both stumbled to the floor, laughing and cursing and punching each other on the shoulder. They finally made it to their bunks. They were sound asleep within seconds. I looked over at Jake. He was gazing at the floor.

The next morning, shortly after dawn, we were awakened by the sound of horses pulling up in front of the shack.

"Jake, get your lazy carcass out here," shouted Willy Venable.

Jake struggled out of his bunk, still suffering the effects of too much rotgut whiskey. He pulled on his pants and stepped into his boots, yanking them on with their mule ears. He'd slept in his shirt, which was wrinkled and dirty. He ruffled his hair and opened the door. The sun struck him squarely in the face, and he winced from the brightness. He didn't step outside.

"Uh, mornin' Willy. What's up?"

"Obviously you ain't. Hang one on last night did you?"

"Uh-huh. Reckon that bottled rattler bit me good."

"Holden and Greer get here like I told 'em to?"

"Yep, leastways they were when the bottle was getting' tipped. You want 'em out here?"

"I want every one of you out here. We got a job to do."

Jake came back into the shack. Holden and Greer were sitting on the edge of their bunks, holding their heads in their hands and groaning. I was particularly happy I hadn't indulged in whatever was in that bottle. Jake told us we were all wanted outside and to get a move on. His eyes were bloodshot, and his speech was still slightly slurred. I was the first one out the door.

"Oh, it's you, is it? Where are the others?"

"They're coming. Trying to get all prettied up, I reckon."

"Hmm. A smart mouth, too. Well, if you live long enough, you can figure you'll get a chance to back up that mouth someday. I wouldn't turn my back on no one, however. Never can tell what might be back there." Willy gave me a sneer that might have sent a chill up my back if I didn't have such a deep dislike for the man. He didn't frighten me, but I knew his words carried a lot of truth, especially about turning one's back on vipers like him.

Jake, Holden, and Greer stumbled from the shack, each shading his eyes from the sun, and squinting to make out Willy.

"All right, men, the idea of taking on your next assignment while you're all clearly hung over–all except for smart mouth, here–doesn't appeal to me, but Bradley says it has to be done. So, you're goin' to do it. Get your gear, guns and plenty of ammunition, and come to the saloon by the back way. You got two hours."

Willy turned and abruptly rode out. Jake and the others looked at each other for a moment, then began the task of trying to get sober enough to ride. It gave me time to think, and maybe probe for anything I could about the Bradley operation. Men who've been pretty well liquored up just a few hours before often prove to be a wellspring of information.

Chapter 18

"What do you figure we're headed for, gents?" I asked as we rode toward town.

"What difference does it make? We're bound to do whatever Bradley wants or face a bullet," mumbled Holden.

"Yeah, and I don't think any of us want to be facing down Willy Venable," said Greer. "I've seen what happens to a man who pushes his luck."

"He pretty fast, is he?"

"It ain't that he's so fast, it's more like him pullin' on you when you least expect it. Back or front, don't matter to Willy, or Joey for that matter. A man wouldn't want to cross either of 'em. They both got long memories," Holden said. "And they're both just naturally mean."

"Yep, mean sure does seem to come natural," said Greer.

Jake rode along silently, a look on his face that was halfway between sadness and despair. I hadn't been able to figure him out from the beginning, and there didn't seem to be any improvement with time, even if it had only been about ten days since we first met. He was a true loner, a man without roots or ties. My curiosity was piqued more every day over what was going on behind those empty eyes.

Jake had reminded me of someone from the moment I first saw him, but I couldn't place where or whom. It was more of a familiar feeling than an actual remembrance, a memory long ago lost or hidden. After my close call with death, it seemed I'd lost some of my previous sensitivity to details. Had I remembered more clearly who it was that had shot me, I might not have been trying to escape past events, and would never have met Mattie. Everything happens for a reason, my ma always said, and you should never try to second-guess destiny. I suppose, in a way I understood her, but the destiny thing was way beyond my comprehension.

As we came into town, I noticed several more horses than usual tied out front of the saloon. We rode around back and tied up there, as per Willy's instructions. We entered the back door that opened into a long hall. Bradley's office opened onto that hallway. Jake led the way, stopping at Bradley's door and knocking.

""Come in." The gruff voice was instantly recognizable as belonging to Bradley. We filed in. Willy and Joey were already inside, along with Amarillo and Snake. Snake's head was still bandaged and he didn't look very good. I wondered if he would ever get back to normal after the beating he took from that Mexican vaquero. He was staring off into the distance, but his eyes seemed to wander, as if he couldn't focus. Drool trickled from of one corner of his mouth. A hand rested in his lap, slightly curled.

"Gents, I've asked you all here to discuss an important job. I hope everyone is ready because we can't afford to make any mistakes with this one."

"Whatever you want, we're ready, Mister Bradley," said Jake. Holden and Greer nodded their agreement.

"That's good to hear, boys. Good to hear." He motioned for all of us to gather closer to the table. Snake remained seated, seemingly oblivious to what was going on.

"How's Snake doin', Mister Bradley?" I asked.

Willy snapped back before Bradley could say anything. "Don't you worry none about Snake. He's in my care, now. Just you take care of yourself and worry about the job at hand. And quit askin' stupid questions."

I disliked Willy in a most intense manner, and I suspect it showed. He, too, held an almost instant disdain for me, unable to even answer the simplest questions without gritting his teeth and spitting out venomous responses. Since he wasn't going to trust me any more than I was going to turn my back to him, we were at an impasse, one that would necessitate my remaining particularly watchful. After Holden's warning, I planned to be especially vigilant from that moment on. I also figured it might be a good idea to avoid asking questions. I'd let Jake take on that responsibility. He seemed not to have incurred Willy's wrath in such a heaping helping.

"All right, boys, it's time to make our move on these confounded ranchers. They seem to be moving in, buying up sections like they were nothin', and the only way I see to put a stop to it is to hit 'em, and hit 'em hard."

"Who do you want us to move on first, Mister Bradley?" Willy said.

"We're going to do this a little different from what we've done before, gents. We're goin' to split up and hit several ranches at the same time. That way, none can come to the defense of another. We'll have 'em so desperate, they'll all be faced with a dead—"

"You want us to just scare 'em, or shoot 'em down like we had to do with Slaughter?" Joey said.

"You cut me off before I could finish, Joey. I meant to

Saving Mattie 159

say, dead-end. *Dead* is the word I want you to put particular emphasis on this time. And, yes, *just* like Slaughter."

It was a good thing no one was watching my expression at that moment or they would have seen a mixture of shock and joy. One, these evil men openly admitted to murder, and two, I'd now heard an admission of their involvement in killing Mattie's family

Clearly it had been done with Bradley's permission and direction. Now all that was left for me to do was figure out what I could about it. About then, I was sure wishing that Marshal Brewster had told me where to find him.

"Which ones do we hit this time?" Willy asked.

"Break up into four men each. Then each group will take a separate rancher. Jake, Amarillo, Snake and Rawhide will hit the Brinegar spread. Willy, Joey, Holden, and Greer, you'll hit the Brewster place. I'll pick up some of the boys at the ranch and go after the Olsons. Any questions?"

Questions? You bet I had questions, lots of them. Questions like how was I going to get word to Marshal Brewster about the danger to his brother's ranch? And how was I going to keep from being part of the attack on the Brinegars? And...

Before I could finish asking myself any number of other questions, all of which needed immediate answers, Bradley stood up and shooed everybody out of his office.

"We'll meet back here after you've all done your jobs." Bradley put on his hat and stuck his revolver in his belt. He came around his desk and took the door to usher any stragglers in the right direction. I was the last one out the door as Bradley slapped me on the back and said, "Good luck out there, gents. I'm countin' on you to teach these land grabbers a lesson."

Outside, I noticed Jake watching my every move, as if he expected me to cut and run. I wondered what he would do if I did make a break for it. Would he go with me or try to shoot me? Was Jake Pardee really part of this scum or had his trail also come to a crossroads, one that he could never turn back from? We were about to find out, because I had already dug in my heels over running some settlers off their lawfully obtained land. I figured to make my move about two miles out of town, well out of Constable Emory's jurisdiction, and far enough away so that shots couldn't be heard in town.

We had ridden for about an hour. And I had yet to figure just how I was going to pull off stopping this raid on the Brinegar spread. I had intended to have my plan in place shortly after we left Bradleyville, but it hadn't worked out that way. We were almost at the ranch's outer boundary, when I was saved from that decision by the appearance of a man sent from heaven. Moses Brewster. He came galloping up from behind. Jake looked around, clearly bothered by the appearance of a stranger just before we were to start our attack on another innocent rancher.

"Howdy, gents, where you headed?" Moses said, reining his horse in a cloud of dust.

The others looked to each other with incredulity. Jake looked puzzled. Snake was still in a daze, but reddened with anger at the interruption, and Amarillo turned sour. He was the one that spoke up.

"What's it to you, mister? Where we're headed ain't no business of yours. You best be movin' on if you know what's good for you."

Moses didn't move, except to brush aside his vest just far enough to reveal the marshal's badge. Jake suddenly froze in place. Amarillo was instantly incensed by the appearance of the law. Snake was slowly moving his hand toward his sidearm. In his condition, I hoped he wouldn't do what I was afraid he might.

Saving Mattie 161

Amarillo eased up a bit. "Why, we're goin' to visit old man Brinegar. Hear he's been feelin' poorly of late. Just wanted to extend our well wishes." He grinned a yellow-toothed grin, as if the marshal would be stupid enough to swallow that story. "Good man, Brinegar, you know."

"Strange. I was by to see him a couple of hours ago. Didn't notice any ailment to speak of. Of course, sometimes a terrible fever can come on a man in minutes, or so I've heard," said Moses. I found myself quietly amused at the way Moses Brewster was feeling out the situation. I couldn't let on, however, so I sat without any outward expression at all, at least as much as it was in my power to do so.

"Maybe we heard wrong, Marshal. I 'spect we should be moseying along. Got lots of work needs tendin' to." Amarillo started to turn his horse around, pulling directly in front of Snake, putting him momentarily out of the marshal's sight.

Snake wasted no time in taking advantage of the situation. He pulled his revolver, and as soon as Amarillo was clear, brought the forty-four to bear on Brewster. The marshal was way ahead of Amarillo. He proved in a flash that he was no beginner in the business of outwitting owlhoots like these. Brewster's Colt blazed flame and smoke as his shot hit Snake squarely in the chest, knocking him backwards out of his saddle.

Amarillo spun around, drawing his gun. But like Snake, it was too little, too late. He became victim number two, falling to the marshal's keen eye and fast gun. Jake sat stunned at the sight. He made no move for his own weapon. Brewster brought his gun to bear on Jake without cocking it.

"Well, mister, which way does the wind blow for you? Is this your day to die along with your friends?" He waited patiently for the words to come from Jake's quivering mouth.

"I-I ain't got no intention, uh, of goin' for my six-shooter, mister. Honest. I'll do whatever you tell me." Then Jake glanced over at me to see if I was the next one to make a foolish move. His shock was evident by the wide-eyed look on his face.

"Marshal Brewster, I was about at my wits ends over what to do next. I figured I was all out of options and might have to draw down on someone. I knew where Snake and Amarillo stood, Jake here was the only one I had no idea which side of the fence he'd fall on. Sure was glad to see you comin' through that cloud of dust, though."

Jake's eyes narrowed as he turned to me. "You threw in with the law? Was that why you kept tryin' to get me to leave the Bradley ranch? I can't believe it." He shook his head.

"I didn't see you as one of these sidewinders, Jake. I thought I saw some good in you, and I didn't want to see you get strung up for murderin' innocent settlers. Brewster, here, gave me an opportunity to right some wrongs. Although, I will admit, I was beginnin' to wonder if he was going to show up when I needed him. Reckon I got my answer."

Jake grunted, still shaking his head in disbelief.

"Jake, you haven't answered my question. Which side you on?"

"I ain't made up my mind yet. I'll let you know soon's I know."

"Ain't no more time for fence sittin', mister. This raidin' and killin' is goin' to stop, even if every blasted one of you Bradley men has to go to your own funeral," Moses said.

"I don't see how Jake can go back to Bradley or explain to the Venables how Snake and Amarillo got shot, yet he didn't get a scratch. Bradley strikes me as a man who expects you to lay down your life in the execution of his orders. I figure Jake's in one of them situations where, whichever way he turns, there's a boulder in his way. Ain't that about it, Jake?"

I watched Jake's face age before me. He had figured on living a life of doing what he was told, no questions asked, and never having to pay a price for it. If he left Bradley, where would he go? That question was painted clearly on his deeply lined face and pursed lips. I waited for his answer with even more anticipation than the marshal.

"Since I made no play, you got no reason to take me in. I'll just go on about my business, if that's all right with you gents." Jake had made his choice. He didn't want a fight, but he wasn't ready to go up against Bradley or the Venables.

I've known men like Jake all my life. Men who straddle a line, never making a choice that requires wrestling with conscience. Here was a shallow man just looking out for himself, and no one else. He had no particular moral code, and didn't really see the need for one, either.

Brewster looked at me for guidance. Jake had never done anything I'd witnessed that warranted him being locked up. I could only shrug, and leave the next move up to Marshal Brewster.

"What were Bradley's orders?"

"He's raiding three different ranches at the same time. This one here, the Olson's, and your brother's place."

"All right, here's what we'll do. You head over to Joshua and Anna's ranch. I'll try to stop 'em at the Olson place. What do you say? It's time we made it clear the killin' is over." The marshal sat straight as he waited for my answer. After what I'd seen and heard from Bradley himself, I didn't have to think too hard on it.

"I'll do as you say, Moses. But what about Jake?"

"I think I have a way to make him choose sides. I'll just take him along with me."

I liked the marshal's plan. Once Bradley saw Jake in the company of the marshal, he was done in these parts, anyhow.

Chapter 19

After spending a minute telling Mister Brinegar to keep a real sharp lookout, and warning him that there could be another attack at any time, I left to cut across country to get to the Brewster place by the back way, a much shorter route than would have been taken by Willy and his bunch. Even so, I urged Chigger to a fast gallop just to ensure a timely arrival.

Coming up on the saucer-shaped valley where Joshua had kept his sheep, I tried to keep an eye out for evidence of where his flock might have been taken. But wind and rain had obliterated any such trail. I kept going.

When I came up to the rise near the back of the Brewtser homestead, I could clearly see I had achieved what I'd hoped for. There was no sign of Willy and his brother, only Anna hanging some newly washed clothing on a line that strung from the shed to the house. That small wash showed just how little Joshua and Anna had to their name. A couple of work shirts, a pair of denims, and a few underclothes that had a distinctly feminine flair were all that swung in the breeze. A peaceful picture, indeed. But I could no longer dally with such comforting thoughts. I had a mission to accomplish, and little time to set things in motion.

I rode in a wide arc to avoid coming up on the house from the rear and surprising Joshua, possibly getting a bullet for my trouble. The incidents of the recent past would make anyone jumpy, and an old man, with a shoulder wound not yet completely healed, could not be blamed if he shot first and asked questions afterward.

"Hello the house. Anyone home? It's me, Rawhide Smith," I called out as loudly as I could, hoping my words weren't carried astray on the wind.

Joshua poked his head out the door, rifle in hand, raising his other hand to shade his eyes and confirm my identity. He stepped out, lowered the rifle, and smiled broadly. He shook his head as he emerged with caution.

"Lordy, it's sure good to see a friendly face, Rawhide. It surely is. Get down off that horse and come inside for a bite to eat."

I first led Chigger to the barn so she wouldn't give away my presence when the Venables came calling. When I came out of the barn, Joshua gave me a questioning glance.

"What'd you do that for?"

"Come inside, Joshua, I have some news. It'll explain why I put Chigger in your barn quick enough." I followed him inside and took a seat at the table. Anna had dished up some beans and made some fresh bread. My mouth began to water the moment I stepped inside. I removed my hat and hung it on a peg just inside the door.

Joshua passed me the bowl of beans after saying a brief prayer. "Now, son, what's this news?"

I took a deep breath and started in, punctuating my tale with spoonfuls of beans. "The Venables are on their way out here right now. They should be arriving in a half hour or so. We have to be ready. There are four of them this time."

"How do you know all this, son?"

"I been workin' for 'em. I got a job with the Bradley outfit so I could uncover something to tie Emmett Bradley to the Venable's raids on your ranch and others, especially the Slaughter's."

"So, what you're sayin' is you got firsthand information that can put those varmints on a gallows, right?"

"That's right. But that doesn't mean it's going to be easy. The law in Bradleyville is as corrupt as Bradley is. That gang of cutthroats controls almost the whole area, and bringing them down won't come without more pain and suffering, I'm afraid."

Joshua's face turned dour and his head drooped. "This ain't what we were expecting when we bought this land. I ain't sure I can put Anna through any more of it. It ain't fair to a hard workin' woman, makin' her suffer the evil that some men seem to thrive on."

"I agree. That's why I had to take Mattie away. I got her settled with the preacher and his wife, like you suggested. I think she'll be safe, at least until this is over. And I promise you, it *will* be over."

"The preacher, huh," Joshua said, rubbing his chin thoughtfully, and nodding. I was puzzled by his reaction.

"Yes, Jericho Pike. He seems to be a righteous man, and his wife, Sarah, took to Mattie right off. You look skeptical. Is there something I should know?"

"I sure hope we were right. But Emmett Bradley, himself, brought that preacher to town, built him a church and a parsonage, and makes sure folks go there every Sunday and drop a few pennies in the basket. He figured a preacher and a church would go a long way toward making the town look respectable. I don't know how beholdin' Pike is to Bradley, or whether he would give Mattie up to save his position in the community."

His words hit me like being tossed from a bronco. What if I'd inadvertently thrown Mattie to the wolves instead of providing a safe haven? I was overwhelmed by that possibility, especially since I'd told Pike Mattie's whole story and revealed her real name, as well. I was cursing my possible bad decision under my breath when Anna spoke up.

"I'm sure the Pike's wouldn't take a chance of endangering the child's welfare for their own gain. Sarah Pike strikes me as a woman of the highest principles. Don't worry about Mattie, Rawhide. She'll be fine."

"I pray that you're right, Anna."

"Now how is it you figure to stop the Venables?" Joshua scowled, probably at the thought of again facing the guns of these desperadoes.

"I'm hopin' to surprise them with my appearance, although not until they get to feelin' confident that they are only goin' to have one man to contend with. They think I'm with three others raidin' the Brinegar spread."

"If that's where they think you are, what's happenin' to Frank and Emily Brinegar?"

"Nothin' ill befell them. Thanks to your brother, Moses."

"Hmm, Moses found you, huh?"

"Yep. At first I didn't know what to make of a marshal that couldn't act in the name of the law. But over at the Brinegar's, he came on strong, ridin' up on us and shootin' two of Bradley's men. He took the other with him to see about stopping whatever was to take place at the Olson ranch."

"When I told Moses about what you did for us, well I think he felt comforted that there would be at least one man around here that could stand up for the rights of the ranchers. He all right?"

"Looked fit as a fiddle to me. And he don't seem to be shy when it comes to havin' to plug a man in defense of his own well being."

"The two of you'd make a real fine pair. Maybe you'll consider gettin' deputized one of these days. This part of the country needs some law, real law, not the kind that can't make up its mind which side of the fence to graze."

"Like Stub Emory?"

"Just like Stub Emory."

Willy and Joey Venable rode in side-by-side ahead of the two other wranglers, Holden and Greer. They rode straight in the saddle, with their expressions making it plain that they intended to drive the Brewsters from their land without further delay. They weren't planning on coming a third time. They knew Joshua Brewster couldn't defend his ranch against such firepower, they probably figured to make an easy day of it. From what I'd overheard Willy say during one of his many moments of bragging, I figured they planned to kill every living thing on the ranch, then burn the house and the out buildings to the ground, just like what they'd done at the Slaughter ranch. I couldn't let that happen, although even with my gun, Joshua likely didn't have a very good chance. I knew we couldn't change the Venables' minds, but maybe, just maybe, I could make them think real hard about their plan, even pray they'd abandon it, at least long enough to get the marshal's backing.

I was in the cabin when I heard the four riders approaching. Joshua sat on the porch, rocking away, cradling his rifle across his lap. I could have sworn I heard him humming. It sounded a lot like an old church song I'd remembered from my youth. I strapped on my Colt, pulled my slouch hat off the peg, and got ready to join the party. I sent Anna out back to the shed with instructions to stay there until the danger was over. She would do as she was told. I was thankful stubborn Mattie was safely in town and out of danger. I could only hope for us.

I stood just inside the door, watching to see how Willy would make his play, when I heard Joshua's gravelly voice. He sounded ten years younger than I knew him to be. He was a man for whom life was a challenge, and he intended to prove he was up to the task.

"What do you boys want?" Joshua challenged. I picked up the rifle I'd brought in from my saddle for added incentive, chambered a round, leaving it cocked. I wanted the Venables and their gunslingers to think hard about what they were about to do.

"You know what we want, old man," Willy said. "We want you off this land. You can go peaceful, or you can get buried here. Make up your mind quick like, before my boys' trigger fingers get too itchy."

That's when I stepped outside.

"Howdy, boys. Nice weather we're havin,' ain't it?" I brought the rifle up and trained it straight at Willy's chest. "You fellas stop by for dinner, or to welcome your neighbors?"

"I told you he didn't seem right to me, Joey. Now it looks like he's throwed in with these damned fools eatin' up all our range," Willy said. Joey nodded. Neither made a move for their guns. "What's your part in all this, Rawhide?"

"I accepted an offer from Mister Brewster here to kinda watch over the place, make sure we don't attract rustlers and such. Nice man to work for. You boys should try getting' on with a more amiable boss man, yourselves."

Willy's expression turned sour, like he'd bitten into a ripe lemon.

"So Brewster here has himself a hired gun, huh? You boys hear that? Rawhide fancies he can go up against all four of us and still be breathin' fresh air," Willy said.

Holden leaned over to say something to Willy just above a whisper.

"Willy, I had had a snort or two, but I saw him practice with that Colt yesterday. He'll for sure get at least one, maybe two of us. The man's good. Maybe we ought to—"

"Shut up, Holden. We're here, and here we're stayin' until this old man takes his woman and heads for California or any other damned place he wants. It must be *someplace* else."

"Fellas, I ain't leavin' so you might as well get on with whatever it is you're plannin' to do. That or get off my land," Joshua said, with determination that belied his frail condition after nearly being killed by this very same bunch.

Willy looked at me for a moment, then to his brother, Joey. "You figure you're good enough to take us all, Rawhide?"

"Nope. I ain't figured nothing. But I can say for sure that when this Winchester gets ready to spit fire and sees you grinnin' jackasses sittin' there like peacocks, why it'll likely go off for the sheer joy of it. If I had to guess, Willy, I'd say you and Joey will go down about a half second apart."

Joshua thumbed back the hammer on his Winchester, a round already having been chambered. The tension in the air was like a heavy weight hanging on my shoulders. I shifted the Winchester to my left hand, freeing my right to draw the Colt. This made the Venables even more nervous.

Right then, Joshua spoke up. I couldn't believe what was coming out of his mouth, or where he came up with such a bodacious concoction of nonsense coupled with a bald-faced lie. It's amazing what a few well-chosen falsehoods can make a man do.

"Sounds to me you fellas ain't never been properly introduced to my nephew, here. Yes, Rawhide Smith's his God-given name, but in Arizona he's better known as the man who cleaned up Charleston, and half the other lawless gold camps. Bet he never told you how many men he's killed, did he? He's modest, but I ain't. It was twenty-four, at last count. I ain't kept track since he stayed a couple months in New Mexico. They say he backed down Curly Bill before the man could clear leather. And you may have heard that no one's ever heard from Mysterious Dave Mather since he left Dodge City, well Rawhide knows what happened to him, firsthand. Ain't nobody gonna see Dave again, either." Joshua leaned back with a satisfied smile on his weathered face. He'd just told two of the biggest whoppers I'd ever heard. In fact, I'd never met either one of those well-known gunslingers. Apparently, neither had the Venables.

Willy and Joey looked at each other. Holden sat silent and unmoving, while Greer appeared to be getting more nervous by the second. There was no telling what would happen next. I knew I wasn't eager to find out that one of those boys actually knew Curly Bill, whom I'd never laid eyes on in my life, or Mysterious Dave, who was still as much a mystery to me as he'd ever been. I had to admit Joshua turned out to be a real good storyteller.

"My advice, old man, is to get packed up and start your journey to someplace else. The next time you see us, we'll have a dozen armed men. Then we'll see how tough you are. You can count on us bein' back. And Rawhide, you're a dead man."

Willy yanked his reins to turn his horse, and the last we saw of them that day was as the four of them disappeared over the very hill Mattie and I had been on, hunkered down behind a boulder, tossing lead their way the day they first attacked the Brewster ranch. That day haunted me still. The idea that men could gang up on an almost defenseless old man and a woman was beyond my understanding. Evil persists in this world; I've always been aware of that fact, but I generally could avoid staring it in the face. Those days seemed to be over. I knew Willy's last words were more than a warning. They were a revelation, a distinct depiction of Satan's rule over this earth. My palms grew sweaty, and I had to swallow to keep my dry throat from closing up. Whatever the pathway of my future, I had the eerie feeling it was getting narrower and narrower.

Chapter 20

I stood on the porch of the Brewster house watching the dust slowly settle from the four men who had just ridden off, wondering how long it would take for Bradley to hit us with every gun he had. Just then Joshua stood up and eased the hammer down on his rifle.

"I can't thank you enough for bein' here, Rawhide. I ain't got the words."

"Oh, I think you got plenty of words. I can't say as how I can figure where you got them though. That was some whoppin' tall tale you fed those boys. Why, I ain't never even *been* to Arizona or New Mexico."

"A little storytellin' here and there don't hurt, does it? It seemed to have a special effect on that mean lookin' one at the head of the pack, don't you think?"

I had to grin. I was getting to like this man more every time I talked to him. He might have been a crusty old rancher, but inside dwelled a good heart and healthy dose of the reality of life. I stepped out the back door and called to Anna that it was safe for her to return. Seeing that we had both walked away none the worse for wear, she was beaming as she came in the house.

"I didn't realize what a couple of tough hombres you two were. But I'm thankful for it," she said as she set to her chores.

"We were lucky, this time, weren't we, Rawhide?" Joshua said.

"Real lucky. The next time, well, I just don't know. Best we set to prayin' lots, that's about all I can say."

"I wonder how Moses is makin' out. He's hard as nails, I'll tell you, but he ain't bulletproof."

"None of us are, I reckon. But now's the time to start plannin' some defense that's more substantial than a couple of tall tales about my expertise with a forty-five. You got any ideas?"

Joshua chuckled at that before his face wrinkled at the seriousness of the situation.

"I had thought that maybe we could gather several families together at one place, make a more substantial stand against these renegades. But it sounds as though Bradley has already out figured us on that point. He'd just go from one empty ranch to the next, burnin' and killin' livestock, so we'd not have anything left to come back to even if we did win some little victory."

"Yep. If he saw you all gathered together, he'd just ride away and let you figure how you're all goin' to rebuild. Then, when you split up, you'd each be weaker than before."

"That's the way I see it, too." He began stroking his chin with a calloused hand, the roughness of his stubbly face sounding like sandpaper. We both sat staring at each other for several minutes, neither willing to spit out a plan.

"You'll stay the night, won't you Mister Rawhide," Anna said.

"I'd like that. Thank you."

"You figure Moses will come by here before goin' his own way?" Joshua said.

"I don't have a notion. The way you say that it sounds as if you and Moses don't get on all that well. That right?"

Joshua looked uncomfortable at that question. He began to squirm in his seat, then he eased out of the chair and wandered over toward the door. He leaned on the doorframe for a moment, looking out as if to make sure we were alone, then he stepped out onto the porch. I hadn't been invited, but I followed anyway.

"I didn't mean to say anythin' out of line. Sorry if I offended you, Joshua."

"Naw. It's nothin' like that. It ain't you. Just brothers bein' brothers, I reckon."

Since I'd never had a brother, or a sister either, for that matter, I had no idea what he was talking about. I thought it best to drop the subject and move on to working on a plan to help the small ranchers. But Joshua apparently wasn't through with the subject of his brother, so I just sat back and listened.

"When Moses rode in here a couple days ago, I figured it was on account of the letter I'd sent him asking what could be done about Bradley. When I told him about you helpin' out and savin' our lives, he appeared more interested in seekin' you out, than he did in helpin' solve our dilemma."

"That's interesting. He *did* track me down right as I was set on leavin' the Bradley outfit. He's the one talked me into stickin' it out for a while longer. I wondered how he knew where to look."

"Yeah. I sent him off in your direction. I figure he was lookin' to find someone to do the heavy liftin' since he ain't a marshal around here."

"He seems like a good man. You ought to be proud to have a marshal in the family."

"I reckon, but it ain't always worked out to the good side of the ledger."

"How do you mean?"

"There were three of us brothers. Hank, the oldest, went down a crooked trail after the war. We were from Missouri, been farmin' there for quite a while. Hank hated the blue bellies, and he got tangled up in a bunch of scum called themselves Quantrill's Raiders. Just a bunch of murderin' trash. They weren't fightin' for the South, like they claimed, just doin' it for what they could steal. Nothin' but outlaws."

"What happened to Hank?"

"He was with another fella got caught robbin' a bank near Springfield. He came out, guns a'blazin', and ran smack into a young deputy sheriff. He was wounded, went to trial, and got sent off to prison. He died there. That deputy was Moses."

"I suppose that put Moses in a tight way with the rest of the family, huh?"

"Yep. Not me, but there *was* resentment between Pa and some cousins who hadn't really figured which side of the fence they wanted to graze. Ain't been but a dozen words pass between us for fifteen years, I 'spect."

"That's too bad. I never had any brothers, so I can't imagine what it's like to come to that kind of crossroad. I'm sorry for you."

"No need to be. Those were hard times. Lots of families in the same situation. Why, you got half the state sidin' with the James boys, and the other half hopin' they catch 'em. I don't fall either way. I'm doin' fine without all that, or I was until Bradley and his bunch decided to kick us off our land."

I was growing weary. I stretched and tried stifling a yawn unsuccessfully. Joshua caught on quickly, rose and suggested we get to bed so that if I wanted an early start, I'd be sure to get enough sleep. I gratefully accepted his suggestion. I stepped off the porch, sauntered across the yard, and into the barn where I planned to bed down in some straw. My head was reeling from the day's activities. It didn't take long before I drifted off to thoughts of what the morning might bring.

I shouldn't have been all that surprised, however, as things seemed all whopper-jawed ever since I met Mattie Slaughter. That wasn't about to change.

It wasn't long after breakfast, while I was saying my goodbyes to Joshua and Anna, when a cloud of dust heralded an approaching rider. I rested my hand on the butt of my Colt just in case it was one of the Venables coming back to follow through on his threats. As the rider approached, I could make out the unmistakable ramrod-straight posture of Moses Brewster. He seemed in no hurry, so we waited until he got off his mount and ambled up to the porch.

"Anna got any coffee, brother?"

Joshua nodded and called to Anna to bring out the coffee pot and some cups.

"Sit and make yourself to home, Moses," Joshua said. "You ain't shot up or nothin', are you?"

"Nope. Not a scratch. If Bradley had known the truth about all those rifle barrels stickin' out of nearly every window in the place, and every openin' in the barn, he sure as shootin' would have started blastin' away. But I confronted him far enough away that I reckon neither he nor his men could make out that they were just sticks and broom handles. Only me, the two Olsons, and Jake had any weapons, and I couldn't take a chance on Jake changin' sides, so I took his revolver away from him and gave him the job of bein' tied up inside."

Moses chuckled at his own humor. So did I. Joshua just stared stoically at his brother, waiting for whatever else was to come. Moses saw that Joshua was neither amused, nor patient, so he cleared his throat and continued on with what he'd come for in the first place.

"Well, anyway, we slowed 'em down for a spell. Not for long, I'll wager, but for a few days until Bradley figures out how he'll gather enough men together to do the job proper."

"What did you do with Jake, Moses?"

"Cut him loose. Nothin' else I could do. He hadn't done anything to make me want to plug him, so—"

"You did the right thing, although it kinda puts him in a tight situation. I'm not so sure down deep in his heart that he's really *one* of them varmints. I saw a good side to him, although he's havin' some trouble recognizing it himself."

"We'll know soon enough. If he runs back to Bradley with the news of how I bamboozled him, the big boss's goin' to be madder than a coyote caught in barbed wire. Bradley might start roundin' up an army to do his dirty work," Moses said.

I thought about the truth of that. I could see that very thing happening. Bradley wasn't a patient man. He was greedy, mean, and ruthless when it came to getting everything he wanted. He wasn't the first of his kind to try corralling a whole county into yielding to his will, and he wouldn't be the last. But this wasn't the time to be studying the whys and wherefores of men's actions. Something had to be done, and soon. When I expressed that sentiment, I wasn't prepared for what was to come.

"And that's where you come in, Rawhide."

"What do you mean by that, Marshal?"

"I want you to come back to Traub with me. Got myself an idea."

"Whoa. I've already had a run-in with some vigilantes from that town. They won't take too kindly to my showing up on their streets anytime soon."

"I'll worry about that. In fact, that could work to our advantage."

"Those men came lookin' for whoever murdered the County Sheriff. How's that going to work to our advantage?"

"Just hear me out. If, after you know all the facts, and I've laid out my plan, you want to skedaddle for New Mexico, I'll not stop you. Fair enough?"

I couldn't think of anything to do but shrug. It seemed a fair offer. Of course at the time, I had no idea what I was being drawn into. Had I known, well, let's just say I'd been better off to jump on Chigger right then and urge her to keep running until we hit California.

"Yeah. I reckon. Say whatever you got to say."

"I had a chance to talk to Jake while we were on our way to the Olson place. He told about how the two of you were mistaken for the ones who shot the County Sheriff over in Traub. He said they took you into town to get Bradley to back your story about working for him."

"That's right. Bradley told them we did and then chased them out of town, or rather, Willy chased them out."

"Yep. But what you don't know was something that Jake learned later, when you were cuttin' yourself out of Bradley's herd, just before I came upon you in the hills."

"You mean where you tracked me down, don't you?"

He nodded an acknowledgement of my more accurate description of the incident.

"Uh-huh. Anyway, he let it slip that when a couple of Bradley's men, named Holden and Greer, came to the line shack where you were stayin', they got pretty drunk, tellin' tales and generally bragging about their exploits. He thought they were all bluster, until they spilled it that they had been in Traub and had shot it out with the sheriff. *They* killed him. Those vigilantes didn't know how close they were to the men they were after. Just your bad luck you and Jake were a fairly close match to the descriptions the witnesses had given of the men who pulled the trigger."

"Holden and Greer..." I had to scratch my head over that one. I hadn't liked those two from the moment I laid eyes on them, but I hadn't figured them for stone cold killers. I wondered why Jake hadn't told me about them. But then there were a great many things I wondered about Jake.

"I can't touch them, but if you go along with my plan, I think they may just get their comeuppance."

"And what is your plan, exactly?"

"Get your things together and I'll explain it on our way over to Traub," Moses said.

"What? I told you, I can't go there. I'll be so full of holes I'll whistle when the wind blows."

"Not if you're ridin' with me. I'm tellin' you my plan will work, if you'll just give it a chance. That's all I ask."

I was shaking my head when he hit me with the one thing he knew would sway me to his way of thinking. Playing fair didn't seem to be one of the attributes of being a Deputy U. S. Marshal.

"You want to square things for that little Slaughter girl, don't you, son?"

"Well, of course I do. That's the most important thing I got on my mind."

"That's what I figured. Now then let's get ridin'. We need to get that badge pinned on as soon as possible. Time's a'wastin'."

"Badge? What badge?" I was completely baffled by his train of thought. I was beginning to think I'd dozed off somewhere along the line and missed about an hour of whatever he was going on about.

"Why, didn't I tell you? You're goin' to be the new County Sheriff."

Chapter 21

The road to Traub was dusty and flat. Not a hard ride, but a hot, tiresome one. Few words were spoken between us for several miles until I had enough questions piled up to start talking.

"Joshua said you had to put your own brother in prison."

"Joshua talks too much. Besides, Hank put himself in prison by followin' the outlaw trail."

He spoke with a bitterness that belied his words. His tone conveyed a subtle remorse for his brother's actions, and I suspect some underlying guilt for being forced into a bad situation. He was guilty of nothing more than doing what he'd been paid to do when he signed on as a lawman. I saw pain in his eyes. Joshua's lack of enthusiasm for his visit didn't help much, either.

"You and Joshua aren't real close I take it."

"I put my own brother in prison. Can't blame the family for bein' a tad cool to the idea." A distinct sadness touched his voice.

But I couldn't help feeling a sense of power in this man. He was decisive and moved to action, yet he seemed dedicated to upholding the law, every bit of it. Sometimes that wasn't an easy task, even for the best lawmen, but Moses Brewster clearly was intent on keeping himself above the temptations that were so prevalent all over the western frontier. I felt here was a man I could trust. That wasn't something I'd felt often these past several years. But my curiosity over what his plan might be to help the small ranchers live in peace and work the land as they saw fit without the fear of being shot or burned out by a greedy outlaw was gnawing at me with a persistence I could no longer ignore.

"Marshal, how about fillin' me in on exactly what it is you are plannin' for my future. Don't it seem proper to tell a man what to expect if you've a mind to saddle him with a badge?"

Moses frowned, then nodded. "Yeah, I reckon that's only fair. Here's the way I see it. Those two fellas, Holden and Greer, work for Bradley, right?"

"Right."

"And if what Jake says is true, they're the ones responsible for gunnin' down the County Sheriff, right?"

"Right."

"Then don't it seem like the right thing to do would be to get a new sheriff, one that will go after those two for their foul deed?"

"R-right, I think."

"I have had a chat with the County Commissioners and they appeared to favor my plan. The sheriff had another six months left on his term in office. They have agreed to appoint a new sheriff for the remaining six months. After that, if the new sheriff works out, he could run for office himself."

"Uh-huh. Where do I come into this picture?"

"You ain't figured that one out yet? I'm surprised."

"I suppose I have, but I'd like to hear it straight from the horse's mouth, no offense."

"None taken. Well, if you've figured it out then you know I want to see you ridin' into Bradleyville with a silver badge on your shirt. The settlers deserve someone who ain't afraid to take on these ruffians on their own terms."

"What makes you think I'm your man?"

"Joshua and I haven't been close these past several years. Kinda went our separate ways. But I know him, and when he says a man has grit, I believe what he says. And that's' a fact."

We rode into Traub mid-afternoon. The one dusty street was empty. It was a dismal, pitiful little one-horse town. Why the County Sheriff kept his office there, one could only speculate. I had the overwhelming impression he hadn't dared to move to Bradleyville and take a chance getting killed. Of course, at least as far as I could determine, Constable Emory wasn't taking too many chances. It was evident that if you sided with Emmett Bradley, all would be well. If not, well you might earn a bullet for your trouble. Emory knew how to play by the rules. Bradley's rules. I could see where I might be walking into a viper's pit, since I certainly had no intention of getting' run over by a blatant criminal like Bradley.

We pulled up in front of a small, clapboard building with a sign that proclaimed it the County Office. We dismounted and Moses led the way, stomping his feet on the plank sidewalk to dislodge some of the trail dust we'd both acquired over the past eight hours. A bell tinkled at our entrance. A man sat on a stool behind a tall desk, making entries into some sort of ledger, or so it appeared. He extended his hand to Moses, then to me. We shook.

Saving Mattie

"Well, marshal, this the fellow you told us about?"

"Yep. Mr. Hodges, meet Rawhide Smith."

He looked at me like he was staring a hole in leather.

"You think you're up to the job, son?"

"I'm not entirely sure what the job entails, sir," He recognized the puzzled look on my face as one of insufficient information, then turned to Moses.

"Don't sound like you've fully apprised this young man of the dangers of sheriffin' around here, marshal. What say we get to doin' that over a drink at the saloon?"

Hodges led the way across the street to one of only five buildings I could see that made up the town of Traub. A livery, a feed store, a general store, and a saloon made up the town, with the addition of the County Office, of course. The saloon was small, dark, and smelled like smoke and spilled whiskey, neither of which was pleasant to the nostrils.

Hodges called for the bartender to bring over a bottle and three glasses. We sat by the window, mostly so we could look across the table and actually see who we were talking to. I took a small sip, winced at its bitter taste, and set if back down. I'd had my drink. I sat back, and prepared to listen to Hodges' explanation of my duties, should they extend an offer to me. And, I suppose, should I accept, although the way Moses had couched his plan, I wasn't certain my choices were many.

Hodges plunged into his explanation of what was expected of a County Sheriff. The keeping of law and order part seemed daunting, but understandable. The part about collecting taxes, well, that part wasn't very appealing. I foresaw a lot of time in the saddle, an increase in my potential for bodily harm, and a crimp in time spent with Mattie, not that I'd done a very good job of that recently.

I was probably in a daze as Hodges pinned the badge on

my shirt, had me place my hand on the Bible, and swear to some things that sounded awfully highfalutin. But, likely while still in a state of disbelief that I'd make a good lawman, I agreed to the terms and signed some sort of official-looking document.

After a restless night on a bed of straw in the livery, Moses and I rode out of Traub at dawn, headed back to Bradleyville and my new destiny, whatever that might be. Considering what had happened to the last man that wore this slightly tarnished badge, I wasn't all that hopeful. The only other Moses I'd ever heard of drove back the waters and led an entire nation out of slavery. I could only hope this Moses had some of the same touch.

We rode into the grassless yard in front of Joshua's log house. Anna appeared at the door with a frown. Joshua was nowhere in sight. I felt a wave of dread come over me.

Moses started to dismount, then hesitated. I stayed in the saddle.

"Where's Joshua, Anna?"

She paused for a moment, then spoke with a voice shaking with uncertainty.

"He went off to find where they took the sheep. Said he'd sat around long enough. Took his rifle and a pocketful of shells. I-I'm a'feared for him, Mister Rawhide. Can you go after him and talk some sense to an old fool?"

"We'll see what we can do, Anna. Calm yourself," said Moses. He wheeled his horse around and we both rode off toward the low hills where the sheep had been kept before being stolen.

I knew what he was thinking. Joshua would start at the last place he knew the flock had been, then start tracking them to wherever they were now. I'd looked the ground over pretty thoroughly already and found no reliable tracks because of the recent rains that had gone through, along with some stout winds blown up before a couple of thunderstorms. But I had a hunch Joshua wasn't really planning on following any trail. I figured he'd go straight to where he felt certain the Bradley men would have moved them. I also don't think he had any great hope of finding any of them alive. He knew, as did I, that Bradley hated sheep.

I pointed out the little valley where George had kept the sheep corralled. Moses sat still for several minutes surveying the land. He slowly urged his mount forward, checking the tracks made by Joshua's old mule.

"He hasn't found any tracks to follow, has he? He's just going after the Bradley gang straightaway. You see it the same way?" Moses said.

"I'm afraid I do. What do we do about it?"

"Go after the old fool, I reckon. And pray we get to him before they catch him out there all alone and plug him."

At least we had Joshua's clear tracks to follow. The mule left a distinct print and the ground was still soft from a recent rain. The tracks seemed to be leading along the same route Jake and I had come when we drove those cattle to the back of the Johnson property. I remember seeing a number of small box canyons along the way, plenty of good spots to hide or kill a flock of woolies. By the time we reached the first set of hills that rose to any appreciable height, we had yet to catch sight of Joshua. I was growing apprehensive of the situation. Moses' expression had taken on the look of a man about to walk into a passel of trouble. All of a sudden I understood what Moses felt. My badge was already growing heavy.

Chigger responded to my urging, stepping nimbly along a rocky, rutted deer path down into the valley. Cattle were spread out for what seemed thousands of acres of grazing land. We were still on open range, but that didn't matter to a man like Bradley who saw it all as his own personal property. While we spotted no wranglers, it was for sure they weren't far away. Still no sign of sheep, however. Mule tracks could be seen headed on down into the midst of those cattle. We pulled up to evaluate the situation. Moses reached into his saddlebags and pulled out a pair of field glasses. He raised them to his eyes and began surveying the valley from one side to the other.

"Don't know whether you noticed or not, but Joshua's tracks have been joined by a couple of horses. Wherever he is, he ain't alone no more," Moses said.

"I saw 'em. Can't tell whether they're trackin' him, or they got him. I'm bettin' on the latter. What are your thoughts?"

"The same. We better get a move on or we'll likely just find where they buried him," Moses growled.

We moved out single file, keeping a watch on any change in the tracks we were following. They led us toward a cut that I recognized. If they stayed on that course, the trail should take us to the line shack where Jake and I were staying. I knew that land pretty well. I saw that as an advantage. At least I knew all the places that would make for a good ambush.

"Hold up, Marshal. Up ahead about a quarter mile is a line shack. That's where some of the Bradley men stay when they're out workin' the herd. We best circle around, staying in the trees or we'll be easy to spot as soon as we hit that clearing up ahead. We'd make good targets."

"All right. You lead the way." He pulled his rifle from its scabbard and levered a round in the chamber. He carried the Winchester across his saddle, ready to bring to bear instantly. I did the same. I preferred the Colt for most uses, but that rifle was a man's best hope at long range. And without venturing out into the open, we were never going to get within sidearm range of the shack.

We remained out of sight, hugging the tree line, until we

were close enough to dismount and go the rest of the way on foot. We tied our horses to some saplings and continued using the shrubs for cover. That was when I saw the most awful sight I've ever seen. Down below, in back of the shack were the bloody corpses of a dozen or more sheep. Moses saw them the same time I did. I heard him mutter a curse under his breath.

We continued on a little farther, hoping to get around to where we could catch a glimpse of the front of the shack, and see who was there. By the front door, three horses were tied to the hitching rail. One of them belonged to Jake. Across the barren yard, near the corral, a man was sitting on the ground, tied to one of the uprights that supported the well. His head was bowed, but I could tell he'd been beaten severely. Blood covered his shirt. He wasn't moving. I didn't need to get closer to tell it was Joshua. His mule was tied to the well post.

The one encouraging sight was huddled off near the tree line, sitting patiently for work to present itself. Joshua's faithful dog, George. He appeared unharmed.

Just then, I heard angry voices coming from inside the shack, then three quick bursts of gunfire. All of a sudden, a man burst out the door, firing back inside as he came. He ran around the rail to a horse, swung into the saddle and rode off in a cloud of dust. Then another man came out, staggered for a few steps, and fell in the dirt. Moses and I looked at each other. We started running toward the man who had fallen. When we came up to him, I drew my Colt and kept a watch on the door. Moses bent over the man, shook his head, and stood up. We both eased toward the open door, keeping out of the direct line of fire of anyone inside. When I neared the doorway, I peeked inside, then withdrew my head quickly. I had gotten a brief look at a man on the floor. He looked to be moving, perhaps trying to sit up. Blood spotted his shirt.

It was Jake.

Chapter 22

Looking around, I saw no others, and we eased into the cabin. Jake looked up and forced a weak smile. He had been shot in the upper chest, near his right shoulder. I could tell he sounded raspy.

"Well, look at my old friend, Rawhide, got himself a tin badge and all. Looks like you got here a mite late, pardner." He coughed and tried to get a grip on the edge of his bunk. I reached out to give him a hand, pulling him to a sitting position, then to his feet. He was wobbly at best, so I urged him to lie on his bunk. I assured him we'd get him to a doctor. He shook his head.

"Holden will be back with the others. You better hightail it on outta here before they get back. I'm a goner anyway."

"Is Holden the one who shot you?" I asked.

He nodded.

"I didn't get a good look, but I assume that's Greer lying out there in the dirt."

He nodded again.

"Well, you got one of 'em, anyway."

He tried to grin, but winced instead.

I peeled back his collar to see the wound. It didn't look fatal to me. Moses just shrugged. I told Jake to lie back and I'd see about getting the bullet out. He didn't look all that happy with the prospect of me digging around in his chest for a hunk of lead, but he did lie back. Seeing that I was looking around for a sharp knife, Moses reached into his pocket and withdrew a pocketknife. When he opened it, the blade was thin and sharp. He handed it to me.

"I'll get some whiskey from my saddlebags. It'll help keep the wound clean. I got some clean cloth, too," Moses said. "You get to diggin'. I'm goin' to take a look at Joshua."

"Sounds like you've done this before."

"More'n once." He went outside for the whiskey and bandages, and to see what could be done for his brother.

Jake looked at me with narrowed eyes. "Well, what're you waitin' for? You gonna get to it or not?"

I struck a lucifer and held it to the blade to sterilize it as much as possible. I bent over and slipped the knife into the wound. The bullet had lodged against bone, thus keeping it from going clear through. I got it out with a minimum of effort, but the blood loss was serious. Since I had no way of sewing him up, I went to the stove and grabbed the poker. I thrust it into the hot coals that had been used to heat coffee. I drew the poker out after a few minutes, placing its red-hot point to the wound. He yelled as the smell of burning flesh rose with a smoky ribbon. He passed out from the pain.

Moses was coming in, half carrying Joshua. He helped him to a bunk. The old man fell back with a groan.

"Did they shoot him?" I asked.

"No. Looks like they worked him over plenty, though. He ain't in good shape, but he'll live. How's Jake doin'?"

"I'm not sure. I had to cauterize the wound to stop the blood. Where're those clean cloths you said you had?"

He went back out and returned seconds later with a half empty bottle of brandy and a handful of cotton cloth.

"Pour some of that brandy on the wound. It'll help keep it clean. Then wrap him in some of these." He tossed me the cloth.

I set to finishing with Jake, then turned to see what could be done for Joshua. I poured some of the brandy on the cuts on his face where he'd taken a ferocious beating, trying to clean him up as much as possible. Moses was right, his brother would show the effects of the trauma bestowed on him for some time to come, but he would live.

"You'd make a fair to middlin' doctor, Rawhide. Ever thought of takin' it up?" Moses said, and then grinned.

"No. And until I had the misfortune of meetin' up with *you*, I hadn't thought of takin' up sheriffin', either."

Jake was out cold, so I sat next to Joshua. He was awake, but in pain. I tried to give him a drink of brandy, but he pushed my hand away. He mumbled something that sounded like, "I won't let the devil's potion poison my insides."

I got up and walked outside. I bent down to get a better look at Greer. He had two bullets in him, either one could have been fatal. I went to the shed next to the corral, and rummaged through a collection of junk until I came up with a shovel. I started digging a hole beside the shack where the earth was softest. I took off my shirt and plunged the shovel into the soil. After an hour, I figured I had a hole big enough and deep enough to accommodate Greer's body, so I dragged him over to it and rolled him in. It didn't take long to cover him up and pat down the earth. I saw no reason to say anything over him, certain as I was that this man was no friend of the Lord.

"Where you been?" Moses asked when I came back inside.

"Buryin' Greer. Coulda used some help."

"Sorry. I been tryin' to talk sense to my stubborn brother. I shoulda stepped outside and lent a hand. It would have done me more good that what I was doin' here."

"Jake come around, yet?"

"Haven't hard a peep. Lost a lot of blood. Maybe he won't wake up."

"That's possible. If he don't, I reckon I'll have to take down my doctorin' shingle." I went to the stove to get some fresh coffee started while Moses snickered at that assessment of my new career.

"Joshua, can you tell me what happened?" I asked, handing him a cup.

His jaw was stiff from the beating, and though his words were mumbled, we could make out most of what he was saying. He'd found this shack when he heard barking, and he came to investigate. He thought he recognized the bark as that of his dog, George. He was right, the little black and white mutt had never given up on trying to keep the flock together, even while the thieves were making off with Joshua's sheep. Joshua was discovered by one of the outlaws when he came closer. George was putting up a real fuss, and Holden came outside to see what was causing the ruckus. That's when he discovered Joshua trying to coax George to move the flock toward him.

He told how Holden and Greer shot every one of the sheep then beat *him* nearly to death, until Jake stepped in and tried to stop it. They tied Joshua up to the post and went back inside, arguing amongst themselves. Said he heard quarrelling, then some gunshots. He blacked out, and that's about when we showed up.

I could feel my first responsibility as the new sheriff creeping up on me.

A trip to town was inevitable, and I knew it. I had the unsettling feeling I would be going alone, and I was right. Moses said he had to get Joshua back to his own ranch where Anna could help care for him. Deep down I knew he was right, but someone had to go after Holden. It was clearly up to me. Those words I'd been asked to repeat back in Traub were now coming back to haunt me with a vengeance.

I helped Moses put Joshua on his mule, then he helped me get Jake on his. I hoped to find a doctor in town that could give him a better chance of survival than I could. He tried to fight me off, but his strength was so sapped from the shock and loss of blood, he was like a child fighting off a bear. I waved to Moses as he rode off, back the way we had come, leading Joshua's mount. The crusty old man lolled from side to side like a rag doll, clinging to the pommel with every bit of strength he could muster. I had to tie Jake on. He wasn't fully conscious.

It was a two-hour ride to Bradleyville, and I could tell the trip had taken its toll on Jake. His face was pasty and his eyes rolled back in his head. As we rode in, I spotted a sign jutting out from a narrow storefront near the end of the main street proclaiming the presence of a doctor's office. I had no sooner dismounted than a man came outside, wiping his hands on a towel, and looking unhappy at my delivery.

"What are you doing here, mister? What happened to this man?"

"He was shot. I tried to patch him up as best as I could, but I'm no—"

"Well, get him inside. I'll take a look. Isn't he one of Bradley's men?"

"Yes. And another of Bradley's men shot him."

I dragged Jake from the saddle, letting him down as gently as I could, and hefted him up enough to half-drag, half-carry him inside. The doctor pointed to a table where I was expected to lay him down.

The doctor looked him over, clucking his tongue all the while, then said, "Well, I must say someone did a fair job on this man, likely saved his life. We should know in a day or two if he'll live, but I'd give him a better than even chance. You patch him up?"

I nodded.

"Bullet out?"

I nodded, again.

"Who shot him? Or did he accidentally shoot himself?"

"Didn't appear to be any accident. But I'm not sure who pulled the trigger. Could have been the man I buried at the site of the shooting."

He finally took the time to look at me. That's when he noticed the badge, and got a quizzical look on his stubbly face.

"Sheriff, huh? Haven't I seen you around town? Don't you work for Bradley, too?"

"I did, for a spell. Not anymore. I'm the new County Sheriff. Rawhide Smith's the name." I stuck out my hand, which he ignored, walking to a table with several bottles of various colored liquids. He pulled the glass stopper from one, doused a clean cloth with the contents, and began rubbing the cloth over the cauterized wound in Jake's shoulder. The label said, "Alcohol."

"Can't say I'm surprised that Bradley was able to buy himself a sheriff, too. Heaven knows he's got the constable on his payroll," he muttered as he tended to Jake.

"I didn't accept the job to do Bradley's bidding, doctor. Just the opposite. I intend to shut him down, maybe get him hauled off to prison. If you're a friend of his, you can pass on that piece of information." My annoyance at being labeled a Bradley man didn't escape him.

The doctor's jaw dropped. He reached out and we shook hands.

"It's refreshing to hear there's an honest man in town. I wish you luck, although I imagine you'll need more than that."

"Surely there's more than one honest man in Bradleyville. Not everyone can be on Bradley's payroll."

He rubbed his chin at the thought. "Maybe not, but there's a heap of them that appear mighty beholding to the man. He only lets me stay around—even though he hates my guts—mostly because he can't find another doctor, and he sure needs one, what with all the wounded men he hauls in here."

"They get shot up a lot, huh?"

"Anybody in the business they're in is bound to get nicked a time or two."

"What business is that? Besides trying to run every other rancher out of the state, I mean."

"Rustling. Murder. Gambling. Bootleg whiskey. About every dishonest endeavor a man can cook up."

"You offerin' any proof of that statement?"

"You think this town needs a dead doctor, do you?"

"Reckon that answers my question. Any idea when I might talk to Jake?"

"He's lost a whole passel of blood. Needs plenty of bed rest. It'll be a couple of days, I'd say, before he's awake enough to give out anything more than a groan," the doctor said. "And only then if we're lucky."

One look at Jake said the doctor was right. He looked like he was already dead. But without him pointing to Holden as the shooter, I couldn't make an arrest. In fact, my being in town was risky. I asked the doctor to let me know of any changes in Jake's condition, and slipped out the back way toward the church.

I came around the parsonage from the side. Mattie was

sitting on the porch with a book in her lap. She looked up as I approached. Her eyes widened and she let out squeal. "Mister Rawhide, you're back! This is wonderful. Let's go have a sasparilla at the store where Sarah gets flour and stuff. Okay?"

I hated to douse her enthusiasm, but the thought of making her a target as she walked alongside me, was unthinkable. It would break her heart, but I had to share with her the dangers that came with my new job.

"I can't, Mattie. Another time. First, I've got to explain something to you, something you may find hard to understand. I've accepted the position of County Sheriff for a few months. My job will mean trying to put the Venables away for what they did to your family. The problem is, I'm going to become a target for every one of Bradley's gunslingers, maybe even Bradley himself. If I get too close to you, you could get hurt, so I'm not going to see you for a little while, at least until things get safer on the streets of Bradleyville. Can you understand what I'm saying?"

She studied on that for a minute before saying anything. I was surprised at how grown-up she sounded when words finally rolled out of her mouth.

"Mister Rawhide, I sure will miss you, but you got an important job to do. I'll be waitin' right here for when you put those varmints in jail. Don't you think I won't." She nodded once to emphasize what she'd said. A proud smile curled her lips, and I knew at that moment I'd done the right thing.

Chapter 23

I knew I was going to miss seeing that little freckled face, but I also knew I had to keep her safely out of the line of fire. I had no doubt that bullets would be flying as soon as I announced to Bradley and his bunch that I was their new sheriff, and that I had a few new rules. They weren't going to like any of those, at all. I'd been compiling them during my ride bringing Jake into town. Emmett Bradley was used to being the one to make the rules. *All* the rules. That was about to change. I could only hope I lived long enough to enforce any of them.

My first stop would be the jail to see Constable Stub Emory. He was leaned back in a chair in front of the jail building, chewing tobacco and spitting short streams into the street. It appeared he was trying to hit a scorpion that had the misfortune to crawl out from under the plank sidewalk.

"Good day to you, constable." I walked up and stood over him. He looked up, forced to shade his eyes from the glare to see who I was. A frown quickly engulfed his chubby face.

"What do you want?"

"I thought it courteous to introduce myself. My name is Rawhide Smith and I'm the new County Sheriff."

"I've heard that name before. Ain't you workin' for Bradley?"

"Not anymore. This lawman job came open due to the other sheriff bein' shot down over in Traub by a couple of yahoos from here. I'm fillin' the rest of his term."

"And just who would them 'yahoos' be?"

"A couple of men named Holden and Greer. I buried Greer about three hours ago, now I'm lookin' to find Holden. You seen him?"

"Can't say as I have. But I'll sure pass on the word that you're lookin' for him. He'll be glad to know that. Willy and Joey will be glad to hear of your new appointment, too."

Emory pulled a pocketknife from his baggy denims and began whittling on a stick of wood. His frown curled into a menacing grin as I walked away. I could swear I heard whistling, too.

As I walked away, I called back, "You may want to make sure the locks are real secure in your jail. I expect to be using a cell or two soon enough." I didn't look back to see his expression.

The saloon was the most likely place to find Holden. He wouldn't be alone. I knew I was walking into a hornet's nest without anyone to back me up. But, on the off chance that none of the Bradley men would gun a man down in front of the whole town, I decided to walk in as if I owned the place.

Once inside, I looked around and saw no Bradley men, only the bartender leaning against the back bar with arms crossed, a couple of cowboys leaning on the bar, engaged in conversation, and three more at a table, casually finishing off a bottle of whiskey. Neither the noise nor the drinking was interrupted by my entrance.

The bartender gave me a squinty-eyed look when he noticed my badge. I walked up to him and asked if he'd seen Holden. Said he didn't know any Holden. The two cowboys looked at each other, turned briefly my way, and shook their heads. They promptly went back to whatever it was that they had been doing before I came in. Nothing would come of my waiting for Holden to appear, so I walked out after asking the Bartender to put the word out that I'm looking for him to anyone who might have knowledge of Holden's whereabouts. The bartender said he'd mention it to Willy, since the Venable brothers seemed to know almost everybody in the county.

I hadn't visited with the preacher since my return, and I thought I should at least say hello. I found him inside the church, standing on a chair, trying to place a picture on the wall. He turned at my footsteps.

"Well, Mister Rawhide, nice to see you." He climbed off the chair to greet me, almost recoiling at the sight of the star. "Wha—"

"Before you say anything, I know it may seem strange, but I accepted a temporary commission to fill the rest of the term of the sheriff after he was murdered. And, yes, I know how dangerous it can be."

He grinned at hearing me answer what he was starting to question.

"Then you must know what you're up against. I wish you Godspeed in whatever task lies ahead. I'll be praying that you be kept safe."

"Thanks, preacher, I'll need it."

"What brings you by? Did you see Mattie?"

"Yes, I did and I told her I would have to keep my distance to keep her out of the line of fire. I think she understood."

"You can rest assured we'll take extra care to keep her safe. Sarah is so taken with her, she's started talking about starting a family of our own. We've only been married one short year, you know."

"No, I figured you'd been married a lot longer than that. You are very well suited for one another."

"Thanks. I think so, too."

"Has any of the Bradley bunch questioned you about where Mattie came from?"

"Nope. I guess they just figured she was family come for a visit. Anyway, none of those ruffians that Bradley employs come to church. That's unfortunate because they're the ones that need the hand of the Lord the most. I fear many of them will be dispatched from this life before they ever even get to know God." He shook his head in disappointment.

"I'm afraid I had to bury a man up near one of Bradley's line shacks early this morning. And a marshal brought down another two, yesterday. I reckon you got your facts about right."

"Oh, dear, that's terrible. Were you involved?"

"No. And I'm not certain who shot the one I buried, a man named Greer. He and another fella named Holden rode together, and right now, Holden is nowhere to be found. If I can locate him, maybe I'll get some of those questions answered."

"We came to Bradleyville a year back at the request of Emmett Bradley, himself. I knew nothing about the man beforehand. Now, I've lived here long enough to realize that an element hereabouts does take a quite cavalier attitude toward the sanctity of life. That realization can be quite distressing. I do hope you'll watch yourself. I'd not like having to tell Mattie something terrible had happened to you."

"Thanks for the good thoughts, preacher, but I don't aim

to make myself any more of a target than I can help. I was a mite reluctant to take the job in the first place, but when I thought about how some of Bradley's men have murdered and robbed and burned out some of the ranchers nearby, I figured I had a duty to try to help. Meeting Mattie under the circumstances I did gave me even more incentive."

"I'm struggling with your implying that Mr. Bradley was in any way connected to the terrible things that have happened to some ranchers. I know he employs some questionable characters, though. Are you *absolutely* certain that Mr. Bradley is behind these evil doings? I wouldn't like to see a man maligned unfairly," Pike said.

"Oh, I'm sure, all right. Straight from the mouth of the devil, himself."

The evening sun had dipped low enough to splash the landscape from a warm palette of comforting colors. Oranges and yellows and purple shadows blessed the quietness, and a soft breeze cleared the air of its stagnant daytime heat. It was a pleasant time of day, one that gave a man a feeling that all was right with the world. That hoped-for ideal was, of course, just the opposite of reality. And I was abruptly awakened to that reality by gunfire erupting from the Big Eagle Saloon.

If this was a ruse to get me to come running, it wouldn't work. The town was the responsibility of Constable Emory, not me. So, I took a seat on a bench in front of the general store and waited. From where I sat, I could see all the comings and goings from the saloon, the jail, and the corral where all of Bradley's men kept their horses when in town. I watched Emory saunter out of his office, stretch his suspenders, and begin a leisurely stroll along the boardwalk, apparently unconcerned with whatever conflict might be occurring at the saloon.

Emory spotted me, frowned, then continued on in my direction. When he got to within a few feet, he stopped, pulled a cigar from his pocket and lit up.

"What do you figure is going on over there?" he said pointing to the saloon with the wet end of his smoke.

"Don't know, don't care. Town's your responsibility. I don't aim to mix in your affairs, constable." I got up and walked off toward the livery to get Chigger ready for the ride back out to the Brewster place. I had no intention of staying in town where I was a certain target after dark, possibly in my sleep should I decide to stay. As I walked away, the constable said nothing, but out of the corner of my eye, I could see him reverse course and head back to the safety of his jail. Smart man. Bought and paid for, but smart.

I reached the Brewster place just after sunset. Anna met me at the door, rifle in hand just in case I was somebody she wasn't expecting. George was curled up beneath the chair on the porch. He wagged his tail briefly, but didn't come to greet me. His muzzle lay on his paws, and his eyes had a forlorn look, almost as if he had somehow failed in his appointed task, and the dead sheep were a result of that failure. I never thought I'd find myself commiserating with a dog, but here I was doing just that.

"Good to see you're still in one piece, Mister Rawhide. Wasn't sure that would be the case with you payin' no heed to the advice of your friends, namely to stay out of that hell hole they call Bradleyville. Moses said you'd taken on the job of sheriff for a spell. Can't say I figure that's a good idea, but I'm sure you know what you're doin', so c'mon in and have a bite to eat. I've saved you some so you won't turn to nothin' but skin and bones." I followed her inside.

"I've come to see how Joshua is doing." I looked across the room to where the old man was sprawled on their bed. Anna had dressed his wounds quite professionally. From the snores and grunts emanating from him, I took him to be sound asleep. "Where is Moses?"

"Said he had business elsewhere. Didn't say no more than that, and then he rode off," Anna said. "'Bout two hours ago."

"Hmm. I wonder what business that might be."

"Couldn't say," Anna said, turning to pull a pot of beans off the stove and spoon up a plateful. She set the plate on the table in front of me, motioned for me to sit, and poured some coffee into a cup. She was jittery, and her face showed she was both weary and afraid of what was yet to come. The toll of all that had befallen them lately was as easy to read as a banner headline on a newspaper. I wanted to comfort her, tell her everything would work out, and that she needed only to have patience. But I couldn't do that without knowing for sure it was true. I still had my doubts.

Joshua was still asleep when I crawled into my blankets in the barn. A full moon illuminated the grassless yard, sending long shadows across it, and splinters of its unearthly glow shot through the barn's loosely constructed siding, giving the impression of a jail cell. I hoped that didn't turn out to be prophetic.

As dawn broke, I crawled out to greet the day. Since Holden and Greer had been with Willy and his brother when they came to threaten Joshua, finding me also waiting with open arms and a loaded Colt, I figured Holden would come back to the Brewster's to get a shot at me. I knew he wouldn't do it in the open. There weren't many places to hide behind that would afford the protection needed to gun down an unsuspecting man with a rifle, let alone a handgun. I kept to the buildings, staying out of the open, in order to make an ambush all the harder.

Anna was cooking up some bacon and kneading dough for bread when I knocked on the door.

"Come on in, Mister Rawhide, door's open." She chucked when I came in.

"What's so funny?"

"You takin' the trouble to knock when you know there ain't but the two of us in here, and we're far beyond needin' privacy. Besides, you're sorta like family, and family don't stand on formalities."

"Thank you for thinkin' of me in that way, Anna. I'm honored."

"Sit and have some coffee. Vittles will be a'comin' shortly."

Instead of sitting, I walked to Joshua's bedside. He was breathing properly, but his face was puffed up and turning several shades of yellow, red, and purple. His eyes were almost swollen shut. Rather than awaken him, I returned to the chair at the table that had sort of become my place. As I pulled the chair out, I heard him mutter something.

"What's happened to George?"

"He's okay, not a scratch. But he's feelin' bad about what happened to you and to the sheep. He'll perk up when you get on your feet."

"It may take me awhile this time, Rawhide. They hurt me pretty bad."

"You'll be up in no time, friend, just a mite sore for a spell, I'll wager."

"You keep an eye on George for me until I'm up, will you?"

"If you think he'll take to me, I will. I rather think he liked havin' Mattie around to scratch his back, though. I might take him into town for a visit once things settle out over this badge I'm totin'."

"Heard about that. You'll do a fine job. Just you watch your back. And that means all the time, not only when you're in Bradleyville. Those rattlesnakes won't let a piece of tin sway them from getting' what they want," he said, his voice weak but clear.

"I'll be careful, Joshua." I stepped outside and called to George. His ears perked up and he ran to me like we were long lost friends. He leapt at me, throwing his full weight against me, almost as if I were a coyote he needed to drive away from his flock. I lost my balance, barely catching myself on the doorframe with one hand before going down completely. I started to chuckle at the dog's humorous move. But before any snicker could escape my lips, it was caught in my throat by a rifle bullet slamming into the porch, right where I'd been standing.

Chapter 24

I rolled aside and scooted for cover behind the door, waving Anna away from the opening. I grabbed the edge of the door and slammed it shut. I had left my saddle in the barn. That was also where I left my rifle. Where had the shot come from? Is there only one shooter or several? I dared not make a break for the barn without knowing the answers to those two very important questions. I checked to make sure the Colt was fully loaded. It was. Now I had to work up the nerve to make some move that would reveal the source of the gunfire. As I pondered how to do that without becoming a duck in a shooting gallery, another shot slammed into the window frame, shattering a pane.

I hastily took hold of one side of the table and flipped it onto its side. I motioned for Anna to get on the floor behind it. Then I crawled over to where Joshua was trying to get up on one elbow to see what was going on. I took hold of his arm and helped him lie down beside her. The table was solid oak and must have been three inches thick. I couldn't have found a safer place to hide the Brewsters with someone throwing lead our way. But now, with them safe for the moment, I had to quickly gather my wits and come up with a plan for our defense.

George had crawled off into a corner, clearly he didn't like being around gunfire. As I thought about it, though, that little black and white mutt had saved my life. Or was it divine intervention? Must have been because as I looked over at George, I also spotted Joshua's rifle leaning next to the front door right under the hat pegs. I grabbed the Winchester, checked it for cartridges, and scanned the room to see if he had any more ammunition. Joshua could see me from where he lay behind the table, and he mumbled, "Above the fireplace, on the mantle."

Sure enough, two boxes of .44 cartridges sat next to a coal oil lantern and an empty canning jar full of seeds of some sort. But getting to the extra ammunition would be tricky because I would have to pass in front of the window, and whoever was doing all the shooting could probably see through what had earlier been panes of dirty glass, but were now empty. The shooter had sent several more bullets our way, taking out the remaining panes of glass, and one of the leather door hinges. If he managed to shoot away the other door hinge, it would take nothing to send the door crashing to the floor, inside. We'd be like three animals trapped in a cave. Bullets could come in unimpeded, bounce around inside, ricocheting off the stove, beams, furniture, or anything else that presented itself to their line of fire. I stayed as low as possible, rising up only to grab the box of cartridges, then scoot across the floor toward the back. So far, no shooting had come from that direction. I reached up to the back door latch when I heard a low growl. I turned to see George looking at the door with a snarl. So that's the reason there had been gunfire only from out front, where the shooter had to be a distance off, likely from the low hill where Mattie and I had first seen the Venables making their run on the place, interrupting their party.

Thanks, again, George. You saved me from walking right into their trap. Doing exactly what they wanted me to do. Probably setting out there behind the shed or the barn waiting for me to come out like it was a spring morning and I was going for a walk. Sorry, friend, no walk this morning.

A small window had been cut into the back wall, only large enough for a single pane of dusty glass. It was hard to see through, but not impossible. I snuck over to it, saw that I was not in the direct line of fire from the front door, and raised up to look out, maybe get a peek at where the guy waiting in ambush was staked out. Even with half of Texas' windblown soil clinging to the wavy glass, I could make out a shadowy figure just inside the barn door, half-hidden by a couple of bales of hay. From the general size and shape of him, I'd have to guess it was Joey, the overweight Venable brother. And since those two traveled almost everywhere together, the shooter must be Willy, not Holden as I had figured it would be.

As I looked around for anything that might come to mind in the way of escape, I noticed what appeared to be a square opening in the back wall, not far from the fireplace. A half dozen split logs were piled in front of it.

"Anna, where does that opening go?"

She snuck a glance around the end of the table. "Joshua cut that so we could reach outside and drag in logs for the fireplace without having to actually go outside if the weather was too bad. It sometimes gets real nasty and a body could get blown over from the storms that blow through here."

"There's more wood on the outside?"

"Yes."

That gave me an idea. If I could pull enough of that stack away to make enough of an opening, perhaps I could get a rifle barrel through and take a few shots at Joey. I might not hit him, but I could make him nervous enough to abandon the ambush idea. While the brothers Venable acted pretty tough, they seemed to shy away from being in the middle when the shooting started. Especially if the odds were too close to even, giving them no guarantee of success without the possibility of harm to themselves. Worth a try.

Keeping close to the floor, I began pulling logs inside. With each one I dragged in, another would loosen and tumble in, too. I soon had enough logs removed to get a fair line of sight to the barn and that chubby figure hugging the doorway.

I slipped the Winchester's barrel out the opening, cocked the hammer, and took careful aim. When Joey shifted his weight to the other foot, I squeezed the trigger. The shot caught him in the right shoulder. He spun backwards with a squeal. I could make out his thrashing about in the shadows. He then called out that he was hit.

"Get me outta here!" he yelled. The shooting from the front stopped. Seconds later, I heard the hoofbeats of a couple of horses pounding the dirt, coming up fast from behind the barn. Then I saw the unmistakable figure of Willy Venable, ramrod straight in the saddle, spurring his horse to a dead run. He had Joey's horse in trail. A moment later, Willy reached the back of the barn. Joey stumbled out and hoisted himself into the saddle. The two of them dug-in their spurs and made a beeline for the protection of the hills behind which Willy had been hunkered down taking his potshots at the house.

I could clearly make out Joey's hulking frame hunched over his horse's neck, weaving from side to side, struggling to stay aboard his mount. The two of them would be long gone in less than the time it took to spill a bucket of water on the ground.

I fired off a couple of wild shots after them just for fun.

I rushed back inside to make sure that Joshua and Anna had come through all the flying lead unscathed. They had. Anna and I pulled and tugged Joshua until we got him back to bed, sat the table upright, and then I set to making repairs to the door hinges and assembling a temporary fix of the window. A piece of brown paper wrapping from the general store, wiped on both side with some bacon grease, would make a serviceable window covering until glass could be bought to restore the window to its original state.

After an hour or so, and with the Brewsters more or less resettled, I began to think about what my response should be to the Venable's attack. The only conclusion I came to was one of confrontation, and I saw that as an unacceptable solution without someone to back me up. There were too many Bradley wranglers—some of whom I'd never even howdied— for one man to go up against. But I knew I'd have no choice but to head for town, if for no other reason than to check on Jake and to see if the doctor was tending to Joey.

"Joshua, I am riding in to Bradleyville. I doubt there'll be any more trouble from Willy with Joey wounded. And I'll be back late this evening."

Joshua grunted something and gave a half-hearted wave. Anna walked me to the barn to saddle Chigger.

"I've never seen him like this before. He's been busted up plenty, but this time, well he seems beaten, ready to give up. I wouldn't mind goin' back to Fort Worth or even Abilene, but not because we're runnin' from a bunch of cutthroats and bullies. I couldn't live with myself, and once he's thought about it, neither could Joshua."

"I know, Anna. I reckon it's up to me to start takin' that

gang down." I mounted Chigger, and reined her around to leave.

"You be real careful, do you hear me? I'll not be real forgivin' of you if you go and get yourself killed on account of us."

I could only smile at the thought as I rode away. One comforting thing about it all was when I looked around and saw George tagging along behind, staying about 25 feet away doing what any good saddle partner would. Watching my back. As I rode, an odd thought drifted through my brain. I wondered if, now that he no longer had sheep, maybe Joshua might consider selling George to me. But just as quickly as it came to me, I put that thought out of my mind when I remembered it was *my* job to set things right, and that included making Bradley pay up for the killing of the Brewster's flock of sheep. I knew there'd be a need for Joshua to give George his old job back once there was money to rebuild, all of which depended upon my success at filling the dead sheriff's shoes, and doing the job right. A picture of Emmett Bradley tied to a plank in front of the jail for all to see, his eyes closed, looking serene in death, flashed in front of me. It was wrong to wish a man dead, I knew, but some thoughts are near impossible to keep out of a man's mind when anger resides there, too. I patted the saddlebags where I kept my tattered copy of the Bible, thinking to myself it was time for a little counsel before my hatred of the Bradley gang overwhelmed me.

I made a wide berth of town and came in from the southwest as I had before. No one would be expecting me to arrive from that direction, if, indeed, they were even on the lookout. I rode straight to the livery, came in the rear fence, and called to the liveryman. He came out with a puzzled look.

"What're you doin' comin' up on a man the back way, er, uh, Sheriff? Don't you know that's what the front door's for?" I dismounted and handed him Chigger's reins. I told him I knew proper etiquette, but that I had good reason to avoid the street. I asked him if Willy and Joey had ridden in recently. He scratched his chin and said he thought he'd seen them about two hours earlier, but that they tied up out front of the doctor's office and went inside. Then he said he heard a gunshot and Willy came out alone and went to the saloon.

A gunshot! Could they have found Jake there and plugged him? I shouldn't have left him there helpless. I hadn't even left him a gun. He was in such bad shape when I brought him in, I didn't figure he could lift a gun, let alone defend himself with it. I had to get to the doc's place. I told the liveryman to water and feed my horse, but keep him saddled in case I needed to ride quickly. He gave me a quick, questioning frown, but shrugged and then walked Chigger inside and began to tend to her needs.

I went to the doc's office by the back way, continuing to avoid the street with its inherent dangers. With Bradley men everywhere, it was paramount that I keep out of sight as much as possible. I told myself that what I was doing just made good common sense. No use walking into a gunfight if it can be avoided. Besides, I needed to get acquainted with those in town with commitments to Bradley, and who might be counted on if push came to shove. So far, those on the side of law and order had been very quiet. Probably a good way to stay alive, so I couldn't really blame them.

At the back door to the doctor's place of business, used for storage, I tried the door handle as quietly as I could, testing to see if it was locked. It wasn't. I pushed ever so gently, praying the hinges had been recently oiled. It swung open quietly and I stepped inside. What I saw made my stomach turn. There, slumped in a chair, his earlier wounds still bandaged, was Jake, now dead for certain from a gaping chest wound, one made at close range. Willy had to have been the killer. Anger rose in me as I stared at the way Jake's body had been pushed into the back storage room as if it was no more important than rubbish to be taken out when time allowed. An understanding about the sanctity of life had completely eluded Bradley and his handpicked gang of cutthroats. My first inclination was to buy about four sticks of dynamite, toss it into the saloon, and clear out the entire nest of vipers.

Pushing that thought aside, I crept to the inner door. I took off my hat and placed my ear next to the door panel. I could barely make out voices coming from the other side. One of them was the doctor, the other, I assumed, was Joey, although he didn't sound like the robust tough guy that I'd met at the saloon that first day in town. It was decision time. Should I walk in and arrest Joey for the attack on the Brewster ranch, or wait? There would be little point in trying to secure Joey in Constable Emory's jail, since he'd be on the street as soon as I was out of sight. I was at a point where I needed some advice from someone more experienced in situations like this. I needed Moses Brewster.

Chapter 25

I slipped out of the doctor's back door and down the alley. I remembered the livery was situated so that a man in the haymow could see all the goings-on for the entire street, from the saloon to the church. When I got there, the liveryman was pitchforking hay into the feeding troughs at the side of each stall. He looked up as I came through the door.

"Back so soon, sheriff? Reckon you'll be wantin' your horse."

"Nope. What I'd like is to sit up there near the haymow door and watch the town's goin's and comin's, if you have no objections."

"Not at all. Help yourself. Reckon you can find your way up there without me havin' to make another trip, right?"

"I'll manage. Thank you."

Then, as I was halfway up the rickety ladder, he called out, "I'll just bet you're in town for the trial, ain't you?"

I stopped and turned my head to him. He was standing at the foot of the ladder, leaning on the pitchfork.

"Trial, what trial?"

"Why the Albert Johnson trial, that's which one. Tomorrow, around noon. They're goin' to try him for stealin' some of Bradley's cattle."

"Do you believe he did that?"

"Not on your life. I think they're all a bunch of lizards, oughta be slitherin' about on their bellies. But you can be certain they'll find him guilty, and probably hang 'im, unless he agrees to leave his land and never come back."

"Who's the judge?"

"A skinny fellow named Paltry. He rides the circuit and makes his stops here about every three months. Be here first thing in the morning. One thing about Paltry, he don't spend time on jawin' and such. Gets right down to business. Don't rightly know whether that's good or bad."

"What do you know about him? Is he honest or is he on the take from Bradley?"

"Naw. He's a good man, but you got to remember, if he hears only from Bradley men, Johnson don't have a chance."

"Johnson got a lawyer?"

"The town don't have a one. Bradley likes it that way so he don't take any chances of losin' to some fast talkin' gent. I'd have to figure ol' Albert's on his own."

Well, Albert was going to have at least one man on his side when he was dragged into that courtroom. That was the least I could do. But I needed to get into the jail to talk to him before the trial, and I surely didn't want Emory around when I did. I had to find a way to distract the constable, and as lazy as the man appeared, that wasn't going to be easy.

"Where do they hold court around here?"

"Over at the saloon. That way, when it's all over, Bradley can stand the whole jury to a couple drinks. A payoff is about all it amounts to."

"You ever been asked to be on a jury?"

"Nope. Don't expect to, neither. Emmett plays his game close to the shirt. No outsiders are welcome. Mostly draws from his own men or a few townsfolk who are known to be beholdin' to the skunk."

"How does the judge come to town?"

"The east road. Drives a buckboard over from Traub."

"I've changed my mind about my horse. Go ahead and bring her up. I'll be back in a few minutes to ride out."

He shrugged his shoulders and jammed the pitchfork into a pile of hay, as I climbed down and headed for the jail, again by the back way. When I got there, I slipped around the corner and into the front door. The constable was lying on a bunk in the second of two cells. He raised up on one elbow as I came in.

"Ah, Sheriff Smith, ain't it? What can I do for you?"

"Nothin' for me, constable, but I hear Emmett Bradley wants to see you about the trial."

"Oh. All right. I'll be back in a minute." He sat up, pulled up his suspenders, boots, and gun belt, and left the shabby little building. As soon as he had closed the door, I turned to Albert.

"Albert, are you aware they're going to put you on trial tomorrow?"

"I figured they wouldn't wait long. Probably hang me the same day. That's the way Bradley likes things, nice and tidy."

"It won't be so tidy, this time. I intend to be in that courtroom, and I think I may have enough evidence to keep you from being railroaded into a rope."

"You'd do that for me?"

"All you have to do is follow my lead. Whatever I say, you agree with. Got it?" I went over my plan with him. The look on his face showed the first hope I'd seen in any of the beleaguered ranchers since I hit this dismal town. I slipped out the door and returned to the livery before the constable came back. I only caught a glimpse of him hurrying back to the jail, huffing and puffing, and cursing loudly. I could only assume he meant the curses for me.

Chigger and I took the circular route out of town, first to the northwest, then turning east about a mile and a half out. That way I could stay behind the trees and hillocks to the north and not be spotted from town. My plan was to go about three miles east to where the creek cuts the main road into town. There's a nice stand of trees that would make for a comfortable place to camp for the night. And that's just what I intended to do.

I was up before dawn, had a fire going, and a tin can full of coffee brewing. I sat on a log awaiting the arrival of any travelers who might like to share some coffee and a little conversation. My hope was that a certain judge might be along at anytime. I didn't have to wait long. I could see dust thrown up from the tall, narrow wheels of a buckboard, its single horse making good time. The driver was slouched back in his seat, likely asleep, allowing the horse to find its own way, a route he'd probably taken many times. As he neared, I called out. He jumped at my voice, reining his horse abruptly. He blinked a couple of times, then leaned forward.

"Merciful heavens, you startled me. I must have dozed off for a few minutes."

"Howdy. Since you're stopped anyway, how about havin' a cup of real good coffee with me. I hate to drink alone." I made sure my badge was easily seen. I noticed his eyes fell to it before he answered.

Saving Mattie

"Reckon I will at that, young man. Coffee might keep me awake until I get to Bradleyville. Thanks for the invite."

We sipped the coffee for a minute before I spoke. I had to be careful to couch my words in such a way as to not try to sway him one way or another concerning the trial. But he made it easy. All I had to do was follow along.

"Where you headed, sheriff? Bradleyville?"

"Yep. I'm goin' to provide some evidence at the trial of one of the ranchers."

"Oh? Well, I reckon I'll be seeing you there, then." He thanked me for the coffee, never revealing his own identity. But from the description, I was sure he was Judge Paltry.

I took my time putting out the fire, gathering up my blankets, and getting Chigger saddled. I didn't want to follow the judge's buckboard too closely. My arrival needed to be a complete surprise to all concerned. Especially to Willy Venable.

About a mile out of town I stopped to pull out my only Sunday-go-to-meeting shirt, freshly boiled by Anna Brewster only three days before. I put it on, stuffing my old blue cotton back in my saddlebags. I spit-polished my leather vest, put it on, pinning the badge where everyone could see it, and spurred Chigger to gallop the rest of the way into Bradleyville.

I stopped at the livery, turned the reins over to the liveryman, and sauntered straight to the saloon, where, if I'd calculated correctly, a trial should be just starting. I slipped into the crowded barroom, staying near the rear while Bradley's leather-slappers tried to make their case against Albert Johnson. Willy got up and claimed he'd seen Bradley cattle on Johnson's land. Then Joey, his right arm bandaged and held in a sling, backed up his brother's story. That was their case. The judge pondered that for a minute, then asked if there was anyone else with any evidence to present. That was my cue. I pushed through the assembly of scruffy looking cowboys, making my presence known so as to hopefully avoid a bullet in the back. When I got to where the judge could see and hear me, I turned to let everyone see the badge.

"Your honor, I have some evidence that you might find most interesting."

"Your name, sir."

"My name is Rawhide Smith, and I am the sheriff of this county." A murmur spread through the room like wildfire. "After hearing of his arrest by Constable Emory, I rode out to the Johnson ranch to see if what had been reported about him was true. I believe I can prove the charges are not only untrue, but simply a fabrication aimed at stealing the Johnson's land."

"That's quite a tall order, young man. I'll look forward to hearing what you have to offer."

I swallowed hard, and started in.

"First of all, right after coming to town, I accepted a job working for Mr. Bradley. I was sent out to a line shack to await my first responsibility. While there, Willy Venable, one of Mr. Bradley's hired guns came to the shack and told us to move some cattle. Another wrangler, Jake Pardee, and I followed that order just as we were told. We drove about forty head to a pasture about four miles due north of the road into town, and about eight miles east, where there were no other cattle at that time. I noticed two things while on that drive: I recognized the pasture as one belonging to Albert Johnson, and also I noticed that not one of these longhorns was branded."

"Is it your contention that these were the cattle that Mr. Johnson is accused of rustling?"

"It is, Your Honor."

"Can you prove that?"

"I believe I can. When we were pushing them east, we

ran into a nasty thunderstorm that spooked the herd. A couple of the longhorns got tangled up in some barbed wire that had been trampled down. They both went down, one against a sharp rock that was jutting out of the dirt, the other suffered a gouging from the horn of the first one that fell. I recognized both of those cattle when I went out to verify Willy Venable's claims. The herd was just where he said it'd be, and just where we had delivered the herd earlier on his orders. The only difference was that those beeves now had brands, fresh brands."

"That's a pretty serious accusation, sheriff," said the judge.

"It's a serious accusation that has been brought against Mr. Johnson, as well, Your Honor."

"Indeed it is." The judge began rubbing his chin. He subtly looked around the room to check the expressions on the faces of Willy, Joey, and Emmett. I could have sworn I saw a slight smirk come across his lips before he continued. "Anything else, sheriff?"

"Yessir, there is." I reached into my pocket and pulled the trinket out. I walked to the makeshift bench, and placed the object in front of Judge Paltry.

"What's this?" he asked.

"That, sir, is a silver watch fob. I found it at the site of a fire that had been built to heat up the branding iron."

"Is there some relevance to this trinket?"

"I believe so, Your Honor. I believe I saw that fob attached to a pocket watch belonging to Willy Venable, himself. Since I don't see such a fob dangling from his vest, I'd say his might be missing."

"Are you saying that this fob proves that Mr. Venable was involved in the branding of those cattle?"

"I am."

"Why couldn't it have been just as easy for Mr. Johnson to have lost it when he was branding those cattle?"

"For one, Albert Johnson doesn't even own a pocket watch. For another, why would he brand those cattle with the Bradley brand if he was intent on rustling them?"

"Mr. Venable, if you still have *your* watch fob I'd like to have a closer look."

Willy's face turned red with fury. He fumbled around, patting his vest, sticking fingers into the pockets, and producing nothing but…a watch. The sheepish look on his face intermingled with his attempt to keep from exploding and drawing his Remington was one worth remembering, if, that is, I managed to get out of this saloon alive.

"Sheriff, based on your testimony, I see no reason to hold Albert Johnson any longer. I find him not guilty. Unless you can prove otherwise, constable, you are ordered to release him immediately. Is there any other business to come before me at this time?"

"Well, Your Honor, I believe it might be worthwhile to look into a dead man in the doctor's back room. His name is Jake Pardee, the same man I rode with in moving Bradley cattle to the Johnson spread, and he has a bullet in his chest. He was at the doc's recovering from a gunshot wound inflicted by another of Bradley's men. I can attest to the fact that when he got to the doctor's office, he had neither a gun nor the strength to pull a trigger."

"Did you see who did the shooting?"

"I saw Willy Venable coming out of the doc's office right after I heard a shot coming from the same direction."

"Well, Constable Emory, since a shooting within the town limits falls primarily on your shoulders, I'd suggest you take Mr. Venable into custody, and then immediately start a thorough investigation."

Emory looked as if a rattlesnake had bitten him. He had been put in an untenable situation, one that could easily end his career as a lawman, and possibly even his life. He swallowed hard, then said, "Uh, yessir."

Judge Paltry smiled knowingly. He was aware of Emory's affiliation with the Bradley bunch, and he didn't appear all that uncomfortable with his decision.

"I'll be back through here in a month. By then you ought to have a case for me to judge. If not, well, whoever is the new constable might." He rapped his gavel on the bar. He arose, gathered up his two law books, and strode through the gathering, not hesitating long enough to listen to questions or arguments proffered by anyone, especially Emory or Willy Venable.

I followed him out. As he climbed into his buckboard, he leaned over and said, "That was a masterful piece of palavoring in there, son. You might want to consider taking up the lawyer business, someday. Meantime, I'd watch my back real careful. There are more poisonous snakes in that building than one man could survive if bitten."

Paltry tipped his hat and clucked his horse to a trot. I went to the jail to ride out to the Johnson spread with Albert, both to see the expression on Vera's face when her husband walked through the door, and to make sure he made it safely all the way home.

The judge had been right; I *had* done a fair to middlin' job that day. Sure had to grin at the thought.

Chapter 26

As we rode, Albert kept glancing over my way. Finally, he spoke up. "Rawhide, there ain't no way I can ever repay you for what you done back there. I'll be forever in your debt." He leaned across and stuck out his long, bony hand. I shook it. It was a strong, hearty shake. His strength was returning.

Indeed, I *did* feel good at how the whole affair had turned out. But I had no illusions about this being the end of the rancher's problems with Bradley. I figured Constable Emory would be out of a job by sunset, and Willy Venable would be out on the street before the judge got completely out of sight, if he even saw the inside of a cell in the first place. And me, I might as well have a wanted dodger out on me. Leading the carefree life of a cowpuncher, sleeping under the stars without a problem in the world, was a thing of the past. And I had this badge and my hatred for Bradley and his gang of cutthroats to blame for it. Not that placing blame was going to keep me alive. Why did I accept this piece of tin in the first place?

While I was plenty glad that Albert wasn't going to pay

for a crime he hadn't committed, that wouldn't let any one of us rest any easier. Emmett Bradley would be madder than ever, and Willy would be thinking of ways to pay me back, none of which I knew I should look forward to. My ability to ride into and out of town unscathed had been severely diminished, and yet that's exactly what I'd need to do if I was to have any chance of bringing Bradley to his knees. And as for Willy and Joey, well, there was certain to be a showdown of some sort in my future.

The joy that Vera showed as we rode in was worth the trip. When she'd finished hugging Albert, she started in on me. I haven't been squeezed that much since I left home several years ago, and my ma wanted to make sure I wouldn't forget her. It worked.

Vera put together a feast fit for royalty that night, and I made up for several of those meals I'd missed before coming upon the Slaughter ranch. Being forced to cook over a campfire didn't seem to cause her any consternation at all. She weathered the added difficulty with not one word of discouragement.

I stayed at the Johnson ranch that night, tossing and turning on a bed of straw in the barn, along with Vera and Albert. He'd had no time to start rebuilding before he was grabbed off the streets of Bradleyville and tossed behind bars, so we all made do with what was still standing. And were thankful for it.

The next morning, I decided to ride over to the Brewster's and see if they'd heard from Moses. I sure could've used a sit down with him right about then. But when I got there, neither of them had seen hide nor hair of the elusive marshal. I sat on the porch in Joshua's rocker, hoping a plan would present itself.

Joshua was improving rapidly from the beating he'd taken

at the hands of Holden and Greer. His spirits were low from finding all his sheep killed, but physically, I knew he'd be his old self soon. I asked him about finding the shack where they'd taken his flock. He said he just followed the most sensible way to herd sheep. Although it took him up a number of dead-ends, he kept at it until he came into a clearing and heard the sheep crying. He was pretty sure he heard George barking, too, but before he had a chance to get close enough to locate the dog's position, he was clubbed from behind. That was all he remembered until he awoke to find he was lying in the dirt with two men grinning down at him. Then they started shooting his sheep, and yelling, "That'll teach you to bring a bunch of woolies to Bradley country, you old fool." After that, they began beating him. He awoke tied to a post.

"Were you awake when the shooting began in the cabin?" I asked.

His gaze wandered off as he tried to recall the events as they happened. He shook his head as if to clear cobwebs from a distant rafter. Then his chin dropped to his chest with a sigh.

"I must be getting' old. It's like a dream, or more rightly a nightmare. I get just a bit here and a piece there, but I can't seem to put it all together. Do you understand, Rawhide, uh, sheriff?"

I had to stifle a laugh. Even my friends were beginning to feel the need to get formal at the sight of this badge. Its presence on my vest seemed to make things uncomfortable for me and everyone else, too. When the job is over, I'm turning in this piece of tin and going on about my way. No need to spend my life getting suspicious looks from friend and foe alike.

"How many of them beat you? Did you get a look at their faces?"

Saving Mattie

"All I remember was two fellas that kept punchin' and whackin' at me. One was a short scrawny man with a mouth full of yellow teeth, and the other was taller, dark hair, kinda curly and greasy. Had a scar on his upper lip. That's about it, I reckon. Yeah, just the two of 'em."

"Sounds like Holden and Greer, all right. The one named Greer, the short scrawny one, was the owlhoot I buried after Jake Pardee shot him. The other man, Holden, well he got away. He was probably the one who shot Jake."

"Who was this 'Jake'? Don't think I ever heard of him before," Joshua said.

"Just a man who couldn't quite figure out which side of the law he was cut out to follow. I kept thinkin' I saw somethin' in his eyes that said he was strugglin' to do the right thing, but that he didn't have the strength. I had hopes for him, but he musta figured it was easier to keep ridin' the wrong trail, and that got him killed. From where Moses and I stood, it looked like he was tryin' to put a stop to what they were doin' to you. Maybe he did finally make his choice, it was just a mite too late."

"Sounds like I owe a heap of thanks to a dead man, too. That the way you see it?"

"As strange as it sounds, yeah, I reckon you could say that."

I watched his face wrinkle up like a shriveled apple as he tried to digest the concept of being beholden to a dead man, and one he'd never met, at that. Neither of us spoke for several minutes. We sat staring out across the wide, dusty yard. A hawk circled lazily above, gliding on shafts of rising heat, seeking his next meal. Life and death all around, and we were just sitting in the shade, taking it all in stride, for the moment even disregarding our own mortal danger.

As the morning faded into afternoon, Joshua began to

sound and move about more like his old self, even as he looked like he'd been trampled by a herd of buffalo. I told him to just be patient and not rush his recovery, but I really didn't think he'd listen. Whether he even responded to my words escaped me as my thoughts dissolved into other things such as keeping a rather gruesome score of the dead versus the damaged, but still living. If I had an accurate count, it appeared that Bradley and his men had been responsible for killing at least four, the Slaughters and the Johnson's hired hand. Then there were the attempts on the lives of the Brewsters, the Johnsons, the Olsons, the Brinegars, the Fulgates, all of which culminated in some spilled blood but so far no deaths. The Bradley gang, however, had suffered several losses. Moses shot and killed Amarillo and Snake Benson. Then Jake killed Greer, and Holden got Jake. I wounded Joey, just enough to slow him down a little, and if that Mexican bunch, the Vegas, were men Bradley might plan relying on, three of them were dead at the hands of Comancheros. The odds seemed to be working more in my favor than theirs. It seemed like the time to make them even more uncomfortable.

I went to the barn and saddled Chigger. When I walked her back to the cabin, Joshua looked at me as if I'd lost my senses.

"Where do you think you're goin'? If town is startin' to appeal to you, have you forgotten there are a passel of souls there that aren't goin' to take kindly to you showin' up? Could get real unfriendly. Why don't you sit a while longer, hang around for supper, and, in the mean time, keep leanin' back in that old rocker? It's healthier than anything you're goin' to find in Bradleyville," Joshua said.

"I know. But it's time to keep tossin' kindlin' on the fire I've already started under that bunch. If I wait any longer, they're liable to start recruitin' some new guns, and that'll just make my job harder."

"I hope you know what you're doin', my friend. Hate to lose you."

"So would I. And no, I don't exactly know what I'm doin', but I'm hopin' to have a plan by the time I get to town." I waved back at him as I rode away, reluctant to leave, but knowing that however dangerous it might become, it was a job that needed doing. And it looked as if I was the one tapped for the task.

I still wasn't brave enough to ride down the center of town, making myself too easy a target, so I retraced my now familiar circling approach. It brought me into the livery from the rear just as before. When I dismounted and called to the liveryman, he scolded me for not using the front door. It seemed he just wasn't having any of my preference for rear entries.

"Just a habit, friend, bad habit. Sorry." I handed him Chigger's reins and walked away. I heard him grumbling something behind my back, but I kept up my pace with no further regard for his disgruntlement.

My first stop would be the doctor. I wanted to know how Jake came to get plugged in his office, and why there hadn't been some attempt by Emory to uphold what little law there might be in this seemingly lawless town. A killing that was so blatantly murder should shake someone's faith in the constable. But who might that someone be? I needed friends, and the place to start looking for them was the doctor's office.

He was bleary-eyed from sucking on a nearly empty bottle of whiskey, a traditional form of self-medication it seemed for those disposed to hiding from their own shortcomings, rather than facing them. He stared at me from his awkward position of being slumped back in a swivel chair, which, it appeared might tilt fully backwards at any moment, potentially dropping him head over heels onto the floor. His bleary eyes said he'd not slept for awhile, and his hand, shaking from alcohol consumption, or perhaps a bothered conscience, struggled to keep hold of the corner of his desk.

"Whadd'ya want, Mister Badge-toter? Nothin' here for you to concern yourself with. Fact is, you've done quite enough already, bringin' that poor Jake Pardee in here, only to get him blasted to kingdom come by that skunk, Willy Venable."

"That's what I've come about. I want you to tell me exactly what happened."

"Don't act like you've a mind to do something about it. That fool constable didn't do anything, what makes you think you can?" He wavered a bit on the chair, grabbing a handful of air to steady himself, then tilted the bottle to his lips one more time. He guzzled the last drop, the tossed the empty bottle into the corner, where it shattered. He bent over to scour his desk drawers for a substitute for the dead soldier. Finding none, he tried to stand. I presumed he was on the scout for a replacement bottle of courage. As he fumbled through cabinets and in drawers, he began muttering, retracing the bits and pieces of the events leading up to Jake's death.

"Pardee was comin' along fine. What you did for him was good enough that he had a chance to survive. 'Bout the time I was figuring on his being able to get around some on his own, in came Willy and Joey with some wild tale about Joey having an accident. That's when they insisted I look at Joey's shoulder wound. I told them to have a seat and I'd look at him momentarily. I went in to look after Jake, when Willy burst through the door. When he saw Jake, he exploded with anger. He drew his gun and shot the man through the lungs. He was defenseless. Had no chance at all. I couldn't do anything but stand and watch. Then they forced me to patch up Joey." He dropped back into his chair with a whoosh, as if all the air had gone out of him. He was morose and bewildered at the same time.

"Would you testify to Willy's killing at trial?"

"And get myself shot for my trouble? Not on your life." His chin drooped to his chest. I could have sworn I heard a sob escape his lips.

"Look, doc, if I'm to have any chance of seeing Bradley and his gunslingers pay for the crimes they've visited on the folks hereabouts, I need to find some citizens who'll stand with me. If others will speak up and back my play, maybe we can send these yahoos packin'. But I'm goin' to need some townsfolk with spine. Am I talkin' to the wrong man, here?"

He shook his head. I knew he felt guilty for not doing something to stop Willy from shooting an unarmed and wounded man. But I wasn't all that sure, even given the chance to see Bradley sent to prison, he'd agree to take a stand. Maybe he just needed time to reconsider. And that's what I told him before I left his office to slip around back and head for the church.

When I got to the church, there was no one around. I looked inside, then went to the parsonage, where I was met with the same lack of life. I scratched my head at where the preacher might be, and where Mattie had gotten off to, when a familiar figure came out the front door of the saloon. A figure I wasn't eager to meet.

Chapter 27

He strode down the center of the rutted street, heading straight for me. His hands were balled into fists, but he didn't appear to be interested in making a play for his revolver. It hung sloppily at his side, tucked under an overhanging belly that attested to too much beer and too little getting up out of a chair. He was also noteworthy for what he was missing: his constable's badge. Stub Emory bore a look of defeat on his puffy face.

"Well, you got me fired, you miserable excuse for a lawman. And I intend to square it with you. The next time you see me, you better be prepared to go for that Colt, 'cause I'll be fillin' my hand. You can be sure of it."

"*Former* Constable Emory, I'd be careful who you go around makin' threats to. It's a real good way to buy yourself a small plot in the cemetery. But I'll take your advice and watch my back because I figure that's where any bullets you send my way will come from. Good day, sir."

I walked away from him at an angle that allowed my

catching sight of any move he might make to follow through on his threat. But he turned and went back to the saloon, hiking up his gun belt as though he'd had some minor victory. Obviously Emmett Bradley had relieved him of his badge, probably for *not* making sure I didn't get to the courtroom to testify on Albert Johnson's behalf. Bradley wasn't a man of great patience when it came to forgiving mistakes made by his hirelings. Why Emory was suddenly brave enough to brace me was a mystery, since he'd shown no backbone before, at least not in my presence. Had he begged Bradley for another chance? Had he promised to make good on his threat to gun me down? Cowards are dangerous because they are apt to carry out their need for revenge while hiding in a darkened alley or from behind a curtained window.

My concern for Stub Emory's bad intentions wasn't the most important thing on my mind at the moment, however. Unless Jericho and Sarah Pike had taken Mattie off for a picnic or something, it seemed strange they weren't at the church or the parsonage. The clerk at the general store might have seen them if they'd left town, so it seemed logical to stop by and see him. He had one customer when I entered, and I acted like I was interested in some shirts stacked on a table near the door until he was through with his transaction. A couple minutes later, the lady brushed past me carrying a package wrapped in brown paper and tied with a string.

"Sir, have you by any chance seen either the preacher or his wife today?"

"No, sheriff, I can't say I have. This is the day of the week they usually come by for flour and such, but so far I haven't seen hide nor hair of either one. Sorry."

"Thanks." I went back outside. I looked up and down the street hoping to see them coming from one of the other stores.

I had an uneasy feeling about their absence, one I couldn't figure. Bradley had no reason to see the preacher as a threat. In fact, he'd been the reason Pike came to town in the first place. I went back to the church, found a seat at the end of the last pew, and sat. For several minutes I just stared at the cross that hung on the wall behind the crudely constructed lectern. Nothing fancy, just a simple country church with handmade pews, and spartan walls. The few windows were plain glass, no expensive stained glass to be seen. It figured that Bradley would build the church to the cheapest standards he could, since his purpose was not to give the community a center for worship, but merely to give the appearance of propriety. But Jericho Pike wouldn't complain about the simplicity of his church. It wasn't meant to be a showplace, but a place to worship, plain and simple. He would view his opportunity to serve the community as a blessing, and if but a handful of people attended each Sunday, so be it, for God would see to it that word spread and the flock grew, no matter how slowly.

Praying had always come hard to me, although I'd been thoroughly instructed at an early age as to its importance. Still, I always wanted to be in charge of my own destiny, do things my way, and not wait for God to solve my problems. Mostly, I had to admit, it was because God didn't always come up with the same solutions as I did. Besides, I saw them as *my* problems, not his. It wasn't until I found myself in some life-threatening situations that I came to realize my thinking was skewed the wrong way. While my religious upbringing had been constant and lovingly applied by my mother, I had to learn the hard way what it all meant. That's when I came to an understanding with the Lord. Things started going a whole lot smoother after that. I can't say I didn't ride over some rocky ground, but I'd learned to listen to the Holy Spirit, finding His counsel always the best way.

Saving Mattie

As I found myself asking God to bring Mattie back safely, the sound of an approaching buggy caught my ear. *Ah, there's Preacher Pike now, probably back from a ride with the ladies.* I got up and stepped outside to see Pike's buggy coming toward me at a terrific rate. He yanked back on the reins. His horse danced and crow-footed to a dusty halt not ten feet from where I stood.

"Sheriff Rawhide, thank the Lord you've come!" Pike yelled, as he jumped from the buggy.

"What is it? Where are Mattie and Sarah?"

"They took them. You have to get them back safely. Please, please, do whatever they say. I can't lose my Sarah. She's all I have. Please—"

"Who has them? What are you talking about?"

"Go inside and I'll tell you, but you have to hurry before something awful happens to them."

I followed Pike into the church. He turned around as soon as we got inside the doors. He slammed them shut.

"I don't want anyone else hearing what I have to say."

"Well, get to sayin' it, then. If it has to do with Mattie and Sarah, then spit it out."

He began mopping his brow with a handkerchief pulled from inside his coat. He shook like someone who'd been recently yanked back from the precipice of death.

"We were in the garden out back. Mattie and Sarah were picking some flowers for the dinner table when Willy and Joey Venable came around the corner. They grabbed Mattie and told us all to get into the buggy. They rode on either side until we were out of town. They took us to a small shack down a narrow path as you go out to the Bradley ranch. When we got there, Willy made Sarah and Mattie go inside. He told me to find you and give you a message."

Pike was out of breath, scared, and shaking with fright

over what might be going on at that shack. The Venables had taken Sarah and Mattie to the same line shack where Jake and I stayed because they knew I could find my way back there.

"What's the message?" I asked, knowing full well what lay ahead for me.

"They said they want you to come alone or they'll kill Mattie and Sarah. By the look in their eyes and growl in their voice, I believed them. They're evil men, Rawhide, and God forgive me, I'm scared to death. I guess I'm just a coward."

"Being scared doesn't make you a coward, Reverend. It makes you human. And there's no shame in that. Sit down and tell me everything you can about what happened."

Here I was in one of those situations I'd always dreaded: needing to act instantly because a life might depend on it and unable, or unwilling, to wait for God's direction. Pike wasn't alone in his fear. My insides were churning and I could almost feel that Colt jumping into my hand. Revenge would be so sweet, I thought, all the while knowing it was dead wrong.

"Did they tell you why they took them?"

"You beat them in court. Stopped them before they could get rid of Albert Johnson. It was apparently important that they acquire his land at that particular time, and you ruined whatever deal they had in the making. They didn't say what that was, but I figure it must have been important, real important, for them to risk the penalty for kidnapping two people."

"Albert's spread sits at the entrance to that long valley that opens into a stretch of open country to the north. To take a herd through there they'd have to cross the Johnson ranch." I scratched my head as I tried to build a case for Bradley's run on Johnson. It didn't make sense. There had to be other ways to get to the northern range.

"Are you suggesting that cattle are the source of something so desperate?"

"No, I think it all comes down to money and control. Bradley wants everything a man can see for fifty miles all around to belong to him. And he'll do whatever it takes to achieve that. You're sure right about one thing, though, preacher. He's evil."

"When he brought us here to start this church, I believed what he said. I thought I saw in him a man who truly wanted to give the community a firm foundation. Now I see him for what he is, and all I can see is disillusionment," Jericho said. He stroked his eye as if a speck of dust had found its way there. "I know I'm supposed to give others spiritual advice, but I'm at a loss to know what to even say to you right now."

"You just keep in touch with the good Lord, preacher, and I'll do everything within my power to get Sarah and Mattie back safe."

"How can you even consider going up against such odds all alone? I feel like I should be there with you, but I know I'd be useless, in the way. I don't even know how to fire a gun."

"Don't worry. I understand. What I need is for some folks who *do* know their way around a Colt. You know anybody around here that might have the guts to stand up to Bradley's bunch?"

Pike hung his head. I knew from the slump in his shoulders that he, too, had little confidence that any townsfolk would risk their lives going up against the likes of Willy and Joey Venable. The town had lived far too long under the threat of retribution against anyone who objected to Bradley's interpretation of the law. The cemetery was full of those who stood up at the wrong time and foolishly spoke their peace. I understood. I hated watching a community exist without the will to fight wrongdoing, but I understood it. Most of these people came here seeking a better life than they'd had elsewhere. They weren't gunslingers. They wanted to be left alone to make a living and raise a family. No one in Bradleyville would step forward. I was on my own.

"I wish there were someone with a backbone in this despicable little town, but there isn't. Of that, I'm quite certain. I've watched it long enough to have a feel for these folks. It's not always a very good feeling, either."

"There must be a few in your congregation who would stand up for right."

"We have only a handful of people in our service each week. Most are older folks. They come, listen, then leave and return home for another week. Most grew up in families that went to church regularly, and now they're just keeping up the tradition. I'm not sure they even listen to what I have to say. Sarah and I have talked about seeking out another church, in another town, maybe up north, Kansas City or Springfield.

"Don't give up just yet. The country needs good folks, decent folks like you and Sarah. It's the only chance we have for survival." I didn't know whether, in his present state of mind, deeply concerned for the safety of his wife, he could understand what I was saying. "We'll get her back."

Without raising his eyes, he nodded with pursed lips, expressing little conviction that I had a chance of succeeding. With a look of defeat, he hung his head to be alone, probably to pray. I hoped he had one for me.

I hurried off to the livery. When I got there, the liveryman was waiting with Chigger already saddled. He had gotten the word that I'd be leaving. Willy probably put the word out.

"How'd you know to saddle my horse?"

"I heard you was settin' out to look for that preacher's

wife and the little girl. Figured you'd be in a hurry." He gave me a gap-toothed grin, and spit a stream of tobacco juice on the ground.

"Who told you that?"

"Hmm, I don't rightly recall. It, uh, mighta been Willy." He rubbed his chin as if he were actually in thought.

"Since you seem to be full of helpful information, who all rode out with the girls?"

Again, he stroked his stubbly chin. I watched as his eyes fell to my right hand. I had begun to slowly draw my Colt. He got the message.

"I, uh, think I remember Willy, Joey, and Holden leadin' the way."

"Anyone else? Think real careful before you speak." Tired of his pussyfootin', I drew my gun and was bringing it up when he stammered, "No. Nobody else. Just them three."

"What about Bradley? You didn't see him?"

"N-no sir. He ain't been around. Probably still over in the saloon. Why?"

"Never mind. If anyone asks if you saw me, I'd better find out you said, 'No.' Understand?"

"Yeah, but—"

I took Chigger's reins and led her outside, leaving the liveryman to ponder my admonition. He was scratching his head as I disappeared around the corner of the building and down the alley. I'm sure he figured I'd be spurring Chigger to a dead run out of town, but I had something else in mind. If Bradley's henchmen were out of town waiting to set me up for an ambush, that meant he was alone in his office. Seemed like a good time for a visit with the big man, himself. I wasn't certain he'd feel the same.

Chapter 28

Once again, the back way would keep me out of the line of fire from anyone watching the main street. I came around from the rear of the building. The Big Eagle Saloon was the last building on the block, attached to several other shops and the livery stable, with the one end open to the alley. By going up that alley, I had an opportunity to see who was inside the saloon by wiping clean a spot on the single, grimy side window. That gave me a view from front to back of the long barroom, allowing a reasonable estimate of whether I'd be walking into a nest of vipers. Fortunately, at that time of day, few cowboys were in town, and the barroom appeared to have but one customer. Stub Emory. I went to the front, stepped up on the plank walk, and, after looking around for any surprises that might be lurking nearby, pushed open the swinging doors. The bartender, Ollie, glanced up from reading some aging newspaper, which, like the sign out front advertising cold beer, looked as if it been around for a long time. The yellowed pages were a dead giveaway. Ollie gave me a disinterested shrug, then went back to his reading after I waved off ordering anything.

I walked closer to where Stub sat bleary-eyed and half-asleep. He struggled to raise his head to focus on whoever was approaching his table. He blinked several times, then realized who it was. His puffy faced twisted into a knot of contorted creases, and he tried to lift himself from his chair by putting both hands on the table and leaning forward. His attempt to acommodate any forthcoming altercation proved unsuccessful and he slipped back into his seat with a groan of frustration.

"Keep your seat, Stub. I'm not here to see you and I'm not looking for trouble. Have another swig on me, and forget you saw me." I turned to walk away, but he apparently was having none of it, his anger overwhelming what little good judgment he possessed. He tried one more time to rise, one hand slipping in spilled whiskey, knocking his glass to the floor. He failed once again to stand, then gave up, motioned for Ollie to bring him another glass and took me up on my suggestion to have another drink.

I pushed aside the curtain that separated the barroom from the back hallway where Bradley kept his office. I listened for any sounds coming from his room, tried the knob as quietly as possible. It wasn't locked.

"That you, Ollie? What d'ya want? Come in and stop scratchin' around out there like some rodent," growled Bradley.

I shoved the door open and let it bang against the wall. Bradley's eyes grew wide as he saw me standing there pointing a Colt .45 at him. His own revolver was sitting on top of his desk, within reach, but risky. His mouth turned to a snarl as he said, "Get out of here, you lowdown double-crosser. I got nothin' to say to the likes of you."

"Could be, but I got somethin' to say to you, Bradley, and you are goin' to listen."

"Forget it. I don't have to listen to anything you got to say. And if you don't back outta here real easy, I'll plug you where you stand. Don't think I can't, either."

"You can try. It'd make my job a heap easier with you dead. But fair warning: I'm a dead shot with a Colt, and I'll pull this trigger the second I see your hand even twitch."

He was being careful not to make a move before he'd gathered his wits about him, likely devising a silent plan to get to his gun before he was blown out of his boots. He must have known I couldn't miss at that distance, no more than ten feet, and that his chances of survival were small. But he was obviously considering his options, nevertheless. Some men are so sure of themselves that defeat is a word that only applies to others.

"Well, what's it goin' to be, Bradley? You goin' to make a move or are you goin' to listen to what I have to say?"

His eyes narrowed. "Speak your peace, and then get out."

"Your hired gunmen, Willy and Joey Venable, and another owlhoot named Holden, have kidnapped Sarah Pike, the preacher's wife, and an innocent twelve-year-old girl named Mattie. You're goin' to help me get them back safe and sound or they'll be dumpin' dirt on your face."

"I don't know nothin' about no kidnapping. I'm a businessman, not a rowdy. Go get them back yourself. Now leave here, and close the door behind you."

"You're the one who ordered those boys to do their dirty work, and you're the one who's goin' to rescind that order. Get up. You and me, we're goin' for a ride in the country."

"I'm not goin' anywhere with you, and that's for sur—"

That's when he made his move. He grabbed for his six-shooter while at the same time trying to duck any shots that might come his way. He got hold of it, and thumbed back the hammer when the room filled with a smoky blast from my own Colt. Bradley fell back against a wooden cabinet, leaving a splatter of blood where he fell against it. He slumped to the floor moaning and groaning. A bloom spread across his shirt and vest near his right shoulder. His gun had spun off his desk and out of reach.

"You ready for our little ride, now, Mr. Bradley?"

He cursed and screamed for someone to help him. I grabbed him by the front of his shirt and yanked him to his feet, just as Ollie burst in the room. He wasn't armed, so I paid little attention to him other than to say, "Get the doc, Ollie. This man fell and hurt himself."

Ollie wasted no time scrambling through the door and down the hall, nearly ripping the hallway curtain off its rod in the process. I shoved Bradley in front of me and toward the barroom. We'd meet the doctor halfway if Bradley didn't bleed to death first. I didn't want that to happen because I needed him as a bargaining chip with the Venables. But I reckon deep down inside, I suppose I really didn't care if a man as evil as Bradley succumbed to my little hunk of lead.

As he stumbled along in front of me, holding his shoulder and moaning that he was bleeding to death, I figured that was as good a time as any to say, "By the way, Bradley, you're under arrest for attempted murder, murder, and kidnapping."

He tried to turn his head to glare at me, but he merely succeeded in running into the wall with his wounded shoulder. He let out a scream at the pain, but kept going. We had just reached the boardwalk when I saw the doctor and Ollie running down the street. The doctor had a black leather bag that rattled as he ran.

"What happened? Who shot Bradley?" the doctor asked, puffing from his jog.

"I did, doc. And I need you to fix him good enough to ride as quick as possible."

"But, but that's a nasty wound. I can't just—"

"You can and you will, doc. Two very important lives are at stake here, and one of them isn't Emmett Bradley's. Now get to work on him."

"I, uh...but...oh, hell. Help me get him down to the office, Ollie," the doctor stammered. "We gotta get that bleeding stopped."

The bullet had gone through the fleshy part of Bradley's shoulder, only nicking the bone slightly. The wound was clean. The doctor had stopped the bleeding and was nearly finished sewing him up within an hour. Bradley kept up a constant flow of foul curses seeming to think his epithets would somehow help his cause. It didn't, and learning from experience didn't seem to come easy for Emmett Bradley, either. He kept pushing threats in my face. The doctor finished wrapping Bradley's shoulder with a clean, white bandage, and helped him get his shirt back on.

"He should be put to bed for a couple of days to get his strength back," the doctor said.

"Sorry, doc, I don't have the time to pamper Mr. Bradley, here. Those lives I mentioned, this man is the reason they're in danger. Any sympathy you might have for him is misdirected."

"I have no more sympathy for him than I would for any man with a serious wound, sheriff. And I am concerned for the two of whom you speak, but there is nothing I can do for them, and I can help this man. I took an oath to do nothing less."

"We can debate the issue later, doc, after I get Sarah Pike and Mattie Slaughter back safely. You can thank your patient for anything that might happen to them. So finish up your work on him and turn him loose. Time isn't on my side."

"And you won't find no one else on your side either, *sheriff*," Bradley said, spitting out the word sheriff as if it tasted like dung. "This town owes me, and it don't owe you nothin'. And I intend to collect. You can count on it."

The doctor got a sour look on his face at Bradley's words, almost as if for the first time he was able to see the man in his true colors. He shook his head and turned back to finish up. After a couple more minutes, he backed away from Bradley.

"Sheriff, he's all yours. Keep an eye on that bandage. If you see any blood getting through, it'll mean he's probably pulled some of those stitches. He can't afford any more blood loss. Try to take it easy."

"Thanks, doc, I'll do what I can to get him to our rendezvous safely. After that, well, only the good Lord can show him mercy. Get on your feet, Bradley. We're goin' for a ride."

I was forced to counter his reluctance to leave town with me by way of a few forceful shoves, but we finally got to the livery. I told the liveryman to saddle Bradley's horse. He did so, taking his sweet time, and with more than a few questioning glances at my prisoner as if to silently ask what he should do. It was clear to me that, even though he had previously expressed displeasure at the way the town was run, this man was one of those beholding to the man whose name the town carried. Bradley was in too much misery to make a fuss at that moment, so the horse got saddled and we got him mounted. As we prepared to ride out, I leaned down to the liveryman.

"If you're thinkin' of gathering up a few of his friends and following us, I'd advise against it, unless you're looking for some of what Bradley got when he tried to go up against me."

The scowl and sudden redness on his face told me he had been considering such a foolish move, but the reminder about Bradley's condition seemed to change his mind. At least I could only pray that my phony bravado would sound convincing.

If any of the townsfolk loyal to Bradley came after us, my situation could quickly become untenable, and Sarah and Mattie would have no chance for survival. I couldn't out-gun the whole population of Bradleyville, small as it was, and getting squeezed between the Venables and a vengeful bunch of Bradley's followers was a frightening prospect. We managed to leave town uncontested. I slapped the rump of Bradley's horse in order to pick up the pace. I had no real plan in mind when I went to Bradley's saloon, but one was slowly forming as we came nearer the line shack where Willy and Joey were supposedly holding their prisoners.

If I was reading Willy Venable's intentions right, he would have Sarah and Mattie in front of the shack, with him using them as a shield to protect his own miserable life. Somewhere up the hill, beneath the cottonwoods, Joey would be hiding with a rifle trained on me. He would likely start firing as soon as I came into range. I had no intention of falling prey to such an obvious setup.

When we came to within a mile of the shack, I made Bradley dismount and start walking. He didn't like that idea from the start.

"I can't walk. I'll bleed to death. Is that what you want? Me dead before you get your precious women back?"

"Can't say as I care one way or another. I intend to get them back with or without you. So plan to follow my instructions to the letter or I guarantee your return to town will be a whole lot less pleasant than the ride out. Now move."

I tied our horses to some trees and prodded Bradley to start walking ahead of me. As soon as I got my first glimpse of the shack, I made Bradley turn right and start walking into the foothills behind the property, circling the shack to give me a better view of the layout. Also, I was pretty certain no one below could see us, and I wanted to get behind Joey. I told Bradley if he made a sound, I would shoot him where he stood.

Hunkered down behind an outcropping of boulders, which formed a sort of catchall for tumbleweeds and other windblown debris, I had a good view of the shack. Willy was sitting on the bench out front, leaning back against the timber sides, smoking a cigarillo. He had put Sarah and Mattie inside where he must have figured they'd be easier to keep an eye on, and with only one door, assure himself of their inability to make a break for it. The door had been left open and I could see inside well enough to see Mattie moving about, apparently unharmed. I couldn't see Sarah.

All I had to do now was locate Joey and hopefully take him down. The circumstances surrounding any plan I was conjuring changed rapidly as the one thing I hadn't counted on was a fly in the ointment called Holden. I'd completely forgotten about him. He hadn't forgotten about me, however. As I rose up to try keeping an eye on Willy and, at the same time, try to spot Joey, Holden came out of the brush behind us, yelling like a banshee and firing wildly. I ducked back behind the boulders for cover, waited for him to get closer, then stepped out and fired one shot.

I hit him squarely in the chest, slamming him to the ground with the impact of the bullet. He was dead before he hit the ground. I knew the shooting would stir things up, and that my desire to secure Sarah's and Mattie's freedom without a lot of bullets flying around to further endanger their lives was now only a dream.

Chapter 29

I crept over to where Holden lay face up, eyes open. I unbuckled his gun belt and took his gun to add to my arsenal. I ejected his empty cartridges and inserted new ones, ready for whatever was to come. I tried to move back to where I had left Bradley, but he had crawled forward into a small stand of trees at the edge of the hill. He was just starting to stand up when Joey burst from *his* hiding place, behind us and further uphill, screaming at the top of his lungs that he had me in his sights, and firing his revolver as fast as he could cock and pull the trigger. Bullets ricocheted off the boulders, digging up clumps of hard dirt, and one of them eventually found its target. Me.

A piece of lead from Joey's .44 ricocheted off a boulder and caught me in the left arm, knocking me off my feet. I went down pretty hard, rolling downhill for several yards, and coming to a sliding stop at the base of a sapling. I only had time for a glance at my bloody shirt, unable to ascertain the extent of my injury, when Joey continued his frontal charge. Like Holden, he fired as fast as he could, throwing lead around as if it were a handful of pebbles. He rushed me and was in a good position to finish me off when I heard it: Click, snap, click, snap, the distinctive sounds of an empty six-shooter.

Joey stopped in his tracks with a bewildered grimace on his puffy face. At first, a look of panic, then helpless acceptance came over him as I stood up and aimed my Colt at his chest. He was no more than ten feet away, an easy shot for anyone who knew enough to pull a trigger. His look changed from resignation to surprise when I didn't take the shot. It wasn't that I didn't want to. He and his brother certainly earned a bullet and much more. But with an empty gun he was no longer a threat. If I were to squeeze that trigger it would have constituted murder instead of self-defense. I told myself I wasn't going to become one of them. I told him to toss his gun away. He did so, tossing it in the dirt with a defeated groan.

From behind me, I heard a low moaning. It was Bradley. When we got to him it was quickly apparent he hadn't been as lucky as I to escape Joey's fusillade with only a grazed arm. Bradley had attempted to make a run for the cabin as Joey started firing. An errant bullet had found its accidental mark, striking him in the middle of his back, and he wasn't doing well. Sprawled face down, he tried to get to his feet, but the effort was futile, and he dropped back into the dirt with a gasp. Blood bubbled out of his mouth with each labored breath.

Joey, watching me carefully for my reaction, moved slowly toward where Bradley lay. He got down on his knees, and started sobbing that he didn't mean to shoot him, and begging for forgiveness. If only he'd asked for forgiveness for his part in murdering the Slaughter family, I might have been more convinced of his sincerity. Bradley tried to speak, but he was sinking fast. One last wordless gasp gurgled from his lips, and he died. I doubted many would miss him.

Joey got to his feet, wiped his eyes, and gave me a look of utter contempt, as if I had been the cause of his misfortune. He made it clear by the hatred in his eyes that he wished me dead and that he intended to do everything in his power to see that happen. Before he could say anything, I decided it was time to interject my demand that he follow my orders from now on or meet the same fate as he'd visited on his boss.

"Joey, I hope you're smart enough to listen to what I'm going to say, and follow my instructions. If you don't, you and your brother will be joining your boss in the happy hunting ground."

"Just say what you got to say. Your threats don't mean anything to me. You got the drop on me now, but if that changes, you're the one who'll be eating dirt."

"Maybe so. I'll try my best to not let that happen. Now, we're going to start down this hill toward the shack. I'll call out to Willy. You'll say nothing. You got that so far?"

"Uh-huh."

I stuck my Colt in his ribs and prodded him on downhill.

"Willy Venable, this is Sheriff Smith. Step outside and let's talk. I have your brother with me, and I'm willin' to make a deal," I shouted to the breeze.

We were greeted by silence, only the rustle of the grass against our boots. I called again, and again, there was no answer. I told Joey to stop moving.

"Don't know where he is, do you? He's just waiting for you to get close enough so he can blow you in half. I'm goin' to like seein' that." A sneer curled his lips. I held up my hand, cocked the Colt, and he shut up.

I pushed Joey ahead of me and we made a cautious approach to the cabin, trying to keep some kind of cover between Willy and us. I didn't hanker to get caught in the open and let him get a clean shot at me. Thinking I would use Bradley as a bargaining chip for Sarah and Mattie. I had the shotgun, but it was only good at close range.

As we approached the cabin, Joey began getting agitated. He was nervously trying to hold back. I saw fear building in him, and I wondered at that moment if the bond of brotherhood might not have been as strong between them as it had seemed. Perhaps Joey knew his brother for the craven coward that he was, and expected he would shoot at whoever entered that door first, which I planned to be Joey.

"Willy, this is your last chance to talk. Nobody has to get hurt. Just come out and we'll work it out."

The silence was palpable. I shoved Joey aside and made a dash for the door. As I burst in, slamming against the leather-hinged door with my good shoulder, I fired a couple of wild shots to hopefully make him seek cover. I made a dive for the floor. My shots were intentionally high so as not to take a chance on hitting Sarah or Mattie. But my precautions had been for nothing. The shack was empty. The corral was empty. The barn was empty. It became clear that when Willy heard all the shooting, and not knowing who was shooting at whom, he must have grabbed his prisoners and lit out for safer ground.

When I walked up to him, Joey was shaking and holding his shoulder where I'd shot him at the Brewster place. He was ashen, pale as a full moon.

"Where'd'ya figure big brother Willy got off to?"

"If I knew, I wouldn't tell you." He was shaking his head from side to side like a child unable to fess up to breaking a plate.

"I reckon it hasn't sunk into that pebble-size brain of

yours that Willy left without regard to whether you were alive or dead. He didn't care what happened to you, Joey. And that's the straight of it."

The realization that I might be right contorted his fleshy face into a shriveled apple.

After retrieving our horses, and hefting Bradley's and Holden's bodies across their saddles and lashing them down, we started out to track Willy. With any luck the light rain the night before would make his tracks easier to follow, especially since he didn't seem to be trying too hard to conceal them. That probably meant he wanted me to ride into an ambush somewhere along the trail, which wouldn't disappoint Joey in the least. From the direction Willy seemed to be riding, I figured he was trying to make his way back to Bradleyville.

With the element of surprise now gone, I had to figure out what might be going through Willy's mind. He had no way of knowing that I had brought Bradley with me to the place of rendezvous, nor could he know that his boss was now dead. Based on the way things were when he left town, Willy's backtracking made sense. When he heard the shooting coming from up the hill beside the line shack, he easily could have been fooled into believing Joey had been successful in killing me, in which case it was time to return his prisoners to town for further orders. He would skedaddle back to seek Bradley's blessing, since he wouldn't make a move without Bradley giving him permission. If Willy thought I was dead, he would be eager to tell Bradley that all his troubles were over and things could get back to normal. That may have been why he took off from the shack without waiting for Joey, to take all the credit, and get his congratulatory pat on the back, as he was used to receiving whenever he completed any of Bradley's nefarious plots.

On the other hand, considering the possibility that I'd killed Joey, he knew he would still be better off to get back to Bradley where he could count on being backed up by whatever hired guns Bradley could cobble together. If that was the case, it still left me with the element of surprise by riding into town trailing Bradley's body. Without someone to tell him what to do, Willy would fight like a cornered mountain lion to save his own skin. That might make him more dangerous than before, and put Mattie and Sarah in an even more tenuous situation. Willy would have no desire to release them, unless he could make a deal.

An idea formed in my head, one that might give me an edge in the coming confrontation. I remembered the day I decided to quit working for Bradley and rode off into the hills. The trail I had taken came out onto a bluff north of town with a view of everything that came or went in either direction. If we took that trail, a much shorter route than what Willy would be taking on his way back to town, I could wait for Willy to ride in and see if he holed up in the saloon, or rode out of town to evade a confrontation. It might also give me a peek at whatever plans he had for his prisoners. Only a very narrow deer trail led down from that vantage point, ending in town near the church at the far northwest end. I'd become a believer of coming into town that less conspicuous way.

When I began leading Joey and our dead companions off the trail we'd been following, Joey suddenly got very nervous.

"Wh-where we headed? This ain't the way to Bradleyville. Where you takin' me?"

"We're goin' a different way, that's all."

"You're plannin' on shootin' me up there in the hills and leavin' my body for the wolves, ain't you?"

"Joey, the wolves wouldn't eat anything as rotten as you. You don't have to worry."

I watched Joey as his eyes darted around, probably looking to identify anything that might assure him he wasn't going to end up as buzzard bait. Easing Joey's mind was the least of my worries. I ignored him, and just let him stew.

When we reached the overlook, the town appeared quiet. I didn't see Willy's horse tied outside the saloon. So, I would wait and watch.

"What're you doin'?" Joey said. He was apparently nervous about our sitting so near the edge of the bluff, because he kept peering over the rim and then drawing back as if he might be sucked off the edge and dropped several hundred feet to his death for his curiosity.

"I'm decidin' whether to shoot you and dump you into that chasm below, or wait until we get back to town and do it." I had no idea he would take so obvious a bluff to heart, but his eyes got big and he started to perspire.

"Y-you wouldn't d-do that, would you?"

"I might if you don't do exactly as I say. Your only chance to come out of this alive is to follow orders and make sure Sarah and Mattie are safe. You follow me?"

"Uh, yeah. But it wasn't my idea to snatch them two. It was Willy's and Emmett's. They're always makin' plans that don't include me, except when someone needs shot." His chest heaved. "I ain't the thinker, Willy is."

"Since you're the one that killed Bradley, how do you figure Willy's goin' to take it when he finds out?"

"H-he ain't goin' to like it none."

"What do you figure he'll do?"

"Might shoot me. He did once before when he didn't like somethin' I did. I couldn't walk on my left leg for near a month. And now you're wantin' to shoot me, too."

"I won't shoot you, Joey, if you do what I say. Okay?"

"Yeah, uh, I reckon that's best. If we get them women back safe, do you suppose you could look the other way whilst I ride off to New Mexico or someplace like that?"

I scratched my chin as if I was thinking over his offer to help. It was all I could do to keep from bursting out in laughter at his suggestion. But at this point, if I had to make a deal with the devil to save Sarah and Mattie, well it might almost be worth it.

"Joey, I don't trust you for a minute. I got this feelin' in the pit of my stomach that you'll turn on me the first chance you get. What guarantee do I have you'll keep your word?"

"How about if I tell you a way into the saloon that only a couple folks knows about? Willy'd never see you comin'"

"All right, tell me about it."

"Do you see that wide building next to the saloon, where the leather goods store and the bakery are?"

"Yeah, what about it?"

"It only goes in about fifteen feet. There's a long hall behind it where you can go all the way from the livery through that building and into the saloon without anyone on the street even knowin' you're there. Willy won't be goin' in that way. He'll go in the front."

"And what'll you be doin' while I'm sneakin' through the secret entrance?"

"I'll be on my way to New Mexico. If that's all right with you, of course." He broke into a gap-toothed grin like a four-year-old who'd gotten caught stealing a cookie.

Before I could say yea or nay, I watched Willy ride unhurriedly into town, leading another horse with Sarah and Mattie on its back. Their hands were tied in front of them. They appeared unharmed, but at that distance, I couldn't be certain. He went straight for the saloon. Anger rose in me like a coming storm. I clucked my tongue to get Chigger moving and motioned for Willy to follow. Just in case he didn't, I pointed the Colt at him to make my request more understandable.

Chapter 30

The ride to the bottom of the cliff took only about fifteen minutes, and for a short time I couldn't see if Willy had left the saloon as it was behind other buildings. I decided to take Joey's secret route into Bradley's office by going directly to the livery. I still hadn't decided what to do with Joey, however. We rode the back way, avoiding the main street all the way to the corral behind the livery. The liveryman—Joey said his name was Tolliver—looked up from forking some hay into a trough. His expression changed from his usual sour to grim when he saw the two bodies strapped across the spare horse. His eyes went from Bradley to Joey, then to me. I could see the fire behind them.

"Did this snake you're ridin' with kill Bradley, Joey?"

Joey's face turned red and he began shifting in his saddle.

"It was more like an accident, Mr. Tolliver. Just an accident. He, uh, didn't do it."

Tolliver shook his head like he didn't believe any of it. The bullet in Bradley's back suggested something other than an accident. He frowned for a second, then went back to his work without another word. I motioned for Joey to dismount, and I did the same, making sure nothing came between us. As big as he was, I sure didn't want to allow him to get into a position where he could jump me, which I knew he would regardless of having given his word. That's just what the devil does. He lies.

I told Tolliver to leave the dead men right where they were, and to say nothing to anybody until I came back for them. He didn't like it, but he nodded his agreement, stabbing the pitchfork into the hard dirt with a thud, then leaning on it. I motioned for Joey to lead the way through the building's secret entrance to the saloon. He held back several times, hoping, I suppose, to delay inevitably having to face his brother unless he could convince me to let him go. He stopped just after we'd entered the first of several doors to a long, narrow hallway.

"All you do is go to the end. The last door goes into Bradley's office. Now that you know your way, you don't need me no more. Why don't I just mount up and ride outta here, now?"

I gave him a quizzical look. "Joey, what makes you think I would trust you to keep your word and not alert Willy to my presence?"

"But you said—"

"I said I'd think about helping you if you helped me. I'll need more proof that you can be trusted than a few directions down a hall."

"W-well, what more d-do you want me to do? I got no gun to even defend myself."

"I'll do the defendin'. You won't need a gun. Now lead the way, and do it quietly."

He grumbled almost all the way down the dark hallway.

Saving Mattie

Every few feet, a small, high window had been installed back when the building was built to let in thin shafts of light, enough so a man could find his way. The windows had been constructed only about a foot square so even the smallest person couldn't crawl through. I assumed that Bradley had ordered them made that way for security reasons. Considering his propensity for making enemies, it seemed a wise choice. Of course, anyone caught in the hallway also had no way to escape, either. That was the one drawback to Joey's secret entrance, and one I was beginning to have second thoughts about, as I heard voices at the other end.

When we got to the door that Joey said opened into Bradley's office, I put my ear to it, hoping for some indication that it was safe to enter. That's when I heard the first encouraging sounds I'd heard for some time. Sarah and Mattie must have been locked in there for safekeeping. I listened for several seconds to be certain they were alone before busting in.

"Mrs. Pike, I just know Mister Rawhide will find us. He says you have to have faith. And I do," said Mattie, her tiny voice trying very hard to be in charge. I could just imagine the steely determination on her face.

"I know, Mattie, but what if he comes too late? That man out there is quite impatient. I've been told over and over that God will protect the innocent, and I've never doubted that. But right now, I'm not so sure of my own faith. And it scares me," Sarah said. "I feel so alone."

"Uh, yeah, me too," said Mattie.

That was enough for me. I tried the door, found it locked, and started to put my shoulder to it when reminded of Joey's presence. I told him to bust in. He shrugged as if it would be nothing, crashed into it with all his weight, and the door flew open. Sarah saw Joey stumble inside and screamed. Mattie ran for the desk and started to crawl under it when I rushed in.

"Mister Rawhide!" she yelled, "you've come. I just knew you would." Then she jumped up and grabbed me around the neck.

Mattie's exuberance couldn't have come at a worse time. Willy must have heard the commotion all the way from the barroom because he came running, slamming through the other office door. He had his gun out. I didn't. I suddenly envisioned my life ending right then and there in a blast of fire and smoke. But an angel intervened at just the right moment in the form of a fiercely righteous twelve-year-old girl.

Mattie let go of my neck and rushed straight at Willy, to his great surprise. She began pounding on him so hard he couldn't get a clear shot. Momentarily put off balance by her sudden attack, he stumbled backward, his gun going off wildly. I had time to draw and yell at Mattie to drop to the floor. She did so without hesitation just before I fired. Willy stood but a moment, a look of utter disbelief on his face, then fell backward into the hallway, a .45 bullet in his heart. After one last gasp, he died. I spun around to fend off Joey, and was surprised to see he'd eased into the closest chair he could find, wiping at his forehead with his sleeve.

When Mattie saw what had transpired, she hugged me, pulling me over to where Sarah stood bewildered and distraught by what she had witnessed. Seeing a man shot down right before their eyes was more than I would ever have wished on two innocent people. Sarah's eyes began to well up and tears cascaded down her cheeks. Mattie put an arm around her waist and tried to comfort her. Mattie wasn't about to shed a tear for Willy Venable, the man she'd witnessed murder her entire family for no reason but sheer meanness. She must have seen his end as justice triumphing over evil. I also felt a great relief, thankful it was over.

I glanced over at Joey, expecting to see anger or remorse over the death of his brother, but what I saw seemed more like liberation. Perhaps through it all, Joey had in some way also been a victim. I escorted all three of them from the saloon, anxious to reunite Sarah with her distraught husband. From the way they hugged and kissed, you'd have thought they were newlyweds. Mattie stood by my side, holding my hand with an iron grip.

She looked up and smiled. "Thanks, Mister Rawhide. And thanks to that God fella, too."

"I think I just heard Him say, 'You're welcome, Mattie.'"

It was over. The dust had finally settled, and the malevolence that had governed Bradleyville was dead and buried. I hoped that the community could rise above what Emmett Bradley had done to them and to their neighbors, and to embrace those who rejected the stench of corruption and supported defeat of the worst kind of evil. That done, the town could grow and prosper.

The name Venable would soon be forgotten, too, and their misdeeds would someday disappear from people's memories like a tumbleweed in a swift breeze. I'm not entirely certain why, but I felt sorry for Joey, and set him free without spending any time in jail for his word that he'd never again set foot in this county, even though he'd earned punishment for his role in his brother's crimes. He actually thanked me for keeping my word, and rode off whistling, wasting no time getting out before I changed my mind. No one questioned my decision. He was a very strange and lonely man. I hoped he could find a way to stay out of trouble now that he was out from under the bad influence of his brother, although I had my doubts.

Before he left, I got him to tell me why Bradley was so set on removing folks from their own land. I was not completely surprised at his explanation. Bradley had wanted a spur rail to come down from the Southern Pacific Railroad. The railroad had expressed an interest because of the vast new business potential, but wanted full control. That didn't fit into Bradley's plans, especially since most of the cattle he would be shipping were stolen. With the railroad putting up the money for the loading pens, they also wanted approval of every shipment, which was their way of ensuring all transactions remained above board. Bradley rightly construed that to mean if they found stolen stock, they'd refuse to ship, and maybe even go so far as to bring in the rangers. That *definitely* didn't fit Bradley's plans. He figured by driving out the small ranchers, he could have more control over what got shipped, since every longhorn would have been his, stolen or not, a major reason why he had left the majority of his cattle unbranded. And with little evidence of his rustling, and no one to say otherwise, the railroad likely would relax their rules after investing so much in building the line. Whether his thinking was sound or not will never be determined. Only time would have told. And time was never a luxury Bradley could afford, thus the ranchers had to be eliminated, one way or another. So now the totality of Bradley's malicious plan has been exposed for all to see. After hearing the full story, the majority of the townsfolk claimed they had no idea what their town's namesake was up to, most unable to accept they had been so gullible.

All I could do now was pray that God would forgive me for my actions in the matter. I take no pride in killing a man no matter how badly he may appear to deserve it. I fully understand that judgment should be left to the Lord above, although sometimes it becomes necessary to hurry things along a little if decent folks are to survive. Perhaps it was God's judgment, and I was merely the means. I reckon I won't know until it's my turn up there to stand before the throne and be judged.

Mattie and me, well, who knows what will come of an alliance between an outspoken twelve-year-old girl and a gunslinger with too many notches on his gun? I do know one thing. I intend to do everything in my power to make certain she grows up happy and healthy and gets a real chance at life.

I decided that since the town had a perfectly good jail, I'd just make Bradleyville the County Sheriff's headquarters, although I was already beginning to hear rumblings over changing the name to something with fewer bad memories. The suggestion I liked best was "New Hope."

My term at being sheriff still had five months to go. That's how much time I'd have before deciding if I wanted to toss my hat into the ring for a full two-year term. I figured Mattie should have some say in it, though. The community had plenty of good folks living there, with more coming in every day, and the Pikes would do all they could to help heal old wounds. For the time being, Mattie would still have the company of Sarah and Jericho, for which I was grateful. She'd grown very fond of the Pikes. I knew the time would come when I'd have to decide whether to take Mattie away from Jericho and Sarah and strike out for someplace new. That is if I decided not to run for sheriff or possibly lose the election. Maybe without Bradley and his gunmen, more families would settle here, families with children Mattie's age. Why, the town might even get a school.

The Brewsters came to town after hearing about the demise of Emmett Bradley and Willy Venable. With the threat of being shot down in their own yard now just a memory, they seemed ten years younger. Anna spent hours at the general store, talking to the other ladies, and perusing all the new merchandise. Joshua had one drink at the saloon, then wandered from the harnessmaker's to the gunsmith, stopping at every liar's bench in between. I asked Joshua if he'd seen Moses. Said he hadn't, but expected he'd turn up again, as unexpectedly as before, just like a bad penny.

"I'd sure like to make his acquaintance again. He's responsible for me getting this badge."

"You thinkin' of thankin' him or shootin' him?" Joshua said with a chuckle.

"Haven't made up my mind yet."

Vera and Albert asked us out to supper as soon as their new house was finished. Several families had volunteered to help build a new one. When a community comes together to help each other, there's not much they can't accomplish.

For the time being, I was still trying to share stories from the Good Book with Mattie. But I had to be honest. That child can come up with more questions than I'd be able to answer in ten years. Rather like tryin' to pull a loaded stagecoach with a pony. I reckon I'd of been better off to sic her on Jericho, and pay more attention to my sheriffin'. But I just couldn't resist a challenge.

~THE END~

About the Author

Phil Dunlap is the author of four previous Western novels. A life-long fan of Western literature, he writes with an eye toward making readers feel they are on the frontier at a time when hardship and danger were the daily fare. The author brings his extensive experience as a journalist to the task of creating characters that are real and believable. Dunlap has been writing professionally for twenty-five years, having been published in such magazines as Plane & Pilot, Sport Aviation, and Indiana Business, as well as being a correspondent for The Indianapolis Star, a Gannett daily newspaper.